Down Mexico Way

To Paul
with the compliments
of the author
Peter

Peter Gordon Williams

Pen Press Publishers Ltd
London

First published in Great Britain by
Pen Press Publishers Ltd
39-41 North Road
London N7 9DP

ISBN 1 900796 77 5

A catalogue record of this book is available
from the British Library

Printed and bound in the UK

Cover design by Bridget Tyldsley

For my wife Jean

CHAPTER 1

I t was September 1863. In that year Robert E Lee's Confederate Army was defeated at Gettysburg; David Lloyd George was born at Chorlton-on-Medlock; Manet painted *Le Déjeuner sur l'Herbe*; Charles Kingsley wrote *The Water Babies*; the Football Association was founded; and the Grand Prix de Paris was first run at Longchamps. Four years earlier Charles Darwin had published *The Origin of Species*, setting out his theory of natural selection.

There was one ecclesiastic, however, who, beneath the carapace of his simple fundamentalism, remained impervious to the turmoil provoked by such heresy.

William raised his eyes to heaven as his father's voice thundered from the pulpit of the tiny church.

'The lustful, the indolent, the avaricious, the Godless, all will burn in the sulphurous fumes of the everlasting fire. The flesh will melt from their bones and their screams will ring out through the vastness of space for all eternity.'

The congregation sat unmoved. William was eager to be off. Ann Wilson had at last agreed to go for a walk with him and he held high hopes that at last he would make some progress with this teasing vixen whose mischievous face and seductive figure had occasioned him many a sleepless night, tormented with the itch of sensuality.

His father reached the furious peroration. 'Imagine you are at the mercy of some medieval tyrant. You are led into the torture chamber. Your legs are placed between two boards and bound tightly together. Wooden wedges are inserted and hammered into place. Your knees and shins shatter. Your legs split open. Mangled flesh, muscle and blood ooze forth. Think not that you can escape from this agony into unconsciousness. Each time you faint they revive you with vile, pungent concoctions.

'There are other tortures: the pulling out of finger nails; the wrenching out of teeth; the gouging out of eyes; the pouring of molten lead down the throat; the tearing out of intestines with hooks of iron; the cutting off and burning of the genitals. Think you the torments of Hell are no more than this? Oh no, you sinful wretches! These are but tortures devised by man's poor wit. How much more terrible will be the torments forged in the mind of a wrathful God? How much more exquisitely cruel will those tortures be? Hell is a sulphurous pit spanned by a narrow bridge that all dead souls must cross to reach Heaven and, unless redeemed by God's mercy, the damned will fall into that pit to suffer for ever the terrible torments of Hell. And they will never end. They will never end. Think what that means. A time span as limitless as the grains of sand on the shore of an infinite sea.'

The Reverend Charles Dawson, his eyes flashing and his round fat face purple with apoplexy,

2

rose on his toes and pointed an accusing finger at the congregation. 'The gates of Hell are open night and day. Smooth the descent and easy is the way. Repent and mend your ways, you miserable sinners, or face an eternity of suffering beyond your worst imaginings.'

He made the sign of the cross and heaved his squat bulk down the pulpit steps to commence the Eucharist.

The service over, William hurried out into the late morning sunshine and caught up with Ann as she passed through the churchyard gate.

'The old fellow was certainly on form today,' William chirped.

'Oh, they've heard it all before, Sunday after dreary Sunday,' Ann said dismissively. 'Those arrows of his launched with such fury fail to find any chink in armour forged by a lifetime of pious hypocrisy.'

'That bit about cutting off one's cock was new. Must have added that in a desperate attempt to alarm some of the more goatish among his parishioners.'

'Must you be so crude?'

'No, but seriously Ann, that part really did alarm me. As a child I wondered what purpose it served apart from pissing through, and anyway girls seemed to manage without one. It was only when I went to public school and was crudely initiated into the furtive world of schoolboy carnality that I realised it could be a source of very great pleasure. A pleasure I hope I will soon share with you.'

'You're disgusting. I don't think I should continue this walk.'

'Only jesting, Ann.'

'Let's change the subject.'

'Fine.'

'What do you make of all that talk of medieval torture – the gouging out of eyes, molten lead, tearing of entrails and so on?' Ann asked.

William answered cheerfully, 'Oh, I take comfort from the more liberal theologians. They believe the pains of Hell are no more than the remorse of conscience – the consciousness of having forfeited the vision of God and the happiness of Heaven. It will involve no physical pain whatsoever. I can live with that.'

Ann shook her head doubtfully. 'I don't know,' she said. 'There seem to be far more priests like your father than those so-called liberal thinkers.'

William and Ann were walking along a footpath across the fields. The accessibility of her young body sent William into a frenzy of frustration.

'Off back to Shackles tomorrow,' he said. 'Clare and Mother at this very moment are busily packing that bloody big trunk of mine. A vast leather thing bound with strips of wood. Even empty it weighs a ton. When Phillips, the science master, spoke of an irresistible force meeting an immovable mass, it conjured up in my mind the sight of Father grappling with that damn trunk.'

'What's life like in a famous public school?'

'Famous! Second-rank, more like. Even if its founders did choose to emulate, very inadequately, the architecture of Eton.'

'But what's life like for a boy there?'

'God - awful, if you must know. The boys live in The Chamber – a long, cold, clammy, carpetless, barn-like room. Each boy has a wooden stall that rises halfway to the ceiling and is furnished with a desk, bookcase and fold-up bed. The room only has one fireplace and in winter term the boys freeze in their horse stalls. One has to take a bath in an old tin tub placed in the centre of the room where one's naked body becomes the butt of crude jokes. One time they grabbed me and lightly toasted my bare buttocks before the fire.'

'You poor thing!'

'Oh, things will be different this year. I'm moving up to Sixth Form Passage where life will be a lot more civilised. No more Chamber for me. I'll be sharing a room with another sixth-former and dishing out the canings instead of suffering them.'

When they came to a wooden stile William vaulted over easily, but Ann's long skirt hampered her movements. She stood astride the stile, affording William a glimpse of her frilly petticoat. Realising that this was his opportunity, he acted.

'Let me help you,' he called and, placing both his hands up her skirt, he lifted her high in the air. They both tumbled to the ground, laughing. He moved his right hand so that it lay between her legs.

'Stop it – you filthy creature! Take your hand away!' she shrieked.

'Come on, Ann. Don't be a prude.'

William gently stroked the smooth flesh of her thighs. Ann struggled feebly and then lay still. Encouraged, he attempted simultaneously to pull down her drawers and undo his breeches. This was his first time with a girl. His clumsiness and over-excitement led to a messy and humiliating climax. Ann rose and stared disdainfully down at the dishevelled, wretched creature at her feet.

'Ann, you darling, I love you,' William pleaded.

'For all the use it is to me, William, you may as well let them cut it off.'

With a toss of her head, Ann laughed and walked away without a backward glance. Yet she could not repress a certain feeling of disappointment at William's performance.

William rose to his feet and pushed his now limp member back into his breeches.

'Bitch! Haughty, humiliating bitch!' he blustered.

When he got back to the Rectory his mother and sister were carefully packing his trunk. He looked compassionately at his mother and sister as they bent diligently over their task. Life with Father had drained all colour from their cheeks and light from their eyes. His sister Clare already had the appearance of the middle-aged spinster she was destined to become; his mother raised her head and gave him a sad smile. He was glad to be escaping tomorrow.

The following morning his father helped him heave the trunk onto the trap while Mother and Clare stood impassively in the doorway. The driver sat holding the reins.

'I trust, my good man, that you will render some assistance to my son when he has to load this trunk onto the train,' gasped Charles.

'Oh yes, your reverence.'

William walked over to the subservient figures in the doorway and kissed them both on the cheek.

'You will write regularly, won't you, William?' his mother whispered.

'Yes, as always, Mother,' he answered. 'Bye, Clare.'

Clare gave a wan smile. William climbed up beside the driver.

'God be with you, my son. Avoid the temptations of the Devil,' bellowed Charles as the pony broke into a trot.

Clare and her mother waved and William raised his hand in farewell.

As he humped his trunk up the stairs to Sixth Form Passage, William thanked the gods that he would no longer have to endure the privations of the Chamber. At the head of the stairs he stopped in front of a door bearing the legend 'Tancred Bowles; William Dawson'. This information dismayed William. Tancred was a second-year sixth-former who was going up to Oxford to read Greats. He was tall and his hair was a profusion of tight blond curls. To William, who had long worshipped him from a distance, Tancred was a Greek god.

'Jesus,' William muttered, 'What's he going to make of short-arsed, nondescript me?'

It was late evening before Tancred strode into the room, flinging a large brimmed hat onto his bed.

'William, isn't it?' he said. 'Pleased to be sharing with you.'

He held out his hand, and William, rising in some confusion from his desk, tentatively placed his hand in its firm grasp.

'God!' Tancred continued. 'What a bore.'

'Coming back to college you mean?' ventured William.

'Good God, no. I'm quite looking forward to this trimester. Old Spear is going to do *A Midsummer Night's Dream* and the chaplain is giving a series of lectures on comparative historical linguistics.'

'Sounds like a barrel of laughs.'

'Well of course, William, if all that is not to your taste, there is always the vicarious pleasure of beating small boys on the bare buttocks with a cane.'

'Oh no. Not at all. I'm not like that,' William stammered.

'Thank God for that. I would hate to share a room with a latent paedophilic sadist.'

'What's the bore then?'

'Pardon?'

'You said "what a bore".'

'Oh, that. Travelling up in the train I met an old buffer who was a former colleague of my father at the Foreign Office. He lives near here and has two daughters nearing marriageable age. He invited me over for the weekend and wouldn't take no for an answer.'

'Could be fun. The girls, I mean.'

'You must be joking. Two simpering, pubescent beauties, all baby fat and sweat.'

'Oh. I see,' William said lamely.

'I've told you what my paterfamilias does for a living. How does yours earn an honest crust?'

'Nothing as grand as that. He's a country rector.'

'Believe all that mumbo jumbo, do you?'

William was taken unawares and answered sharply, 'Yes, of course I do.'

'Well I haven't time to argue. I have to unpack. We'll debate the issue another time.'

When that time came William's beliefs received a severe jolt. They were in the Sixth Form Common Room after vespers, sitting in front of a roaring fire. Tancred sprawled in an easy chair, his long legs stretched out and his feet resting on the fender. William sat tense and nervous on an upright chair facing him.

'You believe all the stories in the Bible?' Tancred asked casually.

'Well my father does. Since he makes his living peddling the stuff, he has to. But I know as well as you that Jonah couldn't have lived three days in the belly of a whale. The poor bugger could never have got down the whale's throat and survived. Moses never parted the Red Sea any more than Canute was able to stop the tide wetting his feet. No, of course I don't believe such stories. But I do believe in Jesus.'

'So you believe in Jesus?'

'Yes, I do and I only wish I could live as he lived – unselfish and pure.'

'Does your belief make you happy?'

William hesitated and looked puzzled. 'Well, in truth I would have to say it doesn't,' he said.

'Believe not and eternal damnation follows. Agreed?'

William nodded.

'Then,' asked Tancred, 'what about all the poor sods who lived before Christ? Doesn't seem fair to condemn them to everlasting torture. What do you say?'

William shrugged his shoulders and was silent.

Tancred returned to the attack. 'This Jesus of yours. Matthew tells us that he was of the seed of

9

David through Joseph his father. But in the next chapter we are told that his father was the Holy Ghost, not Joseph.'

'Christ is a historical figure who instituted the Eucharist and thus founded the Catholic Church. The four gospels state that Jesus died at the Feast of the Passover. They all say that on the night of his arrest he gathered some friends together for a Last Supper,' William parroted. 'That's no story. It's a fact.'

'Is that so? Three of the Gospels claim that the Eucharist was instituted during or after the traditional Jewish Passover meal. This means that every event that follows – the arrest of Jesus, his trial and his execution – must be a work of fiction.'

'Why?'

'Because it's unthinkable that the Jews would have broken their most sacred religious observances in order to put a man on trial at that time.'

'I repeat, I do believe in Jesus, the Son of God.'

'Who is this God?'

'He made heaven and earth. All this,' said William waving his arms vaguely in the air.

'And who made God?'

'Who made God?' stuttered William, his face betraying the fact that this question had never occurred to him before.

'Yes,' persisted Tancred. '*Who made God*?'

'*I don't know*!' yelled William, now utterly exasperated.

'You as a Christian can't answer that simple question. Doesn't say much for your religion. But rejoice. If Christianity is a fairy story, all the prohibitions associated with it are defunct. We can live life exactly as we please and indulge in any pleasure or perversity that takes our fancy.'

Tancred leant forward and gently stroked William's face.

That action had disturbed William and during the next few days he waited, in a state of apprehension and excitement, to see if Tancred would make further advances. However, Tancred behaved as if the incident had never happened.

A few days later, as they lounged in their room, Tancred raised the subject of the Dramatic Society.

'I must insist you join the Dram. Soc.,' he said. 'I'm surprised you're not a member. Where have you been all these years?'

William responded dismissively, 'Oh I'm more a sporting type. Always looked on the members of G.O.D.S. as being a collection of effete show-offs.'

'Indeed!'

'No offence meant. Present company excepted, of course.'

'I should think so. But you must join. Spear has spent all his holiday researching old manuscripts on theatre history, trying to discover how Shakespeare staged his plays. He's going to expound on the results this evening.'

'By the way, what on earth do the initials G.O.D.S. stand for? I can make out "Dramatic Society" but the G and O?'

Tancred shot William an amused glance. 'You are an ass, William. It's not an acronym, it means Gods as in the top seats of the upper circle.'

They both laughed.

It was with considerable misgivings that, accompanied by Tancred, William joined the small group of thespians in the school hall. Old Spear, though only in his late forties, had aged prematurely. Tall with a pronounced stoop, he had lost most of his hair and the few grey wisps that remained hung lank and lustreless about a narrow, yellow-tinged face. His eyes, however, were as bright as those of a bird of prey.

'Gentlemen, gentlemen,' he began in a high pitched whine. 'Welcome to the world of the Playhouse. Shakespeare's playhouse.'

He drew back the curtains that concealed the rear of the hall and revealed a newly constructed stage. When teaching, Spear had the habit of emphasising key words as if they were in bold capitals, underlined and luminous.

'Here we have the *stage* that projects from its background the *tiring house*. As you can see, it is surrounded on three sides by the audience.'

With surprising agility he leapt up on to the stage and pointed excitedly. 'At either end of the *tiring house* we have the *great doors*, which served as entrances and exits for the actors. Note how high and wide they are. This was to allow the easy passage of large mobs or armies, complete with spears and banners.'

He stared upwards and continued, 'Look! Above the *great doors* we have the *windows*. These were used as acting areas.'

He eyed the pupils. 'Who can give me an example where a *window* would have been used?' he asked.

There was an uneasy silence as his gaze raked the gathering. 'Come on,' he said impatiently.

Tancred raised his arm.

'Yes? Out with it, boy!' Spear snapped.

'When Romeo sees Juliet at her window,' said Tancred.

He recited the relevant lines in the most mellifluous and seductive voice:

'But soft what light through yonder window breaks?

It is the east, and Juliet is the sun!'

This provoked a few ribald laughs and a smattering of applause.

'Yes, yes. Give me another,' Spear demanded.

'*The Taming of the Shrew* – Pendant looks out of a window. *The Merchant of Venice* – Jessica leans out of her window to greet her lover Lorenzo in the street below,' Tancred stated confidently. 'Do you want any more, sir?'

'No, that will be quite sufficient. Tancred, isn't it?'

Tancred nodded.

Spear retreated to the back of the stage and, drawing aside a curtain, revealed a shallow inset space in the centre of the Tiring House. Having warmed to his theme, he spoke confidently without a trace of the irritating mannerism that had earlier marred his speech.

'This space is the Study,' he announced. 'Normally hidden behind a curtain which can be opened to reveal certain scenes. For example: in *The Tempest* – Ferdinand and Miranda playing chess; in *Othello* – the sleeping Desdemona; in *Romeo and Juliet* – Juliet lying drugged in her tomb. Above the Study we have the Chamber.'

At this there was a burst of laughter. Spear was perplexed for an instant and then realised the allusion.

13

'Not *your* Chamber,' he shouted, 'Shakespeare's Chamber! This was also used as an acting area. In *Richard II*, the facade of the Tiring House is Flint Castle and the Chamber represents the battlements of the castle. Bolingbroke and his army enter upon the Stage through the Great Doors while Richard and his retinue appear above in the Chamber. Later Richard descends to ground level.'

At this point Tancred interrupted:

'Down, down, I come, like glistening Phaeton, Wanting the manage of unruly jades.

In the base court? Base court, where Kings grow base,

To come at traitors' calls and do them grace.

In the base court? Come down? Down, court! Down king!'

This was said with such noble pathos and awareness of the poetic flow of the verse that it was followed by an awed silence, while Tancred sat feigning complete indifference.

'Very good, Tancred. It's a pity we're doing *A Midsummer Night's Dream*, not *Richard II*,' said Spear, breaking the silence.

'Oh, I'm sure you'll find me a part,' answered Tancred.

'Well let's get on.'

'Excuse me, sir. Would I be right in thinking that the Chamber would have been used in *Anthony and Cleopatra* as the top of the monument?'

This was Oliver, a pretty junior with blond curls and the face of a fallen angel.

Tancred turned to William with a smirk and whispered, 'My! Listen to Olive getting her little oar in!'

'Yes indeed,' Spear said. 'Anthony is lying wounded on the Stage when Cleopatra and her maids appear in the Chamber. The maids heave Anthony up to Cleopatra and the rest of the scene is played in the Chamber. But we must get on.'

Oliver's interruption encouraged Peter, a lad of Falstaffian proportions, to join in.

'But surely, sir, the Chamber and the Study would be too remote from the audience to be used as acting areas,' he piped.

'Nonsense, boy. The size of a theatre like the Globe was such that the distance from the Chamber or the Study to the back of the Gallery would be no more than sixty feet. We really must get on.'

Spear strode up to one of the two pillars that supported a canopy which covered a large portion of the stage. 'These are the Posts and they support the Canopy which represents Heaven and was probably painted with signs of the Zodiac. These Posts also served as stage furniture such as trees. Edgar, in *King Lear*, leads his blind father to "the shadow of a tree." In *As You Like It*, Orlando hangs his verses to Rosalind on a tree.'

'As well as being Heaven, the canopy would be useful to keep the rain off the actors since the theatre was open to the skies,' Peter piped up again.

Ignoring him, Spear moved to the centre of the stage and pointed to the trap door. 'Here we have the Trap Door. It served many purposes. Any suggestions?'

The previous contributions by Tancred, Oliver and Peter encouraged some of the others and ideas were bawled out in rapid succession.

'Hell.'

'Ophelia's grave.'

'The witches' cauldron rising from beneath the ground.'

'The hatch on the deck of the ship in *The Tempest*.'

'The discipline of the mines in *Henry V*.'

Spear raised his arms, 'Enough.' He clambered down from the stage and walking amongst them spoke with a quiet intensity, 'What was the purpose of all these different stages? I'll tell you. With very little in the way of stage props it enabled the production to proceed with rapidity and uninterrupted continuity. None of your laborious scene-shifting and long intervals that so bedevil productions today. Shakespeare used words to paint his scenes and conjured up the settings in the imagination of his audience. That's how we will perform *A Midsummer Night's Dream*. Auditions here after vespers tomorrow.'

Before he started the auditions Spear gave the putative cast a short lecture on the history and the plot of the play.

'*A Midsummer Night's Dream* was written in 1594, probably to celebrate a wedding in a noble family. Some have conjectured that Queen Elizabeth was a guest.

'The plot: Theseus, Duke of Athens, and Hippolyta, Queen of the Amazons, are to marry. As part of the celebrations, Bottom the weaver and a group of tradesmen are planning to perform a play and decide to rehearse in a forest near Athens.

'Hermia is in love with Lysander but her father insists that she marry Demetrius. Her father brings her before Theseus who orders her on pain of death to marry Demetrius. Hermia and Lysander decide to elope and confide their plan to Helena, who is in love with Demetrius. She, to win his affection, tells Demetrius. That night all four lovers steal into the same forest where Bottom and his companions are rehearsing.

'Oberon and Titania, fairy rulers of the forest, have quarrelled and Oberon orders Puck, a sprite, to squeeze the juice of a magic plant into the eyes of the sleeping Titania so that she will fall in love with the first creature she sees on waking up. This results in her falling rapturously in love with Bottom, who has been bewitched and given a donkey's head by Puck.

'Theseus also tells Puck to use it on Demetrius so that he will fall in love with Helena, but Puck, mistaking the two youths, uses it on Lysander instead, who promptly falls in love with Helena. Eventually all the enchantments are lifted. The human lovers are happily paired; Titania and Oberon are reconciled. The three couples are married and Bottom's troupe perform their play.'

William ventured a question, 'What's it all mean, sir?'

A wistful smile lit up Spear's ugly face. 'It's a great celebration of love consummated in marriage,' he said gently.

In the auditions that followed, Tancred secured the dual role of Hippolyta/Titania while, to his consternation, William was given the dual role of Theseus/Oberon. Never having acted before, he felt a nagging apprehension but was secretly pleased that in both parts he would be playing opposite Tancred. Young Oliver was cast as Puck, Peter as Bottom.

During the next few weeks they concentrated on learning how to master the text. In the rehearsals Spear became increasingly relaxed as he communicated his love of Shakespeare to the boys. He explained that actors usually made a mess of speaking blank verse. The secret, he said, was to make the rhythm of the verse an intrinsic part of your being. Then you could mould the lines to the sense of the piece. He conjured up a picture of Shakespeare in the wings, frantically writing the last act of a play while the actors were on stage performing the first act.

When William questioned the feasibility of this Spear laughed and said, 'Well, it mightn't have been quite as frenetic as that. But it is important to realise that Shakespeare didn't write his plays in some ivory tower. He was writing for the commercial theatre. His players were a company who rehearsed and performed six plays a week during the season. Also, he had to tailor the characters to the actors he had available. When William Kemp was his chief comedian, he created comic characters like Bottom and Dogberry but when Robert Armin replaced Kemp, the nature of the comic parts changed. They became more complex and touched with melancholy. We had Touchstone, Feste and the Fool in *Lear*. Another problem, which we also have, is that women had to be played by boy-players. But this provides opportunities as well as difficulties.'

Oliver asked, 'Tell me, sir. Do we know the parts that Shakespeare played?'

Spear shrugged his shoulders and said, 'A tricky question that, but contemporary sources indicate that he played small, elegiac parts like old Adam in *As You Like It*, the Ghost in *Hamlet*, and that he acted them exceedingly well.'

Oliver persisted, 'What part did he play in *A Midsummer Night's Dream*?'

'Duke Theseus, we think.'

At this point, William could not resist asking, 'Did he double as Oberon?'

'I would have thought not, since his duties with the company were onerous enough as it was. So you have one up on Shakespeare there, young Dawson.'

When they had all learned their lines, Spear moved on to the business of acting. He quoted Hamlet's advice to the players: 'Do not saw the air too much with your hand, thus, but use all gently; for in the very torrent, tempest, and as I may say the whirlwind of your passion, you must acquire and beget a temperance that may give it smoothness.'

'Restraint and moderation at all times then, sir,' said Tancred to general amusement.

Spear, however, had one big surprise for them. They turned up for one rehearsal to find a large inverted coloured umbrella suspended from the canopy midway between the posts. Oliver's face betrayed genuine alarm when Spear informed him that he would spend most of the play astride this umbrella, swinging energetically backwards and forwards.

'But surely, sir, Shakespeare wouldn't have used a big coloured umbrella seesawing like that.'

'How do you know?' demanded Spear. 'There at the time, were you?'

'Well no, sir,' stammered Oliver. 'But it doesn't seem...Shakespearianish, if you see what I mean.'

'No. I do not see what you mean. Shakespeare was a showman and he would have used anything that came to hand.'

CHAPTER 2

On the afternoon of April 3, 1814, the Palace at Fontainebleau echoed to the sound of stamping as four Marshals of France, booted and spurred, marched down one of its marble-floored corridors towards the study of Napoleon, Emperor of the French. Each was attired in the campaign dress of a Marshal of the Empire.

Upon the head stood a cocked hat with looped and chastened gold lace trimming and edged with white ostrich feathers, the cockade secured to the hat with a strap of black edged in gold. The coat was a single-breasted tailcoat with stand-up collar, the collar and cuffs ornamented with gold leaf embroidery. A plastron of gold oak leaves covered the chest and flowed down the tails of the coat and the front and back of the sleeves. The buttons bore crossed batons and a trophy of arms. A white silk scarf encircled each man's neck, and the waist sash was of gold, as were the epaulets. Above the sash was the crescent which carried the crossed batons and four stars. White riding breeches and shining black riding boots completed the magnificent uniform.

At their head was Marshal Ney – impetuous Ney, known throughout France as the bravest of the brave. Behind him, matching stride for stride, came the Marshals Moncey, Lefèbvre and Macdonald, their spurs and swords jingling in unison.

Two days earlier the armies of Russia, Prussia and Austria had entered Paris and in his study the beleaguered Napoleon stood peering despairingly over maps scattered across his desk. In contrast to the preening peacocks bearing down upon him, Bonaparte was dressed in a soiled grey greatcoat. His face was lined with fatigue and covered with sweat. A loud peremptory knocking heralded the entry of his Marshals. For a moment they stood confronting him, then Macdonald stepped forward.

'Sire,' he said, 'the Allied armies are entrenched in Paris and have established a provisional government.'

'Yes, yes, but you know I plan to attack Paris and drive them from the soil of France,' Napoleon answered impatiently. 'A man isn't finished when he's defeated. He's finished when he quits.'

He beckoned them towards the desk but the marshals refused to move.

Macdonald, summoning up his courage, said firmly, 'We've decided to make an end to this. We disapprove of your intention to attack Paris. We don't want Paris to suffer the same fate as Moscow.'

'With or without you, I will lead the army against Paris,' Napoleon retorted angrily.

For a moment dismay spread across the faces of the marshals, then Ney spoke. 'The army will not march.'

At this Napoleon shouted, 'The army will obey me!'

'No Sire,' Ney replied. 'The army will obey its generals.'

'And I made all my generals out of common clay,' Napoleon said bitterly.

He instantly regretted that remark and, stepping forward, raised his hands in a conciliatory gesture.

'Comrades in arms,' he began and then addressed each man in turn. 'Lefèbvre, commander of the Old Guard, brave as a lion in battle. Moncey, remember how you proudly bore Frederick the Great's sword in the triumphal procession through Paris after we defeated him at Jena? Macdonald, my dependable old friend. Ney, the man who held the bridge at Kovno; commanded the rearguard of the Grand Armée and led them across a thousand fields of snow. Every man who survived the terrible retreat from Moscow owes his life to your courage and brilliance.'

His eyes filled with tears. Encompassing them all with a sweep of his arm he continued, 'I love you and you love me. We're bound together in that fellowship of blood forged on the battlefields of Europe. Join me in France's hour of need.'

Visibly moved, Ney stepped forward and knelt before the Emperor.

'Sire,' he said, 'our families are still in Paris. How can we sacrifice them and the lives of our men for a cause that even you must realise is lost? Abdicate in favour of your son and the dynasty can yet be saved.'

Napoleon slumped into a chair and sat with his head in his hands. When he spoke his voice was quiet but clear.

'I have not been conquered by men. I have been punished by God. Yes, I know I love power. But it is as an artist that I love it. I love it as a musician loves his violin, to draw out its sounds and chords and harmonies.'

He raised his head and said briskly, ' Go. I will give my answer in the morning.'

The marshals turned and silently filed from the room. When they had gone Bonaparte slowly raised his head.

'No!' he cried as he pulled from his pocket a small, silver-framed portrait of his three-year-old son. He gazed despairingly on those features so dear to him. Would he ever hold him in his arms again? He hoped that Joseph and his mother had fled Paris before the Allied invasion. Could he trust Marie Louise? Would she betray him and take their son to the court of her father Francis I of Austria? He could not bear the thought of his son being brought up under the jurisdiction of his enemies.

For the past two years, fear of capture had made him wear, concealed under his shirt, a small black bag on a string round his neck. The bag contained opium, belladonna and white hellebore. Loosening the neck of his shirt he grasped the bag and pulled the string over his head. He laid the bag on the table and opened it out.

Was this how he wished to end it? All the promise and determination that had characterised him from his time as a pupil at Brienne Academy, where the despised runt from Corsica had outshone the other students and led them in games based on the battles of antiquity, rallying his companions when all seemed lost.

He remembered: the time when as Major Bonaparte he had placed his artillery on the promontory above Toulon and blasted the English fleet from the harbour; the time when as Brigadier General he had saved the revolution by mounting his guns to command the streets leading to the Tuilleries and, as the mob surged forward, had given the order to fire, thus destroying the power of the Paris mob. He recalled the years of struggle; the long roll of victories, culminating in that moment when he placed upon his head the gold laurel crown that made him Emperor of the French; his marriage to Marie Louise and the birth of his son Napoleon Francis Charles Joseph whom, in earnest of glories to come, he created King of Rome.

Napoleon rose to his feet. Within five years after his coronation he had created an Empire greater than any since the days of Rome. All Europe had lain beneath his yoke and the birth of his son had heralded the foundations of a dynasty that he had hoped would last for a thousand years.

He snatched the bag from the table and strode over to the fireplace. He flung it into the fire and watched as a bright flame flared and died in an instant.

'That vision must not die. I will save the succession for my son,' he whispered.

The following morning he wrote out an instrument of abdication.

"The Allied powers having proclaimed that the Emperor Napoleon is the sole obstacle to the re-establishment of peace in Europe, the Emperor Napoleon, faithful to his oath, declares that he is ready to descend from the throne, to leave France and to lay down his life for the welfare of his country, which is inseparable from the rights of his son, those of the regency of the Empress, and the maintenance of the laws of the Empire. Given at our palace of Fontainebleau on this day April 4 in the year 1814."

He summoned Ney, Macdonald and Caulaincourt as witnesses and signed the document. He ordered them to deliver it to the Allied commanders in Paris and negotiate the details of his surrender.

'Gentlemen,' he said, 'my fate rests in your persuasive skills. May they be as efficacious as your military abilities.'

They were not.

Two weeks later a carriage drew up in front of the Imperial Palace at Hofburg. It was late afternoon. Footmen hurried to open the carriage door and lower the steps. A small party of courtiers led by the Austrian Chancellor Metternich advanced from the palace. Marie Louise descended from the carriage followed by a lady-in-waiting who helped the diminutive Joseph, King of Rome, negotiate the steps. Metternich gave a perfunctory bow and escorted the party into the palace. They proceeded down the corridor, Marie Louise and Metternich in front with Joseph toddling behind holding the lady-in-waiting's hand.

Marie Louise turned to Metternich and asked, 'Have you news of my husband?'

'Bonaparte is to be exiled to the island of Elba,' he answered tersely.

'And the succession?'

'The Bourbons have been restored. Long live Louis XVIII of France.'

'And what of my son?'

'He will be brought up as an Austrian aristocrat – as befits the grandson of Emperor Francis I of Austria.'

They stopped in front of a closed door guarded by a gigantic Tyrolean Chasseur.

'Inform the Emperor that his daughter Princess Marie Louise and his grandson, Francis Charles Joseph, have arrived from France and await his pleasure.'

The soldier opened the door and disappeared into the room beyond. Almost immediately Emperor Francis emerged wearing a carpenter's leather apron with the tools of the trade protruding from every pocket. He briefly acknowledged Marie Louise then, brushing wood shavings from his apron, he bent down and stared suspiciously at little Joseph, before lifting him up and carrying him into his workshop. Metternich and Marie Louise followed.

Francis placed the boy carefully on the workbench and continued to study him intently.

'So this is the young eaglet. Ah! The stubborn set of the jaw, the unblinking stare of those black eyes. I see the father in that face,' Francis muttered.

'I want to see my papa,' Joseph piped defiantly.

'Oh no! You'll never see your papa again,' Francis said softly. Turning to Metternich he barked, 'Metternich! We must erase all memory of his father. See he has Austrian tutors and if he speaks French, flog him.'

Marie Louise gave a cry of protest and stepped forward.

'As for you, madam,' Francis said, 'find yourself some comfortable castle well away from court and stay there. I don't want you influencing the boy and reminding him of that monster, his father.'

The Emperor swept Joseph off the bench and thrust him into the startled Chancellor's arms.

'Take him away and start the brat's re-education!' he stormed.

As Metternich carried him out through the door, Joseph glared back at Emperor Francis.

'I want to see my papa. Why won't they let me see my papa any more?' he yelled.

Francis shouted back, 'Remember! If he speaks French, flog him.'

Nearly a year had passed when Metternich brought Emperor Francis some disturbing news.

'Escaped from Elba and landed in France, you say?'

'Landed at Cannes with a thousand men. He plans to march on Paris. Louis is dispatching a large force and intends to intercept him at Grenoble. That should see the end of Monsieur Bonaparte.'

Francis shook his head and said, 'I don't know. That man is a devil.'

At Grenoble Napoleon was confronted by the 5th Regiment of the Line. He stepped out in front of his men and stood facing the levelled muskets of Louis' soldiers. He tore open his tunic and bared his chest.

'Soldiers of France,' he cried, 'you can shoot your Emperor if you dare! Do you not recognise me as your Emperor? Am I not your former general?'

An officer gave the order to fire but old loyalties prevailed. The guns wavered and then were lowered.

A great cry went up, 'Vive l'Empereur!' Those sent out to halt his advance had joined it.

When the news reached King Louis he was lounging indolently among his courtiers.

'My men joined him! Did the devil bewitch them? God help me, I'm surrounded by traitors,' he whimpered, his fat bulk trembling.

He summoned Marshal Ney. 'Marshal,' he pleaded, 'can I trust you?'

Ney cast a disdainful eye over the sycophants and scoundrels who infested the Tuileries and answered, 'Sire, give me the men and I will bring Napoleon back to Paris in an iron cage.'

As Ney turned to leave Louis muttered, 'I didn't ask him to say that.' With a nervous grin he added, 'Napoleon in an iron cage, eh? Well, I wouldn't like such a bird in my room.'

* * *

Napoleon confronted Ney at Auxerre, with predictable results. Opening his arms he said to Ney, 'Michel! Would you destroy your old chief? Come let us be comrades in arms again.'

Ney, with tears streaming down his face, rushed forward and embraced Napoleon. The two armies cheered

'I must send a message to Louis,' said Napoleon.

'And what might that be?' asked Ney.

'Dispatch no more troops against me. I have enough.'

The two men laughed.

Realising the situation was hopeless, Louis fled in panic. Napoleon was carried shoulder high into the Tuileries by the Paris mob and placed once again upon the imperial throne, where he reigned for one hundred days before he was forced to confront the Allied armies led by Wellington at Waterloo.

It was the eve of battle. Napoleon had set up his headquarters at Le Caillou, a pink and white farmhouse. It was a night of torrential rain. He had removed his soaking clothes and lay wrapped in a blanket on a truss of straw in front of a roaring fire. His marshals, including Ney, stood attentively before him.

'Gentlemen,' he said, 'this is a war I did not want. God knows I offered to live in peace with the allied powers if they would but recognise the dynasty I have founded. This they chose not to do. So be it. We have inflicted a crushing defeat on the Prussians at Ligny and I have ordered Grouchy to pursue Blücher's retreating army.'

Ney intervened. 'Sire, would it not be better to keep Grouchy's regiments with our main body and not split our forces in this way?'

A look of annoyance flashed across Napoleon's pale face. For the past few days he had been suffering from the pain of a severe attack of haemorrhoids and as a result his mood was one of extreme irritability.

'We don't want the Prussians turning back and interfering with my destruction of Wellington at Waterloo,' he snapped.

'But what if Blücher gives him the slip and—'

'Enough, Ney!' Napoleon thundered. 'Grouchy's task is to drive Blücher away from Waterloo and then join us. He has orders to march to the sound of the guns.'

Seeing the look of dismay on Ney's face, Napoleon's mood changed. 'Come, Ney. We have ninety chances in our favour and not ten against us.'

Ney gave a wry smile and joined in the laughter.

Late the following day Napoleon and his staff officers stood on a small prominence overlooking the battlefield. The battle had been hard and bloody but it now appeared as if the French were prevailing. One of the officers was looking through a pair of binoculars into the distance.

He called out excitedly, 'Sire! Grouchy is approaching. The battle is won.'

Napoleon snatched the glasses and raised them to his eyes. He saw an army approaching with banners flying. His face turned white and he spoke in a whisper.

'Grouchy? No! It's Blücher. God damn him!'

For an instant Napoleon stood transfixed, seeming incapable of action. He recalled Ney's words of the previous night and his own scornful retort. With a great effort he roused himself from the despair and weariness that was paralysing him.

'I must act swiftly!' he cried. 'Order to Ney. Advance the Imperial Guard.'

Napoleon's fate was sealed when he sent the grizzled and invincible veterans of the Imperial Guard marching inexorably forward with their drums beating the *pas de charge*. As they advanced, line after line of redcoats rose from the ground and poured volley after volley into the serried ranks of the advancing Guardsmen. Under this withering fire they stumbled to a halt and, for the first time in their proud and blood-soaked history, faltered and started to retreat. A cry of incredulity rolled like a great wave through the French army: 'La Garde recule!'

Wellington, sensing victory, waved forward the Allied troops and the retreat became a rout. Napoleon, to cover the withdrawal of his main force, ordered the remaining units of his Old Guard to form squares and check the Allied pursuit. This they did bravely but to no avail. The French were swept from the field. As dusk fell one mangled square remained bloodied but defiant on the field of carnage.

Sickened by the slaughter, a British commander stepped forward and addressed them, 'Men of France. We salute you. The day is lost but you have done more than flesh and blood can endure. Surrender and we will spare your lives.'

But from the depths of that heap of dead and dying men a voice hurled hoarse defiance, 'Merde.'

A fusillade of shots rang out and the voice was silenced.

Napoleon, wrapped in his grey greatcoat, clambered into his carriage and drove off the field and out of history.

Joseph eyed Emperor Francis defiantly.

'Time, my little man,' Francis said kindly, 'for another serious chat. Getting along well with your Uncle Ferdinand, I hear. Saw you the other day rolling him along the corridor in a wastepaper basket. Though, considering you're eighteen years younger than he is, it should have been the other way round. What!'

'He's an idiot.'

'Well, yes, I'm afraid you might be right but he's kind enough.'

'Yes I suppose so. It's Uncle Charles I hate.'

'Oh, be careful there. Charles could one day become Emperor of Austria.' I can't believe I'm having this conversation with a four-year-old, thought Francis.

Joseph looked serious and said, 'I see.' Brightening he added, 'What does that matter to me? I'm going to be Emperor of the French like papa.'

Francis lifted the boy up onto the workbench and placed an arm around his shoulder.

'You know how fond I've grown of you over this last year. For your own good you must listen carefully to what I have to say. Your father has been defeated in a great battle and has been sent to a distant island as a prisoner.' Francis paused and then continued emphatically: 'Note my words. He is finished and you'll never be an emperor – of the French or anyone.'

The boy's eyes filled with tears and his lips trembled.

'Come on, there's a brave lad,' Francis said. 'We'll make an Austrian aristocrat of you yet. What could be more beautiful than the palace at Schönbrunn?'

'Saint Cloud is nicer than Schönbrunn.'

'What could be more magnificent than the Tyrolean Chasseurs?'

'I like French soldiers better than Austrian ones.'

'Tell you what, when you're a little older I'll make you Duke of Reichstadt.'

'You old goat, I don't want to be an Austrian!' Joseph exploded.

He jumped from the bench and ran out of the room. Francis stared after him.

'With your father on Saint Helena and your mother banished to Parma, we'll tame you yet,' he muttered.

Sixteen years had passed. In a room in the palace at Schönbrunn, Sophia, the wife of Archduke Charles, reclined on a divan. She was twenty-six years old and in the full bloom of her dark-eyed beauty.

A court attendant appeared in the doorway and announced, 'The Duke of Reichstadt to visit the Archduchess Sophia.'

Joseph entered. He was twenty years old and six foot in height but in his brooding intelligent face one saw the hypnotic power of his dead father, Napoleon Bonaparte.

Sophia extended her hand. 'Oh Joseph, my dear friend!' she exclaimed. 'What would life be in this barbarous place without your congenial company?'

'Come, flatterer,' Reichstadt laughed. 'It was you who transformed my life when you married Charles. Was it five years ago? Until then my only companions were uncouth Charles and his idiot brother Ferdinand.'

'Oh, Charles is an ignorant bore. The other day I expressed my sorrow at Schubert's death and he just grunted and said Schubert was only a bloody maker of tunes so who the hell cared.'

Reichstadt raised his hands and smiled sympathetically.

'And yesterday,' Sophia continued. 'He caught me reading Heine's new collection of poems and said who would want to read that revolutionary little shit. He then went off to grope one of those fat bitches, the so-called ladies of the court. I've served my purpose – provided him with an heir – so he feels free to indulge in his propensity for coarse loose women. Once in a while, when the mood takes him, he clambers into my bed and brutalises me.'

'I'll always remember the first time I set eyes on you. It was at your wedding. You were dressed in a gown of green velvet with a net of white lace covering your shining chestnut hair.'

He took a step towards her but Sophia rose quickly and moved away with a nervous laugh.

During the months that followed Reichstadt and Sophia grew closer. They would be seen strolling in the gardens of the Schönbrunn – he with his hands clasped behind his back while she glided along, the flounces of her colourful dress floating over the ground. One afternoon, as they sat beside one of the fountains that bejewelled the gardens, she questioned him about the time he was torn from the Tuileries, never to see his father again.

35

A shadow passed across Reichstadt's face. 'At night in sleep my cries still echo down the years,' he said. His voice dropped to a whisper. 'I want to see my Papa. Why won't they let me kiss Papa any more?'

'And your father? What memories of him?'

'I remember the times he carried me in his arms as he reviewed the Old Guard and the times he stood with his arms folded across his chest, watching me as I marched with straight back and toy musket over my shoulder across the lawns of the Tuileries.'

'His final years on Saint Helena?'

'Over the years Metternich attempted to stop all news of my father reaching me but faithful friends smuggled out word. They told me how he would sit for hours staring at a silver-framed portrait of me as a small boy. They said his love for me was the one thing that transcended all his desire for pomp, military glory and power. When he died he had pathetically little to leave me in his will: a collection of pistols; the gold dressing case he used at Ulm and Jenna; his camp beds; the blue coat he wore at Marengo; the sword he carried at Austerlitz.'

Reichstadt, his voice edged with bitterness, continued: 'And Metternich forbade me even those few pitiful tokens of my father's love. He died before his time, killed by the English and their hired assassins. He wished his ashes to rest on the banks of the Seine in the midst of the French people that he loved so much. But they buried him on the island, alongside a stream where he loved to walk. He was dressed in his favourite uniform, that of the Chasseurs de la Garde. The stone covering his grave bears no name, only the words *Here Lies*.'

He smiled and, laying his hand on the sword at his side said, 'But I have this. The sword he carried at the battle of the Pyramids.'

Sophia leant forward and placed her hand on his knee.

As time passed their intimacy intensified. They would drive in a closed carriage along the shady boulevards of Vienna's Prater Park, their hands entwined. He was confined by Metternich, ever suspicious and fearful of Reichstadt's claim to the throne of France, within the boundaries of Vienna and when Sophia was away from the capital they exchanged affectionate letters in which they discussed the latest fashion in music and the arts, and exchanged coded amorous messages.

Sophia had a small salon in the imperial residence at the Hofburg. He would come most evenings, Sophia would make him tea, and they would read aloud to each other and talk of events at court. One evening Sophia was gently reciting a love poem by Heine. She held the book in one hand and with her other hand she played nervously with a gold cross hung around her neck. Her white gown was low cut and the cross brushed against the bare flesh of her half-exposed breasts. She was reclining on a chaise-longue and the folds of her dress delineated the lines of her slender, firm body. Sophia let the book slide slowly down onto her lap and gazed across the room to Reichstadt.

She whispered, 'Oh what lies lurk in kisses.'

Reichstadt rose from his chair and crossed the room to stand before her. He knelt and placed his head on her breast.

'No lies would lurk in my kisses,' he murmured. 'Only my despair and my need for your love.'

Those words released the flood of emotions that burnt within them – his resentment at the contrast between the meaningless life he now led and the glorious future his father had planned for him; her anger at being tied to an uncultured pig. They feverishly tore at their clothes until they were both naked. Reichstadt lay beside her and gathered her in his arms. The contact of their bare bodies calmed their passion and they clung together, seeking solace in this new intimacy. When Reichstadt entered her it was with a tenderness born of great need and tremulous hope.

As they parted she grasped his hand and said, 'Joseph, I will pray that you have given me a son.'

Within two months Sophia announced that she was pregnant again. Charles was ecstatic. 'It will be another boy,' he rejoiced, 'a companion for my beloved Francis Joseph.'

He then went off to make himself more drunk than he already was. Sophia and Reichstadt secretly rejoiced that their love had borne fruit.

Reichstadt's sallow skin and thin body bore witness that his health was not robust but he had always led an active life. Now, however, he developed a slight cough that, with the passing months, grew in severity. One morning, while barking orders on the parade ground, blood poured from his mouth. He was confined to his bed where his condition worsened. Sophia had him moved

38

from the Hofburg to her apartments at Schönbrunn and devoted herself to his care.

One particularly hot day, as she wiped the perspiration from his face, he stared up at the high golden ceiling of the bedroom and gave a faint sigh. 'Do you know what comforts me, Sophia, as I lie here dying?' he whispered.

Sophia bent over the bed and slowly shook her head, unable to speak.

'My father slept in this room, possibly in this very bed, after the battles of Austerlitz and Wagram.'

'And in the arms of the Countess Walewska, I believe,' Sophia said with an attempt at playfulness.

Reichstadt smiled wanly. 'Great men have great appetites,' he replied. 'If it were not for the child you carry in your womb, my father's lineage would end here with the death of this poor body.'

Sophia gathered him in her arms and held him close. 'I promise you the child will be a son and he will grow to bestride the world like a colossus.'

Reichstadt settled back on the pillows, his face illumined with a sad longing. 'I pray I'll live to hold him in my arms.'

The next day he became so ill that it was decided to administer the last sacraments. He was carried in a chair to Sophia's private chapel. Sophia knelt by his side before the priest and they prayed together. The rest of Court looked down from a balcony at the back of the church, unaware of the spiritual yet sensuous bond that made them one.

Sophia's confinement was a long and painful one. Reichstadt was near death but he kept asking for news of her. When a servant entered the room and announced that Sophia had given birth to a boy, Reichstadt was in his death agony and beyond understanding.

As the light of morning filtered through the curtains he started up in his bed and gave a great cry, 'Harness the horses! I must go and embrace my father once more.'

He fell back – those dark eyes staring up at the high gold ceiling – and died.

Dressed in the white uniform of the Wasa regiment – booted and spurred – with his father's sword at his side, he was carried for burial in the Augustiner Church. From a high window in the palace a forlorn figure gazed down at the funeral procession; tears slowly trickled down her pale sad face. She cradled in her arms the baby, Archduke Maximilian, whom the world believed was Charles' second son. But she treasured deep within her the secret that he was the son of her dear, dead lover and the grandson of Napoleon Bonaparte.

CHAPTER 3

News of Reichstadt's death eventually reached a dilapidated castle on Lake Constantine in Switzerland, where Napoleon's stepdaughter, Hortense, lived in exile with her one surviving son, Louis Napoleon. As she sat on the small balcony gazing over the lake, Hortense thought back over the ravelled skein of circumstances that made Reichstadt's death so momentous an event for her son. She was the daughter of Josephine and Vicomte Alexandre de Beauharnais.

'Rose then, not Josephine,' Hortense murmured. 'Her names were Rose and Josèphe. Napoleon took Josèphe, softened it to Josephine, and insisted that should be her name in future.'

After the revolution, Alexandre de Beauharnais had risen to be a general but his dissolute ways had led to imprisonment. Rose had fought in vain for his release and as a result ended up joining him in the Carmelite prison. Hortense's countenance darkened as a shadow of remembered pain crept slowly across her face. She and her brother Eugène had visited their parents every day until one terrible morning they saw on the scaffold outside the prison walls their poor feckless father struggle feebly as the guards thrust his neck beneath the bloodstained blade of the guillotine.

For a time Rose's life had also been in danger but on Robespierre's execution Tallien came to power and, as he was a friend, probably a former lover of Rose, she was released. She and the children went to live in Malmaison, a pretty little house with a bow-shaped garden surrounded with lime trees. There, among the bric-a-brac and chintz, Rose had entertained her friends in the government and it was there that she first met the young Napoleon and was metamorphosed into Josephine.

He was twenty-six and had been made commander of the Army of the Interior. She was thirty-two. He fell passionately in love with her and proposed. She was all Napoleon looked for in a woman – petite, slim, fine skin with kind dark eyes, and a very feminine nature. Josephine, however, found him rather dull and taciturn and could only muster feelings of tepid affection for him. Despite opposition from Hortense and her brother, the marriage took place on the evening of March 9, 1796.

Hortense's reverie was interrupted as Louis Napoleon stumbled onto the balcony. Hortense eyed him fondly. No one could call him handsome, she thought, or graceful, but he was her sweet stubborn boy. He flopped down in a chair swinging his short legs, his feet just scraping the floor.

'You can't beat a fast gallop to clear your head,' he said as he whacked the side of the chair with his riding crop.

'I was thinking of your uncle's wedding night,' Hortense said.

'When Josephine's dog...what was his name?'

'Fortuné. A fawn pug dog with a black face and a tail like a corkscrew.'

'That's right, Fortuné. Didn't the little beggar bite Napoleon on the buttocks as he clambered into the nuptial bed, where Josephine lay passively awaiting his amorous attentions? You've told me about it often enough.'

'The calf, Louis, not his buttocks!' Hortense gave a short laugh and continued, 'All hell broke loose as your uncle, his leg streaming blood, hobbled out of the bedroom with Fortuné snapping at his heels.'

'Probably thought he was defending her from a fate worse than death.'

'Today's news has brought all the old memories flooding back.'

'You know,' mused Louis, 'the relationships in our family are very peculiar. Josephine was your mother and so that makes her my grandmother but because you married Napoleon's brother after she married Napoleon that makes her my aunt.'

'Despite her infidelities Napoleon loved her to distraction, you know. I remember him telling me, "I only win battles but she wins people's hearts." Faced with such devotion she came to love him totally too.'

Louis shook his head slowly. 'Yes. A pity he had to divorce her and marry that stiff-necked Austrian.'

'He had to have an heir and Josephine was incapable of bearing any more children. I believe it

43

was the result of falling from that collapsing balcony in the Tuileries.'

'Well, you know what they say.'

'No. What do they say?' Hortense enquired tartly.

'In politics there is no heart.'

'A typically masculine sentiment. Josephine kept Napoleon's room at Malmaison precisely as he left it, a history book lying open at the very page he had stopped reading. She never gave up hope that he would return to her.'

'Did he ever return to Malmaison?'

'Yes, but that was after Waterloo and Josephine had died the previous May. I was there to receive him, for I could not abandon the man whom I had called Father. The hour of his misfortune was the one for me to manifest my gratitude to him. As we walked in the garden, I remember it was the most beautiful day, he spoke lovingly of Josephine: "Poor Josephine," he said. "I cannot reconcile myself to this place without her. I expect to see her coming down one of these paths gathering the flowers she so loved. She was the most alluring creature. If she could but have borne me an heir, we need never have parted."

'Shortly before she died he had written to her from Elba saying she was always in his thoughts. I was told that, when he lay on his death bed, Napoleon said Josephine had appeared before him but when he went to embrace her she stepped back and told him they would soon be together again, never more to part.'

Louis gave a bitter laugh. 'No one could say the marriages in our family had particularly happy outcomes,' he said. 'Poor old Father wasn't exactly a paragon as a husband or father.'

A nostalgic smile brightened, for an instant, Hortense's sad face and she whispered, 'Ah. You should have known your father when I married him – handsome, talented, so warm and kind in his dealings with people. He was Napoleon's favourite brother.'

She sighed and continued, 'Then some obscure blood disease, the doctors never discovered what it was, paralysed his hands and reduced him to a pathetic crippled wreck. Believe me, Louis, I would have gone on loving and caring for him but his whole nature changed. He became a whining, vindictive hypochondriac who made life hell for us all. I had to leave him.'

'I'm not reproaching you, Mother. I remember what it was like.'

Hortense sprang from her chair with a new-found vitality and started to pace up and down the length of the balcony. 'With poor Rome's death this makes you Napoleon's heir and the rightful Emperor of the French,' she said.

'Try telling that to Louis Philippe. He thinks the throne of France already has an occupant, and that he is that occupant.'

Hortense snorted with contempt, 'The Citizen King! God, when I think of the glory and splendour of the Napoleonic era and compare it with the present court – ruled by that lumpen bourgeois! He travels on public transport and always carries an umbrella around with him.'

Louis looked thoughtful. 'He's popular with the Republicans because they feel he will remain a constitutional monarch,' he said.

'Believe me, he'll change. No man can resist the lure of power. He'll get increasingly authoritarian and corrupt. That will be our opportunity.'

'It will be a long and steep road.'

'Let's make a start.'

'How?'

'From this moment on I'll call you Napoleon.'

They both laughed.

In five years Hortense would be dead and twenty years would pass before Napoleon stood in the Assembly and was proclaimed Emperor of the French – twenty years of frustration and farce.

In October 1836 he presented himself at the barracks of the 4th Artillery Regiment in Strasbourg. The garrison joined him and they marched on the headquarters of the 46th of the line. Here, his claim to be the great Emperor's nephew was scorned by the commandant who loudly proclaimed that he was no more than the bastard son of a captain in the 4th.

Napoleon suffered the indignity of being arrested and deported to America. He returned to France in 1837 to be at the deathbed of his mother and then left for London where Miss Howard, a wealthy courtesan, became his mistress. Financed by Miss Howard, he hired an excursion steamer and, accompanied by nine horses, fifty-five desperados and a stubborn belief in his destiny, set sail for Boulogne.

On landing, they were easily repulsed by Philippe's soldiers and forced to retreat to the shoreline. However, their boat had drifted out to sea and they had to pile into a lifeboat in an attempt to reach it. The episode ended in high farce when the lifeboat capsized and deposited the rebels in the sea. Louis Philippe, exasperated by Napoleon's antics, imprisoned him in the fortress Ham in Picardy. Napoleon promptly escaped and fled back to London and into the welcoming arms of the ever faithful Miss Howard.

In 1848 the moment came that Hortense had foretold. Louis Philippe, his administration having lapsed into lethargy and corruption, was deserted by both the democratic and authoritarian factions and deposed by revolution. Seizing the opportunity Napoleon offered himself as a candidate for the president of the new Republic and was elected by an overwhelming majority. Three years later he converted the Second Republic into the Second Empire with himself as Emperor wielding dictatorial powers. A Napoleon was back on the throne of France.

It was a bleak November day in the year 1852. Albert l'Ouvrier, known as Albert the Worker, made his way through the streets of Paris to the National Assembly – streets that a year ago had resounded to the cries and clamour of riot as the Republicans attempted to resist Louis Napoleon's coup d'état. Elected to the Assembly in April 1851, Albert had played a leading role in that resistance. Many of his comrades were in prison but Albert had been one of the fortunate few who had been granted amnesty and, to show Louis Napoleon's conciliatory nature, he had been allowed to keep his seat in the Assembly.

It was with foreboding that Albert entered the building and took his place among the delegates.

Standing next to him was Pierre Blanc, a fellow member of the small extreme left contingent that maintained a precarious foothold in the Assembly. When Louis appeared the hall erupted. Hats were thrown in the air and shouts of acclamation shook the roof. His large head nodded ponderously above his squat frame as he gazed vaguely through his heavy-lidded eyes.

Albert muttered incredulously, 'How can this caricature evoke such adulation?'

'We are about to be enlightened,' whispered Pierre.

Raising his arm, Louis subdued the clamour and proceeded to speak in that slow, hesitant manner of his.

'Today I stand before you to be confirmed as the Emperor of the Second Empire. Only an Emperor can give France both glory and liberty. The central exponent of history is the great personality called by providence and representing progress. My Uncle Napoleon was the Messiah of new ideas but, despite not being allowed finish his work, he was survived by the Napoleonic concept.'

A great wave of applause swelled up from the body of the hall and Louis paused before continuing, 'What is this concept? It is a social and industrial one. It is humanitarian yet encourages enterprise. It reconciles order and freedom, the rights of the people and the principles of authority. It loves the diligent and needy.'

Albert shook his head in disbelief and, turning to Pierre, said sotto voce, 'Louis might look like an idiot but in that ungainly head resides a subtle brain. He persuades the working class that he's their champion and at the same time convinces the middle class he's their protector against socialism and that all his talk of social justice is no more than Utopian hot air.'

'He's not the first to pull that trick and no doubt he will not be the last,' Pierre answered.

The hall resounded to the shouts of 'Vive l'Empereur.'

Louis tilted his head and stared over the heads of the cheering throng as if at some sacred destiny.

'I entered this hall Louis Napoleon, nephew of Napoleon I; I leave as Napoleon III, Emperor of the Second French Empire,' he declaimed as the cheering intensified.

'All he needs to do now is find himself some trollop as his Empress and the age of Napoleon and Josephine will be back with a vengeance. God help us all,' said Albert.

Albert and Pierre were sitting in a coffee-house talking over the day's event.

'There is talk of Princess Caroline of Austria or one of the Hohenzollern princesses,' said Pierre. 'And I wouldn't think any of them could be called trollops.'

'That's a moot point, my friend. But none of that ilk will as much as pass the time of day with him. The royal houses of Europe think him more of an upstart than his uncle and he realises that.'

'Will he marry a commoner?'

'You've heard of Eugenie de Montijo?'

'Has a sister Paco, married to the Duke of Alba?'

'That's right. Well, they say our Napoleon is infatuated and it won't be long before he marries her.'

'But she's no trollop.'

'No, but her mother was quite famous in Madrid for her illicit liaisons. I believe our little Eugenie is keeping her hand on her pussy until Napoleon makes her his wife.'

A year later Albert's prognosis was proved to be correct when he and Pierre stood with the crowds that lined the route to Notre Dame as the state coach that had carried Napoleon I and Josephine to their nuptials now bore a triumphant Eugenie and a sombre Napoleon III. Eugenie bent forward and waved enthusiastically to the crowd. Her auburn hair shone in the winter sunshine and her large sapphire eyes sparkled with happiness.

'You have to admit she is a good-looker,' Pierre said to Albert.

'From what I've heard of her temperament, she would rather be riding side-saddle on one of the horses than sitting on her bum in that coach,' Albert retorted. 'I doubt if Napoleon will be able to handle a girl of her mettle.'

During the years of frustration that led to Napoleon's final triumph, a child grew to gracious manhood in the court of Austria. The baby, cradled in Sophia's arms as she stood in the high window of the palace and gazed down at the funeral procession of her lover, was christened Ferdinand Maximilian Joseph – Max to the family. Sophia bore two more sons: Karl Ludwig and Ludwig Victor, nicknamed Bubi. Karl was a nonentity while poor Bubi turned out to be a homosexual and ended his days in a distant fortress staffed only by women. The four brothers: Francis Joseph, Max, Karl and

Ludwig, while subject to the strict upbringing of Imperial princes – harsh military drills on sleet-swept parade grounds and cold showers – had the consolation of playing in the lush gardens of the palace at Schönbrunn and in the magnificent royal residences surrounded by the appurtenances of wealth and power.

When Emperor Francis died he was succeeded by his idiot son Ferdinand. The revolution of 1848, that deposed Louis Philippe in France and opened the way to Napoleon's rise to power, also wreaked havoc in the rest of Europe and drove the Imperial family from Vienna – the young Archdukes Francis Joseph and Maximilian riding post-horses either side of the carriage containing their mother Sophia, thus protecting her with their own bodies from the howling mob who were taking over the city.

When order had been restored and the family returned, it became obvious that Ferdinand would have to go. The natural successor was Francis Charles but, aware of his inadequacies, he allowed the crown to pass to his son Francis Joseph. Maximilian was sixteen years old when his brother was made Emperor. Up until that time the two older brothers had been very close. They had shared the same upbringing and studied the same subjects: foreign languages, art, religion, literature, the sciences, law, logic, technology, military matters – all the things that young princes needed to master. Temperamentally, however, they were very different. Francis was obedient, tidy, punctual and emotionally cold. He had no feeling for literature, music or nature. Maximilian was emotional, extravagant, romantic and far more lively and charming than his brother. The difference in their respective appearances was most marked, Maximilian being tall and elegant with dark eyes and handsome features, while Francis appeared desiccated with mean and furtive looks.

Francis was the first to marry, but the choice of bride was unfortunate. Elizabeth of Bavaria was the antithesis of all Francis stood for. She was erratic where he was methodical, wild where he was sober, whimsical where he was calculating. None of this troubled Francis, who continued to rule with a cold efficiency.

While his brother dealt with affairs of state, Maximilian was left to kick his heels around court. For an intelligent and energetic man this was proving to be intolerable, and Maximilian began to embarrass his brother by openly criticising him as being too hidebound and authoritarian. Francis decided that the problem had to be faced and he summoned Maximilian to a formal audience at the Imperial Palace at Hofburg. Maximilian entered the audience chamber only to find Francis surrounded as usual by the officers of his beloved Whitecoats.

'Before you say a word, get rid of these popinjays and let us talk as brothers,' Maximilian demanded.

A look of annoyance flashed across Francis' face but he dismissed the soldiers. Controlling his annoyance Francis attempted a bleak smile.

'There! Alone like the old days. Brother to brother,' he began.

Maximilian gave a sad laugh, 'Brother to brother, eh? It was once. Remember your wooden rocking horse? How you loved that old horse. Remember what you called it?'

Francis looked embarrassed and remained silent.

'I'll tell you,' Maximilian continued. 'Max. That's what you called it. Max. You loved me in those days. We studied together, rode together, played together. When I was in quarantine with measles, who wrote to me every day? From the moment you were made Emperor our relationship changed. No longer could I call you Franz but had to address you as Sire. You withdrew from me and isolated yourself within the coterie of your beloved army officers. You spend your time governing a great nation while I'm left to waste my time on fripperies and court irrelevancies. I'm as intelligent and able as you. So why this disparity?'

'Max, I wish you could understand the sense of responsibility I felt when father relinquished the crown to me. It was as if the heavy mantle of Metternich had fallen on my shoulders. I had to put away childish things.'

'The mantle of Metternich! That's the root of the problem. Your policies are too much like his were – harsh and illiberal.'

Francis responded angrily, 'I know you express those views openly at court. It has to stop. This is why I summoned you here.'

'Then give me something worthwhile to do. Allow me to influence policy in some way. The country will benefit.'

'I gave you command of the navy.'

'Oh come, Sire! Command of a navy that hasn't fired a cannon in anger for three centuries. I know how they snigger at court about the Sailor Prince. Why, the other day Ferdinand greeted me in the corridor with "Hello, sailor".'

A faint smile flickered across Francis' austere face and Maximilian gave a self-deprecating laugh. This broke the tension.

'Would you consider some sort of ambassadorial role?' asked Francis.

'Is this a device to get me out of your hair?'

Francis appeared to be genuinely shocked.

'You know how seriously Austria considers official visits. You will be Austria's representative abroad. That should prove more congenial than the fripperies and irrelevancies that you so despise.'

'Is this your way of disposing of a petty embarrassment by exile?'

In a rare gesture of affection Francis caught Maximilian by the arm.

'The cares of office might have come between us but of course I still love you as a brother and wish to see you content in some useful role. One man must govern a nation if it is to be strong. That is why I can't allow you to interfere, but representing Austria abroad would help me and give you a fulfilling occupation.'

'Where had you thought of sending me?' Maximilian asked cautiously.

'Napoleon and Eugenie seem securely installed in France. This would be the right time to establish good relations with the new regime. After Paris you could move on to Brussels and visit Leopold.'

Emperor Francis duly made a formal request to the French Court that Archduke Maximilian be allowed to make a state visit. The request was graciously granted and arrangements were made for a visit in May 1856. Before leaving for Paris Maximilian called on his mother, Archduchess Sophia. When he entered her salon, the same room where she and Reichstadt had made love for the first time, Sophia was seated reading a book of poems by Heine. Closing the book she rose and greeted him. Sophia, while jealously guarding the position of her eldest son Francis Joseph, reserved her greatest love for Max.

'Sit, mother,' said Maximilian as he gently pushed her back into the chair and sat on the floor beside her.

Sophia laughed and passed her hand through his thick, blond hair.

Pretending to pout she said, 'So you're deserting me, Max, and for what? To visit those two old frumps in Paris!'

'Oh come on, Mother, it should be fun. At least it will be a change from hanging around here watching Francis being masterful.'

'Poor Francis has a profound sense of duty and needs all our support. That wife of his gives him precious little. In court functions she sits at his side hiding behind her fan ignoring everybody. It's as if she's in another world. He never knows where he is with her. One moment she's in a coma and then suddenly she'll leap to her feet, charge out of the palace, fling herself on a horse and gallop wildly away. She returns hours later, the poor horse covered in sweat and she plastered in mud and her hair standing on end!'

Maximilian laughed. 'Don't exaggerate, Mother. You're making her sound insane.'

'Well?'

'No, Sisi is quite interesting. I get on well with her. She tells me tales of her childhood. Of how her father used to go incognito into the countryside, taking her with him. There, in the villages, he played the fiddle and she danced. The peasants used to throw money to them'

'*At* them, more like. I never wanted the match. Her sister Nené would have been a more suitable choice. Untainted by her mad old father. But no, Francis was infatuated by Sisi's dark beauty and that was that. Still, enough of that, let's talk about you. What makes you think Paris will be fun?'

'I hear that Napoleon is restoring France to the glory of the First Empire. He's started a great rebuilding programme. They say it will make Paris the most modern and beautiful city in Europe.'

Sophia snorted and said, 'Believe me, that common lump of clay, Louis, will never fill the boots of his uncle. The man whose destiny that should have been died in my arms at Schönbrunn – dear Joseph, Duke of Reichstadt and Napoleon's only son.'

Maximilian gave his mother an enquiring look and said, 'You were very fond of him?'

Sophia smiled wistfully and said, 'Go on. Go to Paris but remember you will be dealing with a counterfeit Napoleon.'

Throughout his visit those words of Sophia kept recurring to Maximilian and everything he encountered confirmed that verdict. He found Napoleon III at ease in the trappings of majesty and Eugenie, for all her beauty, had the touch of a courtesan. A state ball was held at St Cloud in honour of their Austrian visitor. The gaudy dress and uncouth behaviour of the guests appalled Maximilian.

Towards the end of the evening a person approached whom Maximilian had noticed earlier flitting elegantly in and out of the group of courtiers around Eugenie. Executing a sweeping bow, he asked, 'Your Highness, may such a humble creature as my poor self have the temerity to introduce myself to one of such exalted rank as your Highness?'

'That surely is a question you must answer yourself, as you must be the best judge of your own presumption.'

The stranger stepped back and a look of shock replaced the ingratiating smile that had wreathed his features. Seeing the devastating effect his words had produced, Maximilian felt a twinge of guilt.

'Oh come, sir, what is your name? I am pleased to make your acquaintance,' he said affably.

'Signor José Hidalgo at your service – a poor exile from his beloved Mexico.'

'A troubled country indeed.'

'Ah, your Highness, I wish my friend Gutierrez de Estrada were here. His eloquent recital of my country's woes would move you to tears.'

'Come walk with me in the gardens. I find the noise and bustle here not conducive to serious conversation and I am interested in the situation prevailing in your country.'

Maximilian walked out onto the paved courtyard and down the steps into the cool calm of the gardens. Scarcely able to believe his good fortune, José turned and ran after him.

There they strolled, lit by many coloured lanterns hanging in the trees that bordered the path. The lanterns swayed in a gentle breeze and sent the walkers' shadows dancing in fantastic arabesques across lawns as smooth as glass. Maximilian listened carefully to the foppish émigré chattering at his side, unaware of the malign influence that he was to have on his, Maximilian's, life.

'There are two factions in Mexico,' lamented José. 'The legitimate government headed by General Zuloaga and based in Mexico City, and rebels headed by that nihilist Benito Juárez in Vera Cruz. The country is in chaos.'

'But these people you call rebels, weren't they the duly elected Liberal government?'

Hidalgo raised his hands in horror and protested, 'But they abused that power by passing laws to deprive the most Holy Roman Catholic Church of its sacrosanct wealth and privileges. They had to go.'

'I see. Tell me about this Juárez. He interests me.'

Hidalgo made a disdainful grimace. 'Born in Oaxca, a small state in southern Mexico. Originally studied for the priesthood but soon abandoned that and became a lawyer. Always a man with an eye for the main chance, he became a judge, then governor of Oaxca, then Minister of Justice and eventually President of Mexico until General Zuloaga kicked him out of Mexico City and forced him and his deposed government to flee to the eastern port of Vera

Cruz, where he ferments rebellion against General Zuloaga.'

'But I have heard that he is impeccably honest and a man of simple tastes who has never used public office for personal gain. Quite a distinction for a politician, I would have thought.'

'Lies spread by those who would destroy the most Holy Roman Catholic Church,' Hidalgo said dismissively.

'Catholicism means a lot to you Conservatives.'

'Over three centuries ago, Cortés landed in Mexico with a handful of Spaniards and overthrew a mighty and ancient civilisation. A civilisation that had built throughout the land gigantic temples and palaces overflowing with intricate works of art wrought in gold and encrusted with precious stones.'

'If you are referring to the Aztecs, I can tell you that my brother Joseph and I, during our schooling, studied their history and I believe the Aztecs were not the creators of this advanced civilisation of which you speak, but merely inherited it and contributed little to that inheritance.'

Hidalgo suppressed his irritation at these interruptions and continued: 'That may well be the case, your Highness, as I am sure your schooling was of the highest quality. These people, however, were pagan and worshipped false idols. They practised human sacrifice, offering the hearts of the victims to their gods while eating the legs and arms.'

'Your point?'

'Cortés put an end to such barbarity. He brought the Catholic faith to Mexico. And now that antichrist

Juárez and his Liberal followers seek to destroy Catholicism. They burn our churches, tear down our altars; desecrate our crucifixes and kill our priests. There will be no order in the land until we have routed the liberals and established a monarchy.'

'But you have no native royal family.'

'That is why we must beg some European prince to become our Emperor.'

'You will have to make affairs far more stable before any prince I know would be prepared to take such a throne,' Maximilian said coldly.

Turning on his heel, he walked swiftly away, leaving Hidalgo standing motionless, his tense white face passing in and out of darkness as the lanterns swung gently to and fro. He stared at the retreating figure of Maximilian and muttered softly, 'Au revoir, Archduke. To everything there is a season, and a time to every purpose under the sun.'

The rest of the visit passed off pleasantly and, despite finding Napoleon and his Empress rather gauche, Maximilian felt a certain warmth towards them. They gave him the use of their royal yacht, the Queen Hortense, to travel to Belgium and went to the quayside to see him off. Napoleon, with a tear in his eye, whispered to Maximilian that he had named the ship after his late mother. He then coughed and, shaking Maximilian firmly by the hand, said, 'We are like old friends, are we not?'

When Maximilian arrived in Belgium he was met by Leopold's eldest son, the Duke of Brabant, who was also named Leopold, and escorted to the capital where the King and his other two children, Philippe and Charlotte, awaited him.

Leopold took his position very seriously and considered himself to be the wisest king in Christendom. So when he was alone with Maximilian he used the occasion to initiate Maximilian into the mysteries of statecraft.

'My boy,' he began, 'Shakespeare never made a truer statement than when he said, I quote: "Some are born great, some achieve greatness, and some have greatness thrust upon 'em…" '

Maximilian interrupted. 'Malvolio reading from a letter in *Twelfth Night*, I believe.'

'Yes, yes! But that's not important. It's the thought that counts – if you know what I mean?'

'Yes, of course.'

'That sums up my life. I was married to the daughter of the future King George IV. This meant that when he died, my wife would have become Queen of England and I would have been her consort. But it was not to be. My poor wife, Charlotte, died before George attained the throne and I was left to spend my time as a poor foreigner living in England on a small allowance. Where was the greatness in that? Then in 1830 the southern part of the Netherlands rebelled and formed the new kingdom of Belgium, and whom did they ask to be their King? Why, me! I tell you I thought long and hard before I accepted the crown. I asked myself if I had the necessary intellect and stamina to lead these industrious people.'

'Your majesty gave the correct answer. While the thrones of Europe have tottered all around you, Belgium has remained loyal to its king. What is your secret?'

'Diligence to the needs of the people, hard work and tolerance. When revolutions were sweeping across Europe, I offered to abdicate. The people wouldn't hear of it.'

'I think perhaps a little cunning is also part of the secret.'

Leopold looked puzzled for a moment and then laughed.

'Ah yes! I see what you mean,' he conceded. Assuming a look of great gravitas and laying his hand on Maximilian's shoulder, Leopold continued: 'A monarch is not a free agent in personal matters. He must always take into account the needs of his subjects. The loss of my poor Charlotte was a great personal tragedy for me, you understand, apart from its impact on my prospects. But I realised I needed an heir and that is why I married Louis Philippe's daughter, Louise Marie. This had the additional advantage of forming an alliance with France. Ah! My angelic Louise, how I grew to love her. She bore me three children and, dear sweet creature that she was, insisted we named our third child after poor Charlotte.'

'The death of Queen Louise Marie must have come as a devastating blow.'

'Ah yes. Especially to little Charlotte, who was only ten years old. She and her mother were very close'.

Leopold ended the audience with the promise to continue Maximilian's education in the art of political science at their next meeting. It was a prospect that Maximilian did not relish.

The one person in the court who interested him from the moment he saw her was Charlotte. Her slim figure blossoming into womanhood and her dark, deep-set eyes hinted at the beauty that would come with maturity, though it was not this that attracted Maximilian. It was the thoughtful expression and quiet manner which betokened wisdom beyond her sixteen years. When they did succeed in being alone together, Maximilian was not disappointed.

'I trust we have enough in common to hold an intelligent conversation,' was her opening remark.

Slightly taken aback, Maximilian laughed and said, 'Well if you tell me something about yourself, we might find out.'

'I don't wish to be rude but that is one of the things that worry me about state visits. The visitors can be so deadly dull that I am left tongue-tied and feeling foolish.'

'What subjects interest you?'

'History, especially the lives of the great figures of the past.'

'You will have read *De Vita Caesarum* by Suetonius?'

'Not in the original but in Holland's translation – *Lives of the Caesars*.'

'You should read Suetonius in the original. Only then will you appreciate him fully. His language is concise and without affectation. It loses much in translation.'

'He certainly tells scandalous tales of the Caesars. Can we trust him?'

'Suetonius was chief secretary to Emperor Hadrian and so had access to the imperial archives. Also he lived for thirty years under the

Caesars and so much of his information on Tiberius, Caligula, Claudius and Nero came from eyewitness accounts. Shall I tell you what I think is the most chilling quotation in the whole book?'

Charlotte, her eyes beginning to sparkle with interest, said, 'Yes. Please do.'

'Caligula, in one of his manic rages, saying: "Would that the Roman people had but one neck." '

'Now I'll tell you what I consider to be the most touching quotation,' said Charlotte. 'Vespasian as he lay dying in bed: "Dear me, I believe I am becoming a god. An emperor ought at least to die on his feet." '

Maximilian smiled and said, 'Well at least poor old Vespasian spoke from the heart. A lot of people who utter famous last words do so because they still want to arouse admiration even with their last gasp. I assume that you read contemporary writers as well as the classics?'

'Indeed, yes! I read Heine.'

'Ah! My mother's favourite poet. She takes particular pleasure in his love poems.'

'I liked Die Lorelei, based on the legend of a beautiful maiden who threw herself into the Rhine in despair over a faithless lover. She was transformed into a siren who sat on a rock combing her hair and luring fishermen to their deaths. I believe such a rock exists on the banks of the Rhine.'

'Yes, it is situated near Sankt Goarshausen. The poem is an example of the tension that exists in Heine's love poems. He employs romantic material but is at the same time suspicious of it. This gives his poems a bittersweet quality. I would be wary of his philosophical writings, however. You know he is a friend of Karl Marx?'

Charlotte smiled deprecatingly and said, 'I did not find his *History of Religion and Philosophy* subversive. It appeared to me a call for a new Reformation.'

'But that was written before he met Marx. The poems he has published recently in Marx's newspaper *Forward* are no more than harsh political satire. They struck me as very sour.'

Maximilian was surprised by the knowledge exhibited by such a young woman and was so charmed by her that he sought her company more and more during his visit. On one occasion, while they were out riding, they dismounted and, after tethering their horses to a tree, sat together under its shade.

'We've talked about your interests and what you read but I would like to know you as a person,' Maximilian began.

'My interests and what I read surely define me as a person,' Charlotte answered with a toss of her head.

'To a degree, but events also shape a person. What of your childhood?'

Charlotte looked down and, twisting her hands together, said, 'Ah. The event that shaped my life was the death of my mother. I was ten years old. Until then she was not just a loving mother, she was my teacher and my constant companion. We studied together. We played together. The day she died I stood at the side of her bed and held her poor withered hand. She looked up at me and whispered: "Forgive me, dear child, for the suffering I have caused you."'

Charlotte's shoulders shook gently as, still looking down, she sobbed silently. Maximilian was taken aback and at first did not know how to react. He put a tentative hand on her shoulder. It was the first time he had touched her body and a feeling of great tenderness flooded through him.

Seeking to distract her, he asked quietly, 'What subject did you and your mother most enjoy?'

Charlotte looked up; composing her features she replied, 'Oh, without doubt mathematics, and I'm still continuing with my studies.'

Maximilian pulled a long face and said, 'Not my favourite topic, I'm afraid.'

'I find it fascinating and I particularly like differential calculus. I'll never forget the first time I realised that the differential coefficient of the exponential function equals itself.'

Maximilian laughed and said, 'Hold on. You're way above my head.'

'I'm sorry, but I do so love the elegance of the subject. Did you know that if a function of the real variable can't be integrated, one can convert it into a complex function, integrate it in the complex plane and take the real part of the solution as the integral of the original function?'

Charlotte stopped, looked at Maximilian's perplexed expression and smiled shyly. 'I'm sorry. There I go again,' she said.

As they rode slowly back Charlotte reminisced further about her childhood.

'After mother's death, my aunt Queen Victoria invited me to spend the summer at her seaside retreat at Osborne. She was very kind and went to great lengths to humour me while I was there but I fear I was an unappreciative guest.'

'How did your brothers deal with their loss?'

'My dear big Philippe,' Charlotte said, and her eyes softened as she spoke his name. 'It crushed even his great happy spirit.'

'And your elder brother Leopold?'

Charlotte's face hardened and she spat the words, 'Nothing could pierce that callous nature of his.'

'But I have found him to be most charming,' Maximilian protested.

'Don't be fooled. As a small boy, he delighted in cutting off the limbs of living creatures and in forcing Philippe and me to watch. Believe me, his character hasn't improved with age.'

Charlotte spurred her horse and shouted, 'Come on. Race you back to Laeken.'

Maximilian was content to canter behind and admire the way such a petite figure controlled the great muscled brute of a stallion.

Once back in the palace, Maximilian was subjected to another interminable lecture from Leopold. Maximilian quite liked the old fellow but found his propensity for pontificating at endless length on the state of Europe rather wearying. His mind wandered back to Charlotte. Up until the time he had placed his hand on her shoulder, he had considered her no more than an agreeable person with whom it was possible to have an intelligent conversation. This had been a pleasant change from being subjected to the pompous monologues that her father mistook for dialogue. However, when he had felt her body fluttering beneath his hand like some frightened bird, he had experienced an emotion unknown to him before. It was a feeling of protectiveness tinged with passion. The feeling of sexual excitement was not new to him – his mother Sophia had seen to it that when her sons reached puberty, they were well supplied with compliant females. But the affection was.

That night as she lay in her bed, Charlotte was strangely disturbed. The only men she knew with any great intimacy were her two brothers and her father. Her father amused her; Philippe she adored for his athleticism and sunny disposition, while Leopold she detested. All the other men at court were kept at a discreet distance, so sexual attraction was an unknown country to her. That was until the sight of Maximilian in his uniform of Admiral of the Fleet had quite overwhelmed her on their first meeting; and today, when he had placed his hand on her shoulder, it had stirred emotions she did not know existed. The fluency and warmth of their conversations had reinforced her admiration and the prospect of placing her fate in the hands of a man who until a few days ago had been a complete stranger did not appal her.

Before Maximilian arrived, she had known that her father was scheming to ally the royal house of Belgium with the Austrian royal family. She knew, however, that her father would never force her into a marriage she did not want. Lying there, Charlotte allowed herself a smug little smile as she relished the knowledge that in marrying Maximilian she would not only be satisfying her father, but herself as well.

The following day Maximilian left Brussels to tour the country for a few days. Taking advantage of his absence, King Leopold sent word to Charlotte that he wished to speak to her privately. When she entered his study she found him pacing around the room muttering to himself – a sure sign that he was embarrassed.

'Ah, Charlotte!' he cried. 'Do sit down, my dear.'

As soon as Charlotte was seated he promptly disappeared behind her and she heard him pick up an occasional table and thump it against the wall.

'Urrump,' he continued. 'Comfortable, my dear?'

'Yes thank you, Papa,' Charlotte said patiently.

'Good, good. You know, my dear—'

Leopold circled round in front of her and banged a chair against the wall before vanishing behind her again. He continued, 'You know ever since your mother's death – God bless her pure soul – your welfare has always been close to my heart.'

The table hit the wall again and Leopold reappeared in front of her.

'Of course, Papa, but why don't you sit here beside me. It would be far less distracting.'

'What? Oh yes.'

Leopold sat on the chaise-longue and, leaning forward, held Charlotte's hand.

'What do you think of Archduke Maximilian?' he enquired anxiously.

'Think of him? What should I think of him?' Charlotte asked with feigned indifference. 'He came to visit you, not me.'

Leopold's face fell and, jumping to his feet, he started his perambulations once more.

'Oh do sit down, Father,' Charlotte said. 'I found him charming and intelligent.'

Leopold quickly rejoined her on the chaise-longue.

'You did?'

'Yes I did, Papa.'

'We royal persons are so circumscribed by obligations of state that it is indeed fortunate when political expedience and personal choice coincide.'

'What do you mean, Papa? I don't understand.'

Leopold blurted out, 'I mean it would be excellent for relations between Belgium and Austria if you married Maximilian and since you say you like him, everyone will be happy.'

'But, Papa, saying I find him charming and intelligent does not of necessity mean I wish the intimacy of marrying him.' Then, seeing Leopold's embarrassment and confusion, she added, 'Though the idea is not totally abhorrent to me.'

She kissed her father on the forehead and tripped lightly out of the room, leaving Leopold smiling happily on the chaise-longue.

On the evening of his return to the palace, Maximilian was relaxing in his apartments when he heard a discreet knock on the door. On opening it he was disconcerted to find King Leopold standing alone in the corridor. The King held a finger to his lips and pushed past Maximilian into the room.

'My dear Archduke,' he exclaimed. 'Forgive this intrusion and my conspiratorial air but I need to speak with you privately.'

Seeing Maximilian standing by the still open door he said urgently, 'Please shut the door.'

Leopold assumed his customary air of an elder statesman addressing an ingenue. 'I was telling my daughter only yesterday how the scions of royal households are honour bound to sacrifice the privilege of personal choice on the altar of national wellbeing. It is the price we pay for our privileged position.'

Maximilian was intelligent enough to realise where the conversation was heading and he answered warily, 'And what did your daughter make of that perceptive observation?'

'She said that sometimes political expedience and personal choice coincided.'

'Another perceptive observation. Could she have meant a political marriage where the two persons involved actually liked each other?'

'My dear Archduke, you follow my meaning exactly.'

Before the year was out Maximilian wrote to Leopold from Vienna requesting the hand in marriage of his daughter Charlotte. At the wedding ceremony Charlotte wore a dress of white satin embroidered in gold and a veil of Brussels lace with a tiara of flowers and diamonds in her hair. Maximilian wore the admiral's uniform so beloved by Charlotte.

That night in the bridal chamber, Maximilian waited patiently while Charlotte changed into her nightgown behind a large screen on whose wooden panel was painted a reproduction of Botticelli's 'The Primavera'. He studied the painting with amused interest. It was crowded with the most sensuously beautiful females, but medieval decorum had necessitated the strategic deployment of hands and clothing. A striking feature of the painting was the way it depicted motion across a surface. The streaming hair, the flowing draperies and the contour of an arm all suggested the movement of the figures.

When Charlotte emerged from behind the screen enveloped in an absurdly voluminous garment that seemed to have been designed to extinguish the hottest passion, Maximilian smiled at the contrast with the figures flying across the screen behind her.

'You think I look ridiculous?' Charlotte asked, near tears with apprehension and excitement.

Maximilian laughed and, kissing her on the forehead, said, 'I think you look very sweet dear Charlotte.'

He went over to the dressing table and picked up a small book bound in blue leather. 'My mother asked me to give you this as a secret present from her,' he said as he handed her the book.

Charlotte cautiously examined the book and said, 'Oh! Heine's poems. You told her I liked his poetry?'

'That book means a great deal to her. She and Reichstadt would spend many evenings in her salon at the Hofburg reading from that little book. In giving it to you, she is sacrificing something that she treasures.'

Maximilian gathered Charlotte up in his arms and laid her on the bed. He gently removed her clothing and pressed his face between her breasts. Her heart pounded wildly as she placed her arms around him and dug her fingers into his back.

The following day they went alone to the Church of Laeken and stood before the grave of Charlotte's mother. Suddenly Charlotte sank to her knees and wept uncontrollably. Maximilian lifted her to her feet and attempted to console her. She looked into his face and said, 'Oh Max, how I adore you! The love I feel for you has released all the sorrow I have felt for the death of my poor mother. I can now mourn for her naturally and not feel that grief like a stone in my breast.'

As they walked back to the palace, one of the boats that had taken part in the previous night's celebration floated past. Its coloured lanterns were extinguished but it still carried a huge portrait of Maximilian and Charlotte surmounted by the caption 'FÉLICITÉ' and decorated with bouquets of withered flowers.

CHAPTER 4

Emperor Francis Joseph now faced the problem of what to do with Maximilian and Charlotte. He realised that Maximilian would not be content to spend the rest of his life commanding Austria's third-rate navy and King Leopold had been pressing him to find an occupation more befitting the status of the son-in-law of the King of Belgium. Shortly after the couple returned to Vienna, Francis summoned Maximilian to an audience. An exuberant Maximilian burst in to find his brother in a sombre mood.

'Max, we must talk about your future occupation,' Francis said.

'Well, Francis, Charlotte and I have been discussing that very topic ourselves. She is a very intelligent young woman, far more advanced than her years.'

'Yes, yes,' Francis said impatiently. 'But whatever you and Charlotte think is not the main consideration. What is important is what is best for Austria and I am the one who decides that.'

Anxious not to irritate Francis, Maximilian raised his hands and exclaimed, 'Of course, no one questions that!'

'You are aware of the situation in Italy?'

Before Maximilian could answer Francis continued, 'That mass of petty kingdoms always clamouring for unification. Our ownership of the north must not be jeopardised. Lombardy and Venetia must not be menaced by any half-baked ideas of Italian unity. I thought we had crushed that dream in 1849 with the victory of our Whitecoats, but that mischievous Count Cavour is stirring the pot again and that cousin of his has wormed her way into Napoleon's bed and in her pillow talk speaks endlessly of a United Italy free of Austrian hegemony.'

'Countess de Castiglione – a woman of rare beauty indeed. Why, even old Metternich commented on her long dark curls and flawless complexion.'

'If she succeeds in persuading that ageing *roué* Napoleon to intervene against us, all Italy will burst into flame. I have decided to appoint you Viceroy of Lombardy-Venetia. You and Charlotte will take up residence in Milan. Tour the whole of Northern Italy.'

Francis stopped and then, with the suggestion of a sneer in his voice, continued, 'Let's see what your renowned tact can accomplish.'

That evening in their chamber, Maximilian strode restlessly round the room articulating his intense excitement as Charlotte sat up in bed and gazed lovingly at him.

'You realise the enormity of what has happened?' he exulted. 'For years I have pressed him to ease his iron-fisted grip on the Italian people, only to have him tighten it. He posted troops in the theatres and opera houses to arrest anyone who dared to shout slogans against Austria, and had Italian women flogged in the streets for insulting

Austrian officers. Now he has given me the opportunity to try another way.'

'But why has he done this?' Charlotte asked in a puzzled manner. 'Can you trust him?'

'I can trust him. He's my brother. But why has he done this? I'll tell you. His last visit to our provinces in Italy was a nightmare. Everywhere he went he and Sisi had to be protected from the enraged populace by heavy troop reinforcements. In Venice, when walking from the gondola landing to the steps of the palace, the mob almost succeeded in throwing them into the canal. It has finally dawned on my dear brother that whipping posts, gallows and firing squads are not the answer.'

Charlotte jumped out of bed and threw her arms around Maximilian. 'Oh, Max!' she cried. 'We will win them over. Give alms to the poor, go among the people and help to alleviate their sufferings.'

'I will help them to beautify their cities, improve the water supplies, ease their taxes.'

'But money will have to be raised if we are going to do all these good works. Where will it come from?'

Maximilian hesitated for a moment and a broad smile spread across his face. 'Why,' he shouted, 'we'll organise a lottery of course – a Grand National Lottery! What better way of making money?'

They both fell on the bed laughing.

Two years later they were back in Vienna, their dreams shattered. No matter how diligently the Viceroy and Vicereine had attempted to ingratiate themselves with their Italian subjects, by implementing all the schemes they had talked about so enthusiastically, they had been constantly undermined by interference from Vienna. The result was inevitable: the Italians rose in rebellion and Napoleon – with the cry, 'I must do something for Italy!' – sent his army to support the rebels. After a bloody battle, Francis was forced to sue for peace and pull out of Lombardy.

On their return to Vienna, Maximilian and Charlotte confronted Francis in front of the whole court. Maximilian was white with anger. He knew that Francis Joseph would never give him a position of any authority again and the injustice of the situation infuriated him.

Francis greeted them with a sardonic, 'Welcome home, Viceroy and Vicereine emeritus.'

'And who is responsible for our present status?' Maximilian flung back.

'My dear Max, the answer is self-evident. Your vaunted tact turned out to be mere weakness.'

'My tact was never given a chance to succeed. Some crass, insensitive directive from you undermined every move I made to liberalise the administration. When I asked that Lombardy and Venetia be allowed separate Assemblies to give them at least the illusion of political control, otherwise they would be lost, what was your response? Refusal and a demand that I increase the repressive measures of the army and secret police. I became ashamed to be the representative of such a government.'

Francis coloured and answered angrily, 'That is why I dismissed you and your wife. I could no longer trust the two of you to carry out my orders.

Once I have decided something, it must be carried out immediately and with zeal.'

'And what happened after you had got rid of us? You so aggravated the situation that the Italians rose in revolt and Napoleon came to their aid. Result? Lombardy lost and our hegemony in Italy destroyed.'

Francis sprang from the throne, strode up to Maximilian and yelled in his face, 'For years you pestered me to give you some worthwhile occupation where you could exercise your exceptional talents, but I was doubtful and desisted. Then your father-in-law demanded that I find you a suitable position. It was important to keep in with Belgium so I gave you Italy. That was the reason, not that I thought your so-called liberal attitude would succeed. But I tell you this, never so long as I live will you hold an important position again.'

Maximilian tightened his grip on the pair of white gloves he held in his right hand. He slowly raised his arm and brushed the gloves lightly across Francis' face. He then turned and stalked out of the room with Charlotte hurrying after him.

The court looked on in a stunned silence until Francis ruefully rubbed his face and said, 'If that was a demonstration of Max's famous tact, no wonder the Italians revolted.'

The courtiers surprised by the Emperor's relaxed reaction tittered dutifully but noted the grim expression on his face as he resumed his seat.

Francis was true to his word – Maximilian and Charlotte were condemned to a useless, gilded existence in their castle at Miramar where Charlotte painted and read while Maximilian devoted his time to home renovations and gardening, turning their castle into an exquisite oriental palace with carved minarets of pure white marble, medieval battlements, vaulted arches and flowing fountains. The walls were hung with magnificent paintings; the vast library was stacked with the works of all the great writers since the ancient Greeks and was embellished with their marble busts. Charlotte would complain to Maximilian that they were born to govern, not to waste their lives idling in all this vapid opulence. Consequently they began to grow apart and it looked as if all that lay before them was a slow, arid descent into an embittered and estranged old age.

But events taking place across the Atlantic Ocean would dramatically change that prognosis.

The year was 1863 and the situation in Mexico had dramatically changed from the time when José Hidalgo had spoken to Maximilian beneath the swinging lanterns in the garden at St Cloud. The Conservative leader General Zuloaga had given way to a young handsome soldier, General Miguel Miramon. The civil war between Juárez's Liberals and the Conservatives' illegal government continued unabated with appalling atrocities being committed on both sides. The war climaxed in a bloody battle outside Mexico City in which the Conservatives were routed. Juárez was reinstated as President of the Republic and Miramon fled to Europe, leaving his second in command, the savage General Marquez, to harass the government forces from his lair in the mountains. The civil war had so ravaged the economy of the country that the treasury was empty. Juárez had no option but to suspend all payments of the huge foreign debts to Spain, Britain and France. Napoleon had been waiting for this opportunity. He had long wished to create a French bastion in Mexico and the Conservatives, anxious to acquire a powerful ally, had, through their representatives Hidalgo and Gutierrez de Estrada, succeeded in persuading Napoleon that the Mexican people would support his intervention to restore religion and set up a monarchy.

Britain and Spain joined the French invasion but withdrew from the venture at an early stage. Undeterred Napoleon decided to continue without them and his expeditionary force marched on Mexico City. The Mexican army made its stand at the fortified city of Puebla. The French foolishly made a full frontal assault up a steep slope against a position that was defended by a ditch and a high wall. The French suffered heavy casualties and retreated in disorder. Napoleon sent large reinforcements from France and again laid siege to Puebla. Eventually, when they had used up all their bullets and their food supplies were exhausted, the Mexicans were forced to surrender. The way to the capital was open and it was not long before the French commander rode his horse in triumph through the streets of Mexico City. Juárez and his government were forced to flee to the north and the French rapidly secured central Mexico. The time had come for Napoleon to find a puppet to place on the Mexican throne.

CHAPTER 5

Tancred's disdainful dismissal of Christianity had inflicted a severe blow on William's faith. He had never shared his father's fanatical belief in the infallibility of every word recorded in the Bible but he had found it comforting to think that there was some sort of deity that looked benignly on the fairly good and had prepared a haven for their souls. The thought of black oblivion after death cast a chill shadow over the joys of life. He therefore decided to seek reassurance from the school chaplain.

The Rev Archibald Stammers was a priest who pushed the boundaries of high Anglicanism perilously close to Roman Catholicism. As a young parish priest he had outraged his Low Church congregation by using church funds to purchase a collection of magnificently decorated copes so that he could parade like a peacock in front of the altar with a different cope for each saint day. Nemesis had arrived when he entered a secret conspiracy with the warden's teenage son. Once a month they would lock the church and conduct a High Mass. Archibald, dressed in the most gorgeous of the copes, intoned the liturgy in Latin while the warden's son paraded before the altar swinging a censer on the end of a long heavy chain, sending clouds of sweet smelling incense billowing into every corner of the church.

One day their secret was discovered when a passer-by noticed incense seeping out from under the church door and, thinking that the church was on fire, raised the alarm. A congregation, incensed in more ways than one, petitioned the Bishop to move Archibald to another parish. After many such vicissitudes, an older and somewhat chastened Rev Archibald Stammers found a haven as the chaplain of Shackles College where his addiction to the more theatrical renderings of church ritual, far from being frowned upon, was positively encouraged.

He was completely bald and his pate was a shining white dome. This had the unfortunate effect of making his face appear as if it had been painted on the surface of a hard-boiled egg. His eyebrows were bushy and jet-black, giving the impression that two large black beetles were traversing his forehead. As he sat behind his desk, he exuded an air of contented plumpness. When William entered the room Archibald glanced down at his diary.

'Dawson, is it?' he said.

'Yes, sir,' William answered rather nervously.

Although William knew the chaplain through attending the compulsory church services and the short formal interview each term, this was the first occasion that he had initiated a meeting.

'William Dawson?' Archibald continued.

'Yes sir. William Dawson.'

'Well, sit down, boy.'

William sat on a hardback chair in front of the desk and stared blankly at the chaplain.

This was going to be more difficult than he had anticipated.

Sensing William's embarrassment, Archibald assumed that the visit was to do with the difficulties of puberty in an all boy school. He groaned inwardly.

'Come on, boy. Out with it,' he exhorted.

William stared wildly at the chaplain and coloured.

'No need to be coy here,' Archibald continued. 'Having disturbing thoughts concerning young ladies?'

'Oh no, indeed not, sir.'

'It's nothing to be ashamed of, perfectly natural in a healthy young fellow like yourself. The thing is work hard, play hard and keep yourself pure until the time comes for you to marry. You'll have the rest of your life to indulge in all that stuff.'

'No, sir. It's nothing like that. I don't bother with girls.'

'You don't play with yourself, do you? Take a cold shower every time you feel the temptation. It never fails.'

'It's not about girls or temptation or anything like that,' William cried in exasperation. 'It's about God and the Bible.'

Archibald looked stunned.

'You mean you want to talk about religion?'

'Yes, I most certainly do. That is – talk about religion.'

'I'd have thought you'd have had enough of that with my sermons, what!'

Archibald laughed nervously. He was becoming decidedly suspicious of this fellow. What normal red-blooded lad would voluntarily come and ask for a one-to-one discussion with a priest about religion, of all things.

'I think I've lost my faith,' William confessed.

This touched Archibald. The boy ought to be congratulated, he felt, for at least having a faith in the first place. Most of the barbarians in this place wouldn't recognise a religious concept if it rose up and kicked them in the crotch. He decided to probe.

'What's your background, Dawson? What does your father do?' he asked briskly.

'He's a country Rector, sir,' William responded.

'Well, haven't you discussed this with him?'

'This happened since returning here so I haven't had the chance. Anyway, it wouldn't be any good. Father is very fundamental and would only bawl me out.'

'I see. What brought on this crisis, my boy?'

'I was talking to my friend, Tancred.'

'Tancred Bowles, our resident aesthete and atheist.'

'He pointed out all the absurdities and contradictions in the Bible. But what finally destroyed me was when he asked: who made God?'

Archibald saw a great black hole opening in front of him. But he also saw a path around it.

'My dear boy, take no notice of Bowles. He has a smattering of everything and knowledge of nothing. He partly digests the half-baked ideas of Hume and Huxley and attempts to regurgitate them for whomever is stupid enough to listen to him.'

The chaplain rose and went over to a bookcase in the corner of the room. He selected a large volume bound in leather and handed it to William.

'Here, boy, study this – *The Analogy of Religion* by Bishop Joseph Butler. A great work of moral philosophy. He confounds the sceptics and ponders scrupulously the basis of man's knowledge of his creator. He will banish your doubts far more effectively than any poor words of mine.'

He then hustled William out of the room and, as the bewildered boy staggered down the corridor under the weight of Bishop Butler's thoughts, Archibald called after him, 'Don't forget to bring it back once you've finished with it.'

During the next week, William conscientiously attempted to understand the Bishop's arguments as he attacked those whose approach to God was to reason rationally from nature rather than from faith in the doctrine of revelation. He did his reading when Tancred was busy elsewhere but one evening Tancred returned early and caught William with his head in the book and a perplexed expression on his face.

'Who gave you that?' he demanded.

'The chaplain.'

'Don't waste your time on Butler. He's a man of the past. You should be reading men like Huxley.'

'Huxley? Who's he?'

'You're a dead loss, William. Thomas Henry Huxley is a biologist and the chief supporter of Darwin and the theory of evolution. You've heard of the theory of evolution?'

'Of course I have,' William said angrily. 'Says we're all descended from apes.'

'Well, there's a bit more to it than that but it will do to begin with. I have a copy of his latest book –

Man's Place in Nature. I'll lend it you. If you've got any brain it should banish the notion of God having any place in the universe.'

'You admire this chap Huxley?'

'Darwin is a rather timid character so it falls to Huxley to take the battle to the sceptics. Last year there was a meeting at Oxford of the British Association for the Advancement of Science, where Huxley defended Darwin's theory. His main challenger was Bishop Wilberforce, who, in a speech characterised by unfairness and spleen, facetiously referred to Huxley's grandfather as "that old ape". When Huxley rose to reply he started his speech by saying that he would prefer to have a poor ape as his grandfather rather than a man of high intelligence and great influence who used these attributes for the mere purpose of introducing ridicule into a serious scientific discussion.'

'My father admires Bishop Wilberforce but I've never heard him mention Huxley.'

'Read *Man's Place in Nature*, there's a good boy. Your ignorance cramps my conversation.'

This remark stung William into a sustained effort to read and digest Huxley's essay.

A few nights later he looked up from his reading and said to Tancred, 'Listen to this.' He proceeded to quote from the book: ' "Some experience of popular lecturing has convinced me that the necessity of making things plain to uninstructed people was one of the best means of clearing up the obscure corners in one's own mind." '

William raised his head and said, 'How's that for intellectual arrogance?'

'What do you mean? Sounds rather self-deprecating to me. At least he's admitting that there are obscure corners even in his mind, but the important point is, has he succeeded in clearing out all that religious cant from the corners of *your* mind?'

'He talks of the scientific method. Can you explain that in simple terms?'

'Put simply, it's a systematic method for the pursuit of knowledge.'

'I grasped that. But how does it work?'

'It involves three steps. One: the recognition and formulation of a problem. Two: the collection of data through experiment and observation. Three: the formulation and testing of a hypothesis that answers the problem and fits the data.'

'So when he states that the structural differences between man and the gorilla are not so great as those which separate the gorilla from a monkey, that is based on observable data. And the scientific method then leads him to the conclusion that man is descended from the great apes.'

'Exactly! And has he convinced you?'

'Well, the deployment of the scientific method is certainly more credible than the blind faith of my father.'

'Good. Once you've grasped the maxim that there can be no knowledge of anything beyond experience, you're on your way to becoming a rational human being.'

The next day William returned Butler's tome to the chaplain and assured Archibald that his faith had been fully restored by the Bishop's inspirational words. Archibald expressed his satisfaction at such an efficacious outcome and, as he closed the door on William, sent up a fervent prayer that he would not be troubled again by importunate youngsters worrying about the state of their immortal souls.

William, rejoicing in his complete lack of faith, was able to throw himself wholeheartedly into the rehearsals of the play and speculate tantalisingly on what Tancred had in mind when he had spoken of indulging in any pleasure or perversity that took their fancy. His years at Shackles had inured him to the bullying that occurred by day and the insidious air of repressed sensuality that pervaded the Chamber by night.

He had been troubled by Oliver's demeanour in the last few rehearsals. The boy had appeared pale and listless, totally unlike his usual blithe self. He had a suspicion that the cause was a burly fifth former named Jake Thorn, who was playing the part of Demetrius. He had observed Oliver casting apprehensive glances at Jake, who smiled back mockingly.

This night William decided to return to the Chamber an hour after lights out. Shielding the flickering flame of his candle with his hand, he entered the Chamber and made straight for Oliver's stall. The sound of his approaching steps had warned Jake and when William lifted the light high to illuminate the scene, it revealed Jake scrambling out of Oliver's bed, his face flushed with embarrassment.

'What the hell do you think you're doing, Thorn?' William hissed.

Jake had regained some composure and, staring defiantly at William said, 'And what gives you the right to come sneaking in on chaps in the middle of the night?'

'Answer my question. What were you doing in Oliver's bed?'

'I was never in his damned bed.'

'I saw you scrambling out.'

'No you did not. All you saw was me standing at the side of the bed. I was never in his bed. Ask Oliver. He'll tell you – if he knows what's good for him.'

Looking down at Oliver's pale, tear-stained face, William realised that the boy would never tell the truth about what had happened.'

The whole dormitory was awake and staring with intense interest at what was going on. William realised that, without Oliver's testimony, he would not be able to prove Thorn's guilt to the school authorities but the sight of the stupid triumphant smirk on Jake's face drove him to seek a way of teaching the bastard a lesson. He stepped forward, landed a right-hand blow squarely on Thorn's nose and then smartly took a step back, in true pugilistic fashion. Taken by surprise, Thorn slumped on one knee with blood spurting from the afflicted protuberance. He recovered quickly, however, and rose menacingly to his full height. Uttering dire imprecations, he lunged wildly at William but, before further blows were exchanged, someone pushed between the two protagonists, forcing them apart.

An insouciant voice said, 'Steady on. No brawling in Chamber please.'

It was Tancred who, intrigued by William's stealthy departure from their room, had followed him and arrived on the scene in time to witness the confrontation.

'You must settle this in a civilised manner,' Tancred continued. 'Tomorrow is our half day so we can organise a proper boxing match behind the woods out of sight of the school. No bareknuckle boxing, I'll get boxing gloves. You are both gentlemen, not street fighters.'

'Will you fight?' Thorn snarled.

'Till you beg for mercy, you pederast,' William answered calmly.

Back in their room Tancred remarked, 'That brute Thorn is a big lump. I was afraid he was going to pulverise you back there. That's why I stepped in and proposed the boxing match. At least wearing gloves should limit the damage. But if you like I can inform the Master, he'll stop it.'

'No, I would lose face and anyway he needs a good thrashing,' William said.

'But he's too big for you. It's you who'll get the thrashing.'

William smiled and said, 'I have an older cousin who occasionally stays with us at the Rectory. He's an officer in the Guards and a bit of an amateur boxer. My father is very fond of him and, since the gentry are taking to the sport, raised no objection when the fellow initiated me into the mysteries of the noble art. Felt it would make a man of me.'

'So Thorn is in for a bit of a surprise?'

'He's way above my weight but let's hope craft will triumph over brawn.'

'Only tomorrow will tell.'

When Tancred and William, together with a group of sixth formers, arrived at the site the boys had already lined up in a perfect square to form the ring. William removed his jacket and tie and handed them to Tancred who passed them on to one of their party. William then undid his collar and rolled up his sleeves. The boys parted to allow him and Tancred into the ring where Thorn was waiting. Glancing around, William saw Oliver's worried face at the back of the crowd. Tancred supervised the putting on of the gloves, and William noticed that the leather was of a shining blue hue and bore no blood or perspiration stains – no more than one would have expected from a person as fastidious as Tancred, he thought.

Tancred was taking his position as organiser very seriously and before battle was allowed to commence he addressed the combatants: 'Each round will be of three minutes duration, I will be the timekeeper. The fight will end when one of the protagonists says he has had enough. You will box under the London Prize Ring Rules: no kicking, biting, gouging, butting or hitting below the belt. At the first sign of any such behaviour, the match will be stopped and the perpetrator will be disqualified and his opponent declared the winner.'

He retreated to a corner of the ring and, after ostentatiously consulting his watch, gave the signal to start. Thorn, confident in his superior power, immediately made a mad charge in an attempt to bring matters to an abrupt conclusion. Remembering his cousin's instructions, William skipped smartly to one side and caught Thorn with a right-hand to the side of his face as he lumbered by. Enraged, Thorn turned and shot out his left hand, William ducked and countered with an uppercut that hit him solidly on the chin. A cheer rose from the crowd, confirming William's belief that Thorn was detested by the rest of the school who, cowed by his bullying, took pleasure in seeing him defeated.

Thorn now realised that William would be no walkover, so he changed tactics and started to box. Though he could not match William's skill, his superior reach and more powerful punches redressed the balance and William knew he was in a fight. In the second round, Thorn caught William with a vicious jab to the solar plexus that knocked him right off his feet and left him winded and gasping on the ground.

'Had enough?' Thorn asked, leering down at him.

The crowd was silent, fearing the worst.

Lying there, William realised that his only hope was to tire his heavier opponent by making him chase round the ring.

'I haven't started yet!' cried William, struggling to his feet and wiping his gloves on his shirt.

During the following rounds, William back-pedalled around the ring, peppering Thorn's face with lefts and rights. This infuriated Thorn, who pursued William with reckless abandon, oblivious of the fact that his face was becoming a mass of bruises and small cuts. William also noted that Thorn was breathing with difficulty through a blood-clogged nose. He decided the time had come to finish him off. The hurt he had received from the blow to his solar plexus was still vividly in William's mind and he thought it would be poetic justice to deliver a similar punch as the *coup de grâce*.

When the opportunity arose, William gathered up all his remaining strength and planted a full-blooded blow just above Thorn's bulging waistline. Thorn stood for an instant goggle-eyed then, bending double, vomited over his trousers before toppling over onto his back, where he lay motionless. Tancred hurried into the centre of the ring and bent over him.

'Are you all right, Thorn?' he shouted anxiously.

Thorn painfully forced himself into a sitting position and grunted.

William walked over and, staring contemptuously down at him, demanded, 'Do you wish to continue or have you had enough?'

Thorn wiped the blood and vomit from his mouth and murmured, 'Enough.'

Lowering his face until it was level with Thorn's, William hissed, 'Sleep in your own bed in future.'

Back in their room, Tancred smiled sardonically and said, 'William, my boy, you'll have the devil's own job to shake off that little blighter now, you know.'

'What on earth do you mean?'

'Didn't you see Oliver's face after you slayed the ogre?'

'No.'

'Oh, those big innocent eyes filled with adoration. He's yours. Take him, William. After all, you've abandoned your faith so you're free to indulge in any form of pleasure or perversity that takes your fancy.'

'When you uttered those words before, I had the impression that you would figure in that perversity.'

Tancred appeared disconcerted and looked out of the window. 'Sorry to disappoint you, William, but I feel my role in life is to be the corrupter and not the corrupted,' he said softly.

At the next rehearsal William kept a wary eye on Oliver and tried to avoid being alone with him. He resented Tancred's suggestion that he should take advantage of the gratitude that Oliver naturally felt. To William's surprise, Oliver seemed equally reticent and during breaks in the rehearsal kept well away, though William did spot, on a number of occasions, Oliver's pale face peering thoughtfully at him from a distance.

Spear was hammering home the fact that Shakespeare was fully cognisant of the relationship between punctuation and the intelligent speaking of the lines.

'How do we know that?' asked William, who enjoyed the rehearsals and found Spear's insights into Shakespeare quite stimulating.

'Study the Prologue of Peter Quince and the comments made by Duke Theseus and Lysander on his delivery of it,' said Spear.

Spear went on to quote the relevant passage, 'Duke Theseus says: "This fellow doth not stand upon points." Whereupon Lysander replies: "He hath rid his Prologue like a rough colt; he knows not the stop. A good moral my Lord: it is not enough to speak; but to speak true." Duke Theseus goes on to comment: "His speech was like a tangled chain; nothing impair'd, but all disorder'd." '

'But the folios could have been riddled with printers' errors,' said William.

'If the craftsmen of the printing-house were capable of recording with flawless accuracy the deliberate mispunctuation of Quince's Prologue, they were surely able to observe the playwright's intentions elsewhere,' Spear retorted sharply.

Spear had given much thought to the part music would play in his production. His research had convinced him that the music had to be an integral part of the play. It should not be shared only by the playwright and the audience to the exclusion of the characters on stage. Therefore, it should only be used when the dialogue or action called for it. For example, the horns would sound to herald the arrival of the Duke's hunting party and later to wake the sleeping lovers. The music should come from different parts of the playhouse and the musicians should often appear on the stage. He decided that the instruments available to Shakespeare would have been drums, horns, trumpets, cornets, flutes, pipes, lutes and the human voice.

Spear was having problems with David, the boy playing Helena; he knew his lines well enough but delivered them in an unmodulated manner that killed all meaning. This was especially evident in the scene where a contemptuous Demetrius threatens to leave her to the mercy of the wild beasts of the forest.

William was standing with the small group of players observing Spear as he attempted to illustrate how Helena's response should be delivered.

Spear took centre stage and declaimed,

'The wildest hath not such a heart as you:
Run when you will, the story shall be chang'd:
Apollo flies, and Daphne holds the chase;
The Dove pursues the Griffin, the mild Hind
Makes speed to catch the Tiger. Bootless speed,
When cowardice pursues, and valour flies.'

He turned to David and demanded, 'Do you think Apollo would run away or that doves would pursue griffins or hinds go hunting tigers or cowardice pursue while valour flies?' he demanded.

'Well... no, sir... I s-suppose not,' David stammered.

'Then you must convey to the audience that these are paradoxes. And how do we do this?'

At this point Spear stopped and, putting his face close up to David's, hissed, 'By introducing contrasting levels of pitch into our voice. Not by speaking the lines in a flat monotone, as you persist in doing.'

William felt a gentle tap on his arm and, on turning, found Oliver standing at his side.

'You are no Demetrius. You didn't run when you faced Thorn,' Oliver said, looking up at William. 'I haven't thanked you for saving me from him.'

Embarrassed, William placed an arm around Oliver's narrow shoulders, 'Oh, think nothing of it,' he said. 'Bullies like him need to be taught a lesson.'

He had thrown out the remark in an offhand manner but the contact with Oliver's frail body and the sincerity of the boy's gratitude had induced in

William a sudden surge of tender protectiveness such has he had never known before.

'I hope that we can become firm friends,' Oliver said, holding out his hand.

Dazed by the strange emotions seething within him, William shook the proffered hand and said, 'Yes indeed, why not?'

Since the day of the fight, the relationship between Tancred and William was one of polite tolerance. William harboured a hurt resentment at Tancred's cool rebuff of his advances while Tancred felt that his mask of cynical hedonism had been removed to reveal a creature who, despite his brave words, was in thrall to conventional morality. This tacit hostility lent an air of credibility to the heated exchanges between Oberon and Titania.

Oliver was having difficulty with the part of Puck and during one rehearsal Spear took him to one side.

'What's the problem?' Spear asked gently.

'Well sir, I don't understand what sort of a creature Puck is.'

'But the point is that he is not one creature.'

'I don't follow you, sir.'

'He is a clown but he is also the devil. See his dark side – "Sometime a horse I'll be, sometime a hound/ A hog, a headless bear, some time a fire/ And neigh, and bark, and grunt, and roar, and burn/ Like horse, hound, hog, bear, fire, at every turn." He is the demon of movement, he is as quick as thought – "I'll put a girdle round about the earth in forty minutes." He is a blind cupid. Oberon is the one who devises the plan but it is Puck who sprinkles the eyes of the lovers with berry juice and, by blundering, produces the cruel mayhem.'

'So I can change as the mood takes me?'

'You change as Shakespeare takes you,' Spear said sharply.

This exchange gave Oliver confidence and he started to swing to and fro, and hop in and out of his umbrella with great gusto. The burgeoning friendship between William and Oliver gave their scenes together a warmth which so pleased Spear, he directed William that, after greeting Puck with the words, "My gentle Puck, come hither", he should kiss Oliver on the forehead.

As the time for the dress rehearsal approached, Spear had to consider the question of costumes. He knew from his researches that Shakespeare used contemporary, that is Elizabethan, costume but would add a touch of period colour. This had tempted him to consider using modern dress but he realised that he would be committing an anachronism by dressing the players in a fashion which could never have entered Shakespeare's conception. He therefore determined to play safe and use Elizabethan costumes.

One thing he was sure of was that Shakespeare's players would have had an extensive wardrobe of magnificent costumes from which to draw. This he had gleaned from eyewitness accounts of the performances, which remarked on the astonishing grandeur of the costumes. He also knew that vast sums of money were paid to achieve that level of opulence. In addition, the nobility, slavishly following the ever-changing fashions at court, would give away to the players opulent garments that they might have worn only once or twice.

Having made his decision, Spear bullied the bursar into providing the necessary funds. There was great excitement when the costumes arrived and much laughter and teasing as the boys tried them on. William and Tancred each had two different costumes according to their dual roles. Theseus, as befitted a Duke, was clothed in a heavy brocade tunic embroidered with precious stones, and the finest hose, while upon his feet were gold-buckled shoes, the predominant colour being a pale blue. Oberon's costume was equally resplendent but the colour was black laced with flashings of silver. A pair of diaphanous wings discreetly folded on his back indicated the fact that he was King of the Fairies. The costumes for Hippolyta and Titania were typical of those worn by a noblewoman of the Elizabethan court, the distinction between mortal and fairy being made by the different colours and the discreetly folded wings.

Spear had given much thought as to how he should dress Ariel. The result was a costume of stunning simplicity. When Oliver shyly appeared before them, he was naked from the waist up apart from a tunic of transparent gossamer. A pair of golden voluminous silk trousers, caught tight around the ankles, covered his legs, and his feet were bare.

Tancred viewed with derisive amusement the growing intimacy between William and Oliver. But he felt that in some way he was responsible for

William's present behaviour and, though he now found it difficult to tolerate the fellow, he decided to warn William of the danger he was running. They were walking back to their room after a rehearsal when Tancred caught William's arm and forced him to a standstill.

'I know we haven't exactly been hitting it off lately,' Tancred began. 'I evidently haven't lived up to the image you had of me.'

'You're like a sounding brass, all noise but signifying nothing,' William said scornfully. 'Who was it told me that now I had lost my faith we could indulge in any pleasure or perversity that took our fancy?'

Tancred flinched and said sadly, 'There you go again. William, you should have realised that I'm a cerebral creature. My rebellions are all in my head. I'll pass the bullets but don't ask me to fire them. Anyway, since you've used my words against me, who was the person who, when challenged that he might be a paedophile, repudiated the idea with great indignation? "Oh no. Not at all. I'm not like that." '

'I'm certainly not a paedophile.'

'Then why are you and Oliver always hanging around together? Good God, you sneak into town and take afternoon tea together in the King's Hotel, like an old married couple.'

'You, with your twisted mind, can't envisage a friendship between a senior and a junior that is innocent and purely platonic.'

'Come on, William. A bit of horseplay in the Chamber after lights out is one thing. It's part of the public school ethos. But this mooning around in broad daylight is unhealthy. What do you talk about over your muffins and tea?'

'Our families. He's a lonely boy, you know. His father is in the colonial service and so his parents are out in India. He only gets to see them once a year. We talk about what we want to do with our lives. It's all perfectly above board. Ever since I rescued him from Thorn, I've felt very protective towards him.'

As he said this, William knew that he was not being honest with Tancred or with himself. That instance when he had put his arm around Oliver's shoulders, he had not only experienced a rush of tender protectiveness, there had also been a frisson of sexual excitement. During the last rehearsal, when he had kissed Oliver on the forehead, he had felt a desire to gather the boy up in his arms and press that lean, firm body to his breast.

'Well, I've done my duty,' Tancred said. 'Stop this relationship, it can only lead to disaster. Your young life is a blank canvas, don't start the painting with a false brushstroke.'

He turned and walked rapidly away, leaving William standing alone. A boy, who had been watching them from a distance, moved tentatively towards William. It was Oliver.

Tancred's prescience was to be vindicated all too soon.

The dress rehearsal had gone well and everyone was in a high state of exhilaration, except Spear, who knew that a successful dress rehearsal normally boded ill for the performance proper. The cast had gone backstage to change out of their costumes but William and Oliver lingered in the study. It was here that Spear had placed the bank 'where the wild thyme grows' and where 'sleeps Titania, sometime of the night'. He had made the bank by covering a nest of cushions with a drape of green velvet and strewing it with all the flowers in season at the time. The curtains were closed and the intimacy of the small space and the fragrance of the flowers enhanced the emotion that the performance had aroused.

Oliver lay down on the bank and provocatively stretched in imitation of Titania sleeping. The excited babble from the changing room had died and there was a strange stillness, indicating that every one had left and they were alone in the building. William looked down on the fair-haired Oliver. He perceived, for the first time, how the delicate nostrils and the bright green eyes gave him the look of a small, wild forest animal.

Seized by a sudden madness, William lowered himself onto the bank and feverishly removed Oliver's tunic. With shaking hands, he undid Oliver's trousers at the waist and slid them off. Oliver was not wearing underclothes and so his completely naked body was exposed to William's gaze. He had just reached puberty and so his body was touchingly virginal. The contrast between its clean, hard beauty and his recollection of the intimidating voluptuousness of the unresponsive Ann Wilson sent a pang of longing through William's being. He tore off his clothes and, putting his arms around Oliver, clutched him to his breast. He felt Oliver tremble like a plucked harp string. To his surprise, he found that he was not gripped by any feelings of lust but was filled with a deep satisfaction that, by holding Oliver in his arms in this way, he was the protector of something unique and precious.

It was at that moment of revelation that they heard voices outside the study. The headmaster had been unable to attend the dress rehearsal but had decided that Spear should now take him on a guided tour of the set.

Spear's high-pitched whine pierced the air. 'Behind these curtains, Master, we have what was known in Shakespeare's day as the study.'

This was followed by the headmaster's deep, authoritative *basso profundo*: 'Yes, yes! I'm not a complete ignoramus you know, Spear.'

'Indeed not, Master.'

'Just tell me what use you have put it to.'

'The bank on which Titania sleeps. Look.'

With those words, Spear drew back the curtains with a flourish.

CHAPTER 6

The carriage rumbled up the long circular drive to the Castle of Miramar. Gutierrez de Estrada poked his head out of the window and stared in disbelief.

'God man,' he said to his companion, 'it is an Austrian Archduke we're visiting, not some oriental potentate?'

José Hidalgo looked puzzled and answered, 'What do you mean?'

'Well, Pepe, take a look yourself.'

The building they were approaching would not have looked out of place in Baghdad but outside Trieste it was wildly incongruous. It was built out of the purest white marble and adorned with slender, pointed towers. On alighting at the ornately sculpted entrance, Estrada and Hidalgo were ushered into a medieval world of battleaxes, coats-of-arms, suits of armour and minstrel galleries. It was when they entered the great hall and saw through the large window the terrifying drop to the waters of the Gulf of Trieste that they appreciated the dramatic position of the castle.

Maximilian and Charlotte had decided to receive their visitors in the more informal ambience of the great hall rather than the throne room. Maximilian was aware of the purpose of their visit and did not wish to confer too official a status on the proceedings, as he was determined not to give an answer to their request until he had given the matter more thought.

The formal introductions over, Hidalgo, with an ingratiating smile, broached the purpose of their mission.

'Your Highness will no doubt recall our last meeting?' he asked.

'In the gardens at St Cloud,' Maximilian answered. 'You spoke of the distressing situation existing in Mexico at that time.'

Hidalgo shook his head sadly.

'Ah yes. The country divided and in chaos, with Juárez challenging the legitimate most Holy Roman Catholic government.'

He paused and smiled broadly. 'But all is changed, as you know. The French have driven Juárez and his rabble from Mexico City and forced them to flee to the far north. Our country is restored.'

'I congratulate the French on their victory and rejoice with you on the restoration of orderly government. I do not see, however, what this has to do with me.'

Gutierrez de Estrada, who had been sitting on the edge of his chair, barely able to contain his impatience, rose to his feet.

'Your Imperial Highness,' he said in a voice rasping with emotion, 'on that glorious morning in May when General Forey rode into Mexico City, the sun glinting on the helmets, breastplates and swords of his gallant men, the future of Mexico was assured. Never again would that anti-christ

Juárez, his army a defeated, bedraggled remnant cowering in the far north, desecrate our lovely country. Ever mindful of the wellbeing of the Mexican people, the Emperor of the French ordered the general to set up an Assembly of Notables, drawn from the common people of Mexico. Their task was to choose a form of government for Mexico.'

Here, Gutierrez de Estrada looked straight at Maximilian and announced, 'The Assembly has made its choice. They voted for a monarchy and named you, Archduke Ferdinand Maximilian Joseph, as the man they wished to be their sovereign.'

Before Maximilian could reply, Gutierrez went down on one knee and declaimed, 'Royal Highness, as soon as Emperor Napoleon, that powerful Prince who has restored liberty to the afflicted people of Mexico, heard the decision of the Assembly, he dispatched José Hidalgo and myself, two poor servants of our nation, to beg you to accept this crown. The Prince believes that without you all that he has achieved will be lost. May it please your Imperial Highness to answer our prayers and accept our choice, so that we may carry the joyous tidings back to a country that awaits them with such hopeful anticipation.'

Maximilian rose and went over to the window where he stood gazing out across the Gulf to the Istrian coast.

'Gentlemen,' he said, 'I would be less than frank if I did not tell you that I am aware you have already consulted various heads of state, including my dear brother, as to my suitability for this high honour.

The fact that you are here must mean that I have their blessing. How very flattering.'

The irony behind these words was lost on Gutierrez but not on Hidalgo's sensitive antennae. He hastened over to where Maximilian stood and spoke urgently to the stiff imperial back.

'Your Highness! It was not to question them as to your suitability. The whole of Mexico and the mighty Emperor of the French were convinced that you were the one man who could bring stability and prosperity to Mexico. No, it was to enquire whether they thought you would consider our heartfelt plea.'

Maximilian turned round and said brusquely, 'I have a number of matters that need urgent attention. We will meet this evening for dinner. In the meantime, the Archduchess will show you around the palace.'

Maximilian retired to his study while Charlotte, smiling benignly, led the two Mexicans out of the great hall to start an exhausting exploration of the palace and its extensive grounds. Hidalgo pranced along at her side, feigning great interest as she expounded on the myriad features of the building and its environs. Gutierrez lagged behind, his mind in a ferment of speculation on what Maximilian's decision would be. They visited the comprehensive library adorned with the busts of every great thinker and writer from Aristotle to Goethe. They ascended the massive oak staircase and traversed terraces adorned with sparkling fountains and limpid pools filled with exotic fish. They leaned over balustrades and gazed down from a frightening height at the foaming sea. Leaving the building, they wandered through gardens carpeted with flowers and delineated with masses of shrubbery and elegant trees. It was a walk made all the more delightful by the groups of graceful statuary stationed around every corner.

'You know, the Archduke planned and supervised the building of this palace himself,' Charlotte said proudly.

Hidalgo raised his hands in admiration and exclaimed, 'His Highness is a man of many talents and the location is so...'

He struggled for the right word.

'Spectacular,' Charlotte suggested.

'Exactly,' sighed Hidalgo.

Gutierrez scowled and groaned under his breath.

'The story of how he came to choose this place is quite romantic,' Charlotte said. 'When a very young man, long before he met me, he used to sail single-handed in a skiff along this coast. These waters are notorious for the sudden squalls that can blow up from nowhere and one day he was shipwrecked on the beach below. If it had not been for some local fishermen, he would undoubtedly have perished. They rescued him and gave him shelter. He vowed that he would build a magnificent palace on this spot and, when he married, make it home for himself and his bride.'

Hidalgo turned to Gutierrez and said, 'Isn't that a romantic tale, my friend?'

A look of disbelief passed over Gutierrez's face and he startled Charlotte by asking bluntly, 'You and his Highness are no longer involved with affairs of state, so how do you occupy yourselves?'

Charlotte coloured at the undisguised insolence of the question and said, 'I spend most of my time reading.'

'Poetry and such like, no doubt?' he said dismissively.

'Well, yes, but mathematics too.'

'Mathematics? You do surprise me, Your Highness. I would have thought mathematics too practical a subject for a lady of your refined tastes. Has it not been said that mathematics is the journeyman of the physical sciences?'

'I fear, sir, that you are behind the times. It is true that in the 18th century it was considered that mathematics should serve the scientific and technical needs of a nation. For example, projective geometry – where a three-dimensional object is described by its orthogonal projections onto horizontal and vertical planes – was very useful in the design of forts, gun emplacements and machines. Calculus was developed to solve the problems of determining areas and volumes and the calculation of tangents to curves. Newton used it in his investigation of the planetary orbits. But a widening gulf has opened between mathematics and the physical sciences. It no longer has to rely for its validity on its application to science and has become a subject in its own right. This means that it has developed higher standards of rigour and evolved in directions that have little to do with applicability. It deals now with concepts and has become an art form. One might ask the question: where does mathematics end and philosophy begin?'

'I stand corrected. Might I ask how your husband, the Archduke, spends his time?'

'Look around you. He has devoted himself to perfecting our home.'

Gutierrez spoke deliberately: 'And do you think that is a suitable way for a man of your husband's ability to spend the rest of his life – locked in this gilded cage?'

Gutierrez had taken a risk in being so brutal and he waited apprehensively for Charlotte's reaction. Hidalgo shuffled uneasily, horrified at his companion's presumption.

The question had been a shrewd one, however, as Charlotte had long been troubled by the frustration she sensed festering in Maximilian at his incarceration at Miramar.

She answered calmly, 'For a man who was once Viceroy of Lombardy-Venetia it is of course disappointing to be excluded from all decision making, especially at a time when Austria is beset with problems. But the Emperor has seen fit to decree it so and my husband and I, as his subjects, must bow to his will.'

Sensing his opportunity, Gutierrez pounced. 'Mexico offers the Archduke a glorious way out of this terrible sterility. It holds up before him the golden crown of an Emperor and begs him to seize it with both hands and place it on his noble head.'

'My husband is a man of honour and would only take the crown if he were certain that the people of Mexico wished him to rule them.'

'But the Assembly chose him unanimously,' Hidalgo protested.

'But how can my husband know that they represent the will of the poor peasants?' Charlotte rejoined.

After a moment's hesitation, Gutierrez said forcefully, 'We will go out into every town in Mexico gathering signatures for a petition begging Archduke Maximilian to become our Emperor. We will collect hundreds of thousands of signatures. Will that not show him that he is the overwhelming choice of the humble citizens of Mexico?'

That evening at dinner, Hidalgo and Gutierrez formally made the proposition that Maximilian would be presented with irrefutable evidence, in the form of a petition endorsed by the ordinary men and women of Mexico, that he was indeed their choice. In the light of this undertaking, Maximilian graciously consented to consider thier request.

The following morning as they drove away from Miramar, Hidalgo grasped Gutierrez' sleeve and asked anxiously, 'How can you be so sure we'll be able to collect enough signatures? The peasants support Juárez.'

Gutierrez smiled grimly and said with a chuckle, 'We'll send the French troops into every stinking hamlet and beat the signatures out of the unwashed bastards.'

During the next few months, while they waited for the arrival of the petition, Maximilian and Charlotte threw themselves enthusiastically into the task of learning about the country they hoped they were soon to rule. Books on the topography, climate, history and culture of Mexico flooded into Miramar. They would take it in turn to read to each other.

One afternoon Charlotte was describing the main features of the land mass, as Maximilian listened with his usual intensity.

'Most of Mexico is an immense, elevated plateau, flanked by mountain ranges that fall sharply off to narrow coastal strips in the west and east,' she began. 'The two mountain chains, the Sierra Madre Occidental to the west and the Sierra Madre Oriental to the east, meet in a region called La Junta in the south east. The most prominent topographical feature is the central plateau that constitutes more than half the total area of Mexico. The coastal plains are flat and sandy.'

'The rivers,' Maximilian interjected. 'What does it say about the rivers?'

Charlotte glanced down the page and read, 'The longest river is the Rio Grande, which extends along the Mexican-US border. Other important rivers are the Balsas Pánuco, Grijalva, Usumacinta and the Conchos.'

Charlotte stopped, let the book slide onto her lap and said sadly, 'You know Max, this reminds me of how excited we were when Francis made you Viceroy and look how all our high hopes came to nothing.'

'That's why I insisted on them proving to me that the majority of Mexicans want me to have the crown. In Italy we were doomed from the start no matter how enlightened my policies were. They hated Austrians and wanted us out of their country. In Mexico I must be sure before I set foot on that elevated central plateau that I am welcome. Old Leopold, pompous bore though he is, had the right idea when he wrote,' here Maximilian mimicked Leopold's voice, 'My boy do as I did. Don't let them see you chasing after the crown, rather let them chase after you. It worked for me as you can see.'

'I don't trust Napoleon. He wants you there to protect French interests. Will he stick by you if things should go horribly wrong?'

'We'll be in Paris shortly. Then will be the time, when we're face to face, to secure a copper-bottomed guarantee. Leopold is most insistent that I get a written statement, signed by Napoleon, as to the length of time the French troops will stay in Mexico and their numbers.'

When Maximilian and Charlotte arrived in Paris they were enthusiastically received by Napoleon, who saw Maximilian as the key to removing the heavy burden of French involvement in Mexico while still retaining control of the region. The crucial meeting took place at Versailles where Napoleon, with Eugenie at his side, faced Maximilian and Charlotte.

Napoleon rose from his chair and striding across the room grasped Maximilian's hand.

'Maximilian,' he said. 'I cannot express how overjoyed I am that you are going to complete the work that I began. Peace and the Holy Roman Catholic Church now reign in Mexico and you, as Emperor, will ensure that remains the case.'

'Oh, my dear boy,' Eugenie trilled, 'at last you will have a position in the world worthy of your exalted Habsburg lineage and a task deserving the attention of your exemplary talents!'

It suited Eugenie to ignore the rumours that Maximilian was Reichstadt's son, since this would impugn the legitimacy of her husband's claim to be Bonaparte's sole heir.

She turned to Charlotte and gushed, 'My dear Charlotte, you and Max will make such a handsome couple in your robes.'

Charlotte flushed with annoyance and said, 'I look forward to using my poor talents in support of Max, as I did when he was Viceroy of Lombardy-Venetia.'

Maximilian, who had been standing tensely at Charlotte's side steeling himself for the task of extracting satisfactory guarantees from Napoleon, now spoke.

'Your Majesty,' he began. 'Mindful as I am of the great honour you do me and my wife, I would not be doing justice to the cause you hold so dear to your heart if I did not ask for certain assurances that I feel are necessary for the success of the enterprise.'

Napoleon smiled and said, 'France has devoted immense resources of money and troops in order to hand you a country purged of troublemakers and eager for your jurisdiction. What more do you want?'

'Documents, signed by your Majesty, stating the number of French troops to remain in Mexico after my coronation and the length of time before you recall them.'

'France cannot go on sustaining the heavy expenditure needed to sustain an army in Mexico. The idea is to develop an indigenous Mexican army, otherwise the French soldiers will be looked upon as an army of occupation and that will cause rising resentment and strengthen the hand of Juárez and his rebels.'

'Yes, yes. But there must be an interregnum to allow the formation of a disciplined Mexican army. At present they are a subversive rabble.'

Napoleon closed his hooded eyes. There is too much at stake here for me to lose my temper, he thought. He slowly opened his eyes and gazed reassuringly at Maximilian.

'Of course, there will not be an immediate withdrawal of French troops. I'll draw up a document detailing the specific numbers and the time they will stay. Believe me, it will lay all your fears to rest. Trust me.'

When Maximilian left Paris he carried in his portmanteau a letter signed by Napoleon in which the Emperor pledged unequivocally to keep twenty five thousand troops in Mexico until a credible national army was formed. In addition, eight thousand men of the Foreign Legion would remain for a period of eight years. He left behind with Napoleon an undertaking to accept the Mexican throne if Gutierrez delivered the signatures he had promised.

He and Charlotte were in high good humour when they arrived back at Miramar. All they had to do was wait until the Mexican delegation arrived and then they would be freed from an idleness that, however luxurious, was crippling their spirits. The elation was short-lived. Francis had received a communication from Napoleon in which the latter revealed that Maximilian was prepared to accept the Mexican Crown. Francis promptly wrote to his brother informing him that he must renounce irrevocably all his rights and inheritances as a member of the Habsburg family.

Maximilian and Charlotte were on the terrace at Miramar when the missive arrived. As he read it, Maximilian's face went white with rage and when he had finished he handed it to Charlotte without a word.

Maximilian waited tensely as Charlotte read the letter before he burst out angrily, 'It's monstrous. We must go to him immediately.'

Charlotte raised her hand and said calmly, 'No, Max, not immediately. If we are to make him change his mind, we must show him how this places you in an impossible situation.'

'And how do we do that?'

'Write to Napoleon. After all, you have both exchanged solemn undertakings. Yes, write to Napoleon and wait until you receive a reply. Then I believe we will have something worthwhile to take to your brother.'

On receiving Napoleon's reply, Maximilian and Charlotte left Miramar by carriage and drove to Trieste railway station where they boarded their train to Vienna. At the Hofburg, Emperor Francis and his mother Sophia awaited their arrival. Francis had wished to conduct the audience in the formal surroundings of the throne room but Sophia, anxious to heal the rift between her two sons, had persuaded him to meet them in one of the private sitting-rooms. When Maximilian and Charlotte entered the room, they found Francis and Sophia sitting uneasily together on a chaise-longue. Francis, with an imperial wave of the hand, indicated that they should sit on two upright chairs that had been placed facing him. After a moment's awkward silence the battle commenced.

The altercation followed the pattern of the fourth movement of Beethoven's String Quartet No 10 in E Flat, with Maximilian and Charlotte as the first and second violins, respectively, Sophia as the viola and Francis as the cello. Vigorous, staccato playing sounded from all four instruments: a dreamy and melodic solo from the viola; a virile solo from the first violin; a duet from the second violin and cello; a meandering pianissimo over the cello's insistent bass; a crescendo leading to final unison.

Francis: 'Archduke.'
Maximilian: 'Your Majesty.'
Francis: 'Sister-in-law.'
Charlotte: 'Your Majesty.'
Sophia: 'Max.'
Maximilian: 'Mother.'
Sophia: 'Charlotte.'
Charlotte: 'Mother-in-law.'
Sophia: 'My children, I appeal to you both. Once you were loving brothers, why is there now this dissent? Francis, do you remember the time when you and Max were small boys and Max was in quarantine with measles? You were heartbroken and wrote to him every day telling him all the things you had done that day. Two brothers could not have been closer. And when you grew to manhood, do you remember the time when that revolutionary struck with his knife and seriously injured you? Didn't Max rush across the country to be by your side? And didn't he build a church on that very spot and dedicate it to your safe recovery? Could actions speak more loudly? You cannot disinherit such a loving brother.'
Maximilian: 'Mother has spoken of the way I hastened to your sick bed after the attempted assassination. Does that not prove that the love I

felt for you as a boy still burns fiercely within me? With the consent of your Majesty, I pledged my word of honour to the people of Mexico. When I did, there was no question of the conditions you are now seeking to impose on me. A nation has called on me to lead them to a future of peace and prosperity. To obey that call I must leave my beloved country and the tranquillity of my beautiful Miramar, a home I have built with love. Do not make my sacrifice more cruel. Return the love that I have shown to you.'

Francis: 'To be honest with you, Max, I was always a little suspicious of the alacrity you showed on that occasion, you were not wont to move so fast.'

Sophia: 'Shame on you, Francis, for such ignoble thoughts.'

Charlotte: 'Your Majesty, you cannot make Max sign away his birthright.'

Francis: 'I can only give my consent if your husband signs a document renouncing all claims on the throne of Austria and all his inheritances as an Archduke of the House of Habsburg.'

Charlotte: 'Please, Francis, think of my unborn children. You must relent and give us the assurance that should the Mexican enterprise fail, then at least Max and I, together with our future children, will have a place back in Austria befitting our rank.'

Francis: 'Charlotte, please understand that the protection of the dynasty is my one aim in life. What if I should die, how could Max, a thousand miles away, act as regent for my son Rudolph? What if you and Max have children and years in the future they decide to come home from Mexico and challenge my children for their inheritance? No! He must sign away all his rights as a member of the Habsburg family.'

Maximilian: 'I will not sign. If necessary I will board a French ship and sail for Mexico without your permission.'

Francis: 'Do that and I will erase your name from the lineage of the House of Habsburg. As far as Austria is concerned, it will be as if you never existed.'

Sophia: 'No, Francis, you could never do that to your brother. It would break my heart.'

Francis: 'He must sign or refuse the crown of Mexico.'

Sophia: 'I beg you, Francis, do not make my son sign a document that disinherits him.'

Maximilian: 'I have a letter from Napoleon concerning this matter.'

Francis: 'You wrote to Napoleon?'

Maximilian: 'Listen to what he has to say: "Reluctant as I am to interfere in a quarrel between you and your exalted brother, I must make the following observation. You entered an agreement which, in honour, you cannot abrogate. In what esteem would you hold me if, when your Imperial Highness had already landed in Mexico, I were to renege on the commitments I had made to you and withdrew all French troops from Mexico?" '

Francis: 'Napoleon wrote that?'

Maximilian: 'Yes. Here, take it.'

He leaned forward and passed the letter to Francis who studied it closely, a worried frown on his face.

Francis: 'You shouldn't have involved Napoleon in a family matter. It's treachery. As if I haven't enough worries on the diplomatic front, you have to go and force me into confrontation with France.'

Maximilian: 'It doesn't have to be like that. Make reasonable provision for my family and me. Then I will be able to honour my commitment to Napoleon.'

Charlotte: 'Dear Francis, we are your family and ask only what is our due – no more, no less.'

Sophia: 'My one wish is to see my sons in amenity. I plead with you Francis not to break your mother's heart.'

The look of a trapped animal passed across Francis' face and he reluctantly succumbed.

Francis: 'In no way will I allow Austria to become involved with this Mexican adventure. But I will make Max and Charlotte a yearly allowance and guarantee that should they ever have to return to Austria they and any children they may have will be given a position befitting that of members of the House of Habsburg.'

Sophia: 'Bless you, Francis.'

Francis: 'So, Max, you can become Emperor of Mexico and you, dear sister-in-law, Empress. That should please your patron Napoleon and get him off my back. And mother, I trust you will be content and that your heart will remain intact for the foreseeable future.'

Sophia: 'I am content.'

Francis: 'I will have the necessary document drawn up and deliver it in person to you, Max, at

Miramar, where we can both sign it. That is my final decision.'

He rose to his feet and looked at each one in turn. They immediately responded by standing. Maximilian stepped forward and offered his hand.

Maximilian: 'I agree, brother.'

Francis took Maximilian's hand, held it for an instant and then turned away.

Charlotte: 'Max will not betray your trust. He was born to fulfil a great destiny. He will make you and Austria proud of him.'

* * *

Before Maximilian and Charlotte left for Miramar, Sophia received them in her apartments at the palace. Whenever she looked at Maximilian she saw the face of her dead lover Reichstadt and was moved to the verge of tears by the memory of her lost love. She was torn between her burning desire to see him attain a destiny worthy of Napoleon's grandson and a mother's fear for the safety of her child.
'Come here, Max, sit on the floor beside me as you used to,' she called as they entered the room and stood awkwardly before her.
Maximilian gave his wife an embarrassed smile and complied. Sophia leaned forward and held his head between her hands.
'I remember one particular day when your father lay on his death bed,' she said, her voice muted

with sadness. 'It was particularly hot and I had to wipe the perspiration from his poor face. He whispered, 'If it was not for the child you carry in your womb, my father's line would end with the death of this miserable body. I gathered him in my arms and made him a promise. I promised him that the child would be a son and that he would grow to...'

She paused and gave a self-deprecating laugh before continuing, '...bestride the world like a colossus. He settled back on the pillows, his face illumined with a sad longing and said, "I pray I'll live to hold him in my arms." He died a few hours before you were born.'

'Come, Mother, this is not the time for such morbid memories,' Maximilian exclaimed as he struggled to his feet.

'No, no, not morbid,' Sophia said quickly. 'For I know that you are going to accomplish the promise I made and it fills me with joy. Forgive a mother's stupid fears for the safety of a beloved son. You and Charlotte set out for Italy with such high hopes and look how that ended – in disaster. But now, alone in a distant land populated with a wild and barbarous people, depending on the protection of a capricious ally, you both could lose your lives.'

'Mother, things are so different. Then I was venturing into a country that hated all Austrians and wished to drive us from the soil of Italy. But I go to Mexico because the people have chosen me to be their Emperor.'

'But how can you be sure of that?'

'Because very soon Gutierrez will present me with a petition signed by hundreds of thousands of

Mexicans – wealthy landlords, humble peasants – all begging me to take the crown.'

'France, Gutierrez and his crew, can you trust them?'

Charlotte, who had remained silent during this exchange, clenched her hands and with messianic fever said, 'While there is breath left in my body, I will hold these people to the pledges they have made.'

Sophia smiling fondly at Charlotte said, 'Ah my dear child, I have always found it hard to envisage the time after my death when Max would still be in this world and I would not be there to protect him. I will die happy, knowing that Max has you by his side.'

For the second time Gutierrez de Estrada and José Hidalgo approached the castle at Miramar. This time, however, they were not alone, for behind them in a convoy of coaches travelled a formidable delegation from the Mexican Assembly.

Gutierrez glanced down at the large leather case resting on the floor of the carriage and said, 'Better see that all the blood has been washed off that petition before we present it to our future Emperor.'

Seeing the horrified look on Hidalgo's face, he laughed and said, 'A joke, man. Don't you recognise a joke when you hear one? Anyway, any cleaning that was necessary would have been done on the spot.'

On arrival, the delegation was ushered into the throne room where Maximilian, in his favourite uniform of Admiral of the Fleet decorated with the orders of the Golden Fleece and the Grand Cross of Saint Stephen, and Charlotte, resplendent in a gown of crimson silk with the black ribbon of the Order of Malta, were seated on thrones placed on a high dais.

Gutierrez stepped forward followed by two fellow émigrés carrying the bulky petition which they deposited at the foot of dais and then moved back into line.

'Noble Prince,' he declaimed, 'the petition lying at your feet is proof that the Notables and commoners of Mexico avow their eternal love and unshakeable fidelity. In their name I offer you the crown of Mexico.'

Tense and white-faced, Maximilian rose and stepped down from the dais so that he stood directly in front of Guiterrez. His voice when he spoke trembled with emotion.

'Honourable representatives of Mexico, you have proved to me that I am indeed the man you wish to be your leader. I accept the crown and pledge before you all to devote the remainder of my life to the service of the Mexican people.'

Guiterrez knelt before Maximilian and proclaimed in a loud voice, 'Archduke Ferdinand Maximilian Joseph of Austria, with the power invested in me I declare you Emperor of Mexico. God save His Majesty Maximilian the First. God save Her Majesty Charlotte, Empress of Mexico.'

A great cheer arose from the assembled dignitaries and the Mexican flag was unfurled from the battlements of the castle.

That evening, before the banquet called to celebrate the day's events, Maximilian and

Charlotte were alone in the library. Maximilian sat in a chair while Charlotte stood at his side, cradling his head on her breast.

He was near tears as he mumbled, 'All my life I have flitted from one diversion to another like some demented butterfly – poetry, history, art, architecture, military tactics – and proved a mediocrity at them all. I have travelled aimlessly over Europe like some bored dilettante. The one time I attempted to play a significant role – in Italy – it ended in a fiasco. Now I have taken on the role of Emperor. I should have given this more thought. To be responsible for the welfare of millions of people – the idea terrifies me! Charlotte, I know I am not capable of holding high office. Charlotte, please go and tell them that it has all been a mistake. Tell them I am not the man they think I am. Tell them I am not worthy.'

To Count Bombelles, who observed the scene from an open doorway, Charlotte was the picture of serenity. The calmness was born of an inner determination that she would not allow this foolish weakness of Maximilian to ruin her dream of the glory that awaited them both.

Speaking as if to a child she said, 'Not worthy! No man is more worthy of this crown or more fitted to administer the power it represents.'

'But I am no leader. I don't have the ruthlessness.'

'Mexico does not need ruthlessness now. The battle has been won. The nation is at your feet and looks for wise governance. It needs a ruler who can bring conciliation, a ruler who has sensitivity. You, Max, are that man.'

'Oh, Charlotte, how I wish I had your faith in my abilities.'

'The events of today have exhausted you. You need rest.'

Charlotte looked directly across the room to Count Bombelles and said, 'Karl, go and inform our guests that his Majesty has a slight indisposition and unfortunately is unable to attend the banquet. Empress Carlota will preside in his stead.'

'Carlota?' Karl said quizzically.

'Yes, Carlota. I wish to use the Spanish form of my name in future and this is the right time to tell them.'

The following morning Maximilian and Carlota walked in the gardens at Miramar. Spring had flung off the leash of winter and the flowers were beginning to bloom, the trees turn green and the birds sing. Maximilian had not slept and was as apprehensive and tearful as he had been the night before. Carlota spoke urgently but gently.

'I know you love the beauty and tranquillity of this place but have you been truly contented here?'

'Is it so small a thing/To have enjoyed the sun/ To have lived light in the spring/To have loved/To have thought, to have done?' Maximilian pleaded.

Carlota smiled indulgently and said, 'Oh Max, you're incorrigible. It's no good quoting Arnold at me. How many times in the past have you told me how frustrated you felt? How you, the grandson of a man before whom the princes of this world trembled, longed to be worthy of such a heritage? Well, now you have the chance. Grasp it with both hands before it passes beyond your reach forever. A Bonaparte founding a new empire.'

Three days later, on April 13, 1864, Emperor Maximilian and Empress Carlota set sail for Mexico.

CHAPTER 7

Shame is an isolating and alienating experience. The victim is exposed to the searing scrutiny and ridicule of others. The first impulse is to escape or hide but where this is impossible all that can be done is to face it out, pretend it is not happening. Shame, like physical pain, hardens the sufferer. William jumped to his feet and with assumed nonchalance attempted to pull on his trousers. A foot became snagged in the material and he went sprawling, providing Spear and the Master with a new perspective on his predicament. The Master was the first to speak

'Dawson, isn't it?' he barked. 'Cover yourself, boy!'

Oliver whimpered and curled up, covering his face with his hands.

The Master bent down and peered at the pathetic ball of quivering flesh.

'Why, it's young Oliver Fortiscue!' he exclaimed.

He turned in fury to William, who had hastily re-robed in the doublet and hose of Theseus and looked a decidedly dishevelled Duke.

'How dare you abuse an innocent lad like young Fortiscue? Mr Spear, conduct this miscreant to the sick bay and hold him there. I will join you after I have attended to this poor child's need.'

He waved dismissively and knelt down beside Oliver, where he gently helped the boy to dress. William and Spear walked in silence to the cell-like room dignified by the ludicrously inappropriate appellative 'sick bay', its only amenities being a truckle-bed and a rickety locker. Spear sat on the bed and wearily smoothed his lank hair back over his balding head with a yellow, dark-veined hand.

'Dawson,' he said sadly, 'I can't hide from you the deep disappointment your behaviour has caused me. That you should use the performance of a play that celebrates the sanctity of the love between man and woman as the occasion for an act of indecency destroys my faith in humanity.'

'But sir,' William protested. 'There was no such act.'

'No such act? Why, boy, you were both naked and in each other's arms!'

'You don't understand. I felt no lust but a feeling of chaste love and protectiveness towards Oliver.'

'You're right, I don't understand and you can be sure that the Master will definitely not understand. As for protecting young Fortiscue, you can leave that to the Master.'

'What do you mean?'

'Fortiscue's family are of ancient lineage and the boy's father is one of the country's top diplomats. The Master is very proud of the fact that Sir Fortiscue placed his son in Shackles.'

In his highly wrought state, the unintended pun caused William to emit a short laugh.

'This is no laughing matter, boy. In his mind you are the one to blame while Oliver is the innocent victim of your depravity. Why do you think the Master ordered me to bring you to the sick bay? He'll tell Oliver to forget about the incident and he'll keep you here in isolation under the pretence that you have measles or some other such infection.'

'But he can't keep me here indefinitely.'

'No, but long enough for him to inform your father that he is expelling you for gross moral turpitude and that in the interests of all the parties concerned it would be better if the matter was kept secret. Then he'll send you home to face your father's wrath. Situations like this have arisen before and he's always concealed them.'

'But my father won't accept that.'

'Oh yes he will. No father wants his son branded publicly as a degenerate. A clergyman, isn't he?'

'Yes.'

'Well, there you are, my boy. It's a pity it happened after a rehearsal of *A Midsummer Night's Dream* though. It was hard enough getting the Master to agree to our performing Shakespeare in the first place – he considers him a subversive. Now we'll be back to nativity plays and dramatisations of the work of Samuel Smiles. With a hey, and a ho, and a hey nonino.'

As he stared down at the defeated weary figure sitting on the bed, William recalled the wistful smile that had brightened Spear's face as, in answer to Oliver's question on the meaning of the play, he had said gently, 'It's a great celebration of love consummated in marriage.'

He remembered Theseus's words to Hermia, 'To live a barren sister all your life/ Chanting faint hymns to the cold fruitless moon.'

William forgot his own desperate situation and felt genuine pity for old Spear.

A week later William stood outside the closed door of the Rectory with the ubiquitous trunk upright beside him. Spear's prediction had proved cruelly accurate. William had not been allowed to set a foot outside that sick room. Food had been brought to him by matron who also provided him with a chamber pot for his other physical needs. The school had been informed that William Dawson was suffering from a particularly virulent strain of measles and would have to be kept in isolation until he was fit enough to travel home.

While William was under no illusion that his father would kill the fatted calf to welcome home the prodigal son, he hoped that the Rector would feel a certain solidarity with his son concerning the manner in which William had been condemned and Oliver exonerated. After all, it reflected badly on the status of the Rector vis-à-vis Sir Fortiscue. Muttering a prayer under his breath, William tugged at the bell-pull and heard the bell tinkling deep within the house. He glanced around to the right where the bay window of the Reverend Charles Dawson's study protruded into the forecourt and saw the stolid figure of the man himself standing motionless gazing into the distance, completely ignoring the obvious presence of his son on the doorstep.

The door opened a fraction and Gwener peered suspiciously through the narrow gap. The parish was not a wealthy one and so could not rise to the luxury of a live-in housekeeper. The establishment had to be content with a daily help and Gwener, a woman from the village, fulfilled that role. Her family was Welsh and impoverished, the father earning a meagre wage as a farm labourer. Gwener grew up as a living embodiment of their penury. Her body was small, thin and wasted; her face had the feverish eyes and desperate look of a ravenous animal. Mrs Dawson saw to it that she was well fed but the years of deprivation had left their indelible mark. William had not known whether to laugh or cry when Gwener had proudly told him that her name was Welsh for Venus.

'Why, if it isn't Master Dawson,' she said in her lilting Welsh accent.

The sound of her voice brought back memories of tales from the Mabinogi, wild, magical stories that Gwener said her mother had told her when she was a child. One in particular had transfixed William, that of Prince Llew Llaw Gyffes whose mother, with her dying breath, had placed on the young prince a curse that he should never take to wife any daughter of man. A magician fashioned a woman from flowers, named her Blodeuwedd, and brought her to Gyffes. William could still hear Gwener's voice as she described the scene. Blodeuwedd walked towards Gyffes naked as the flowers of the dawn with the dew still upon her chaste breasts. Gyffes took her to wife but she brought no joy to his bed. No blush coloured her pale cheeks; ice flowed through her blue veins; he held in his arms a creature cold and alien.

Fate may have given Gwener a stunted body but her voice was melodious and her mind full of grace.

She threw open the door and said, 'Welcome home. Come on in, *cariad*.' Then, on seeing the trunk: 'I'll help you in with that old thing.'

She hurried down the steps and hurled her diminutive figure against its bulk.

'It's all right, Gwener,' William remonstrated. 'I can manage.'

'What the Reverend was thinking of when he bought this hen glamp I don't know,' Gwener said as she tried to put her arms around the trunk.

Between them, they dragged the trunk up the steps and into the hall.

'Thank you, Gwener. We'll leave it here for now,' William gasped. 'The family expecting me home?'

A look of uncertainty passed across Gwener's face and she answered, 'The Reverend received a letter the other day and said you would be home soon but not a word of why. Holiday or something, is it?'

'No, not a holiday. I'm home for good.'

'For the night.'

The voice was loud and emphatic and came from the entrance to the study where the Reverend Charles Dawson stood framed in the doorway.

'You, sir!' Charles barked. 'Come here. Gwener, go bid Mrs Dawson and my daughter to attend me in my study.'

Gwener hurried down the passage to the parlour and burst in on Mrs Dawson and Clare. They both looked up, startled.

'Master Dawson has arrived home and is in the study with the Reverend and the Reverend asks you to join them,' Gwener blurted out.

'Oh dear,' cried Mrs Dawson. 'What can be the matter?'

Gwener shrugged her shoulders and left the room, muttering worriedly to herself, 'Beth sy'n bod ar y Parchedig, dyna'r cwestiwn!' (What's the matter with the Reverend is the question)

What transpired in the study was swift and brutal. William in his worst imaginings could not have envisaged a denunciation so devastating and a rejection so callous. Charles Dawson informed his wife and daughter that the degenerate creature who stood shamefaced before them had once been his son but had now committed an act of such gross indecency, the nature of which was too obscene to reveal to their innocent selves, that he could not be allowed to remain in the family home lest he infect them with his monstrous depravity.

William protested his innocence and his mother went down and pleaded on her knees but to no avail. William would be allowed to stay the night but must then pick up his trunk and leave the house, never to return.

The following morning, Charles summoned William into his study. The anger of the previous day had gone to be replaced by a studied aloofness.

'Have you given thought to where you will go and how you will make your way in this harsh world?' Charles asked coldly.

William attempted an ingratiating smile and said, 'I've lain wide awake all night pondering those very questions.'

'And did you find satisfactory answers?'

'I'm afraid not, Father. I never thought that I would face such questions so early in my life.'

'Nor did I expect to find that I had nurtured such a viper.'

William, close to tears, made a last desperate effort, 'Father, I am your son. Why won't you at least listen to my version of what happened? It was not sordid or vile. Oliver and I were innocent of any indecent thoughts or actions.'

'Naked in each other's arms – not indecent? Enough, not another word – do not add to your iniquities by lying about them.'

William threw up his hands in despair and turned to leave the study.

'Wait!' Charles ordered. 'I have a proposition to make. I understand that America is a land of opportunity. I am not a rich man but, if you solemnly pledge never to communicate with this family again, I will give you a sum of money. It will not be much but should be sufficient to pay for your passage to America and sustain you until you find work.'

William's first reaction was one of fear and he felt his knees buckle. He steadied himself by placing his hands on the desk. The thought of leaving not just his family but his country to journey across a vast sea to a land of which he knew nothing filled him with dread. Then he felt a frisson of excitement. He was young and a new life lay open before him. A life he could live as he wished without regard to the strictures of others.

'I agree,' he said.

'You vow that you will never attempt to contact this house again?'

'I so swear'

Charles unlocked a drawer of the desk and drew out a bundle of notes. He counted out twenty pounds and handed them to William.

'I don't suppose it would trouble your conscience to learn that this money constitutes the bulk of my savings,' Charles said.

William, unable to reply, headed for the door but when he reached it he turned and said in a bewildered way, 'But, Father, how do I get to America?'

For an instant, his son's helplessness pierced Charles' armour and touched his heart.

He stumbled forward and said, 'Get to America? Well, let me see...Yes, yes, I have it, go to Liverpool and take a steamer from there.'

Recovering his composure, he raised his right hand and said, 'May God have mercy on you. I will pray for your soul.'

William bowed his head under this harsh benediction and left the room.

Waiting in the hallway he found his mother, Clare and Gwener. The only one capable of speech was Gwener.

'The Reverend sent me to the village first thing to order the carrier. He's here already.'

William kissed his mother on the forehead and the tears ran down his face into her eyes where they mingled with the tears welling there. Clare flung her arms around him and moaned softly. He kissed her on the cheek and gently smoothed her long black hair.

'Come, *cariad*, I'll help you with that hen glamp,' said Gwener her voice rough with emotion.

When Gwener and William had loaded the trunk on to the cart, Gwener gave him a hug and said,

'I'll look after them. You watch out for yourself. It's a hard old world out there.'

'Thank you, Gwener, for your wild Welsh tales. The image of Blodeuwedd will live with me forever.'

William leapt up beside the driver and looked for the last time at his home. He saw his mother and sister clinging together in the open doorway and he raised his arm in farewell.

As the cart clattered down the road he heard Gwener shout, 'Pob bendith!' (Every blessing.)

Liverpool was the second most important port in Britain, the first being London. That it attained such prominence was due to the slave trade. Manufactured goods from Merseyside were exchanged for slaves in West Africa, who were in turn traded for sugar, molasses, spices and other plantation crops in the West Indies. The docks extended along the Mersey for seven miles and Liverpool stood at its centre.

William's first task on alighting from the train was to dispose of the detested trunk. It was all that remained of a life he was putting behind him and anyway it was far too cumbersome to lug around the town. He was fortunate to find a ship's chandler only a few hundred yards from the station entrance. He exchanged the trunk for two sturdy kit-bags, which he stuffed with his belongings. The items for which he had no room and considered superfluous to his requirements he sold to the chandler for a few pence.

With the kit-bags slung sailor fashion over his shoulders, William stepped out on to the streets of Liverpool in search of a night's lodging. He inspected a number of places offering accommodation but was repelled by their squalor and the filthy bed linen. Just when he was despairing of finding anywhere suitable, there rose before him a building of gigantic proportions, bearing in letters three foot tall the inscription ADELPHI HOTEL. He cautiously climbed the steps leading to the entrance and peered into the lobby. It was starting to get dark and the oil lamps had been lit, the flames flickered in their large glass bowls and cast a warm glow over the plush red upholstered furniture and the polished oak reception desk. Casting caution to the wind, William flung open the glass-panelled doors and strode boldly in. There were two female clerks behind the desk, both in identical black calico dresses with white lace cuffs and collars.

The younger one eyed William with an amused look and, turning to her companion said, 'Halloo, don't look now but the fleet's in.'

'I didn't know the press gang had taken to snatching babes from their mothers' arms,' the other sniggered.

Undeterred, William heaved the kit-bags on to the desk and produced a one pound note from his pocket.

'I require a room for the night,' he demanded, in as deep a voice as he could manage. 'I sail for America in the morning.'

Suitably impressed, the girls gave him the key to his room and asked him to sign the register. As he marched off he turned his head and ordered haughtily, 'See that the porter brings the luggage to my room.'

That evening William ate in the hotel restaurant and then consulted the list of sailings prominently displayed in the lobby. He noted that an *SS Scotia* was due to sail for New York at two o'clock the next day. He was faced with the problem of how he was going to spend the rest of the evening. The meal and the postprandial glass of brandy had filled William with an unaccustomed boldness. Seaports were notorious for the prostitutes that thronged their streets. It was time, he thought, for him to lie with a woman and lose his virginity.

His quest led him to the uncobbled streets near the docks. He walked past rows of squalid houses whose gaping doors sent feeble shafts of light out into the night. Foul smelling fumes rose from cesspools and mingled with the creeping sea fog. Drunken sailors cursed, vomited, urinated and brawled around him. Cheap whores, shawled and dishevelled, called from doors and dark lanes. One stepped out in front of him and raised her skirts. The thickly applied rouge and smeared lipstick made it difficult to gauge her age but, from the slightness of her figure, William thought her no more than a child.

'How's your middle leg?' she cackled. 'Want me to polish it? That'll stiffen it for you.'

William pushed her aside and fled. She stared after him and let out a screech of laughter.

'That's right,' she shrieked, 'go back to mother, you shitbreeches! What's wrong with yer, all prick and no pence?'

Back in his hotel room William lay curled up on the bed, his confidence destroyed and all joy in his newly acquired freedom gone. He fell into a fitful sleep.

He was standing on the deck of a sailing ship. A fierce wind blew through stark rigging devoid of sails while all around the sea lay black and stagnant. Above him, spread out against the sky, glowered the face of the Reverend Charles Dawson. At his feet, stretched naked on the splintered planks of the deck, the white body of Oliver writhed sensuously. As he gazed down, the image of his friend changed to that of the young prostitute he had encountered earlier, her red lips fixed in an obscene grin. Suddenly, with a loud shriek, Old Spear leaped from the crows-nest brandishing a cane and started beating William savagely about the head. William was driven to the stern of the boat where he slipped and fell into the sea.

When he resurfaced he found, to his surprise, that the ship was now some considerable distance away. Luckily he was a good swimmer and he struck out with vigorous strokes towards the boat. He had nearly attained his goal when he saw gliding towards him over the surface of the water a woman of ethereal beauty. Her body swayed like the stalks of daffodils in a gentle breeze, her face was a rose bud opening to receive the sun, her hair flowed as do the branches of a weeping willow trailing in a stream. When she reached him she gathered him up in her arms and pressed him to her body. Her limbs were of steel and her breasts of polished marble. Holding him in an inexorable grip, she sank slowly through the dark and slimy water. William, legs and arms thrashing frantically, gasped for air as his lungs filled with water. He woke screaming and tore away the sheets that were smothering him.

It was a chastened William who, the following morning, presented himself at the harbour office to buy his ticket. The clerk informed him that the steerage fare was four pounds and that this only bought a space on deck – if he wished to sleep with a modicum of comfort he would have to provide a mattress himself. Helpfully, the clerk told him that the purser carried a stock on board and that William could hire one for a reasonable fee.

William was standing on his allotted deck space when the ship's doctor came around on his inspection. He was a little taller than William and of slim build. His weather-beaten face was fringed with a short greying beard and his eyes were bright blue.

'Where's your mattress?' he demanded. 'It's illegal not to have one.'

'Give me a chance, sir, I've only just got on board,' William answered plaintively. 'I'll be seeing the purser shortly.'

'Get a blanket too. The nights can be very cold.'

The doctor studied William more closely.

'How old are you?' he asked.

'Sixteen. Why?'

'Where are your parents?'

'They're dead. Why?'

'You're going to America on your own?'

'Yes.'

'What do you plan to do there, for God's sake?'

Strangely, the question of how he would earn a living in America had not, until this moment, occurred to him. William hung his head and was silent.

The doctor looked concerned and said, 'What's your name?'

'William, William Dawson.'

'Dr Frank Howard. Jump to it, William, and get a mattress and blanket. I must carry on with my rounds but I'll come back and see you later.'

It was a few days before he found time to redeem that promise and, when he did visit steerage, he invited William to come up to his cabin. The stateroom was large and the furnishings consisted of a narrow bed, a desk, a wardrobe, a sofa and screwed firmly to the wall two small bookcases. Doctor Howard sat on the bed and waved a hand towards the sofa.

'Go on make yourself comfortable,' he said. 'I know the *SS Scotia* is renowned as a luxury steamer but I don't think that epithet can be applied to the steerage deck.'

'Thank you, Doctor,' William said sinking gratefully into the cushions.

'Call me Frank.' He added with a wink, 'Except of course on those occasions when you seek my help professionally.'

'Have you been at sea long?' William asked, attempting to make polite conversation.

'Practically from the moment I qualified. I joined the service in the era of sailing ships.'

'How does your wife manage your long absences at sea?'

Frank laughed and said, 'No wife for me. I'm a loner.'

William glanced around the cabin and saw that it exhibited the obsessive neatness of a dedicated bachelor. For the rest of the voyage Howard allowed William to share the comfort of his cabin during the day but was scrupulous in seeing that when darkness came William was banished to his mattress and blanket in steerage. While Frank was around the ship carrying out his duties, William made use of the small but eclectic library contained in the two bookcases. Frank had catholic but discriminating tastes. William noted Thomas Carlyle's *The French Revolution* and all three volumes of John Ruskin's *The Stones of Venice*. Fiction had its place, too, with Jane Austen's *Pride and Prejudice*, Anthony Trollope's *The Warden*, and George Eliot's *Adam Bede*. Robert Browning's *Dramatic Lyrics* and Alfred Tennyson's *Idylls of the King* represented poetry.

When Frank was present he would light up his pipe and they would discuss what William had been reading. Discussion was not the correct word to use: monologue with interruptions would be a better description.

Frank had great respect for Jane Austen, whose novels he felt chronicled the emergence of regency society into the modern world. *Pride and Prejudice* showed how intelligence could triumph over the opacities of social custom. Her novels had been published anonymously and it was only after her death that her identity was revealed.

When William asked why Dickens did not have a place on his bookshelf, Frank commented that, while Thackeray attacked the upper classes, Dickens showered mawkish sympathy on the lower classes.

When questioned on his choice of poets, Frank said that Tennyson and Browning represented the creative diversity of contemporary poetry. Tennyson was the suburban Virgil – idyllic and refined – while Browning, though grotesque and colloquial at times, was a distinctive modern voice.

Frank had an encyclopaedic knowledge of the history of transatlantic navigation. His eyes lit up as he spoke of the clippers, those long graceful three-masted ships with projecting bows and exceptionally large spreads of sail. He explained how by 1840, when Cunard launched four paddle steamers with auxiliary sails, it was clear that the last glorious days of the pure sailing ship were at hand, though some still plied the Atlantic. Now, Frank concluded, paddle power was being superseded by the screw propeller and he predicted that, in the mad scramble for speed, ships would get bigger and bigger and engines more and more powerful. In past years there had been fierce competition between the British and American lines but after the outbreak of the American Civil War in 1861, Confederate raiders sought out and sank Union ships. This meant there was a reduction in the number of American ships on the Atlantic route, leaving the seas clear for the British.'

One afternoon, as Frank sat on the bed with his back propped up against the pillows and William lounged on the sofa, William asked if Frank knew of somewhere he could lodge while he was in New York.

'Go up Fifth Avenue towards Central Park until you see a large timbered house standing on its own. The name is the Shamrock and the landlady is Mrs Mulligan,' he said. 'I've stayed there often. She's a widow and Irish but a good enough soul who gives bed and board at a reasonable price.'

'Do you think there'll be much chance of employment in New York?' William asked. 'Or will the war have devastated the place?'

Frank smiled and said, 'No, the South has fared much worse than the North. Mind you, at first the Confederates were quite successful and at one point General Lee was so successful against the Union forces that he threatened the capitol Washington. Things are vastly different now with the Union armies under Grant and Sherman driving down into the South. In June last year there were was an outbreak of rioting in New York, some thousands of rioters, mostly impoverished Irish immigrants protesting against a new draft law that allowed people to buy their way out of the draft, swept through the city doing the usually things rioters do in America. You know – looting, burning and hanging Blacks from streetlights. But everything's back to normal now.'

'I don't really know much about the war but is it all to do with the emancipation of slaves?'

'Indirectly. Although Lincoln hated the institution of slavery, he was elected President on the ticket of non-interference with slavery where it already existed, which was largely in the Southern states. I would guess that these states didn't trust him and so seceded from the Union. The Northern states then went to war to preserve the Union.'

'So the North is going to win?'

'Inevitable. The contestants are so unevenly matched – in population, economic resources and mineral wealth.'

'I shouldn't find any difficulty in finding employment in New York, then.'

'No, but if I were you I'd take the railroad out to Washington. This war will have established Washington once and for all as the capitol of the United States and it should grow rapidly. It'll be the place of opportunity for a young man of enterprise.'

'Don't suppose you know of good lodgings there?'

Frank laughed and said, 'Yes, another widow, Mrs Surratt of 541 H Street.'

The fifteen-day journey passed pleasantly without major mishaps, apart from the occasional outbreak of seasickness among the passengers. The *SS Scotia* was due to dock the next day and this was the last time Doctor Howard and William would be together. Life had turned sour for William. His friend Tancred had tried to destroy his belief in God and then proved to be all mouth and no action; the Master's judgement had been dictated by expediency; his father had brutally rejected him and his glimpse of depravity on the streets of Liverpool had frightened him. He felt that Frank was the only person he could trust.

'Tell me, where does evil come from?' he asked. 'Is each and every one of us born into this world with our own little seed of sin.'

Frank looked startled for a moment and replied, 'You mean is there such a thing as original sin?'

William nodded.

Frank smiled and said, 'No, William. We are all born innocent and in love with the world. We think it is made for us and our wishes. Then we suffer the humiliation of disillusionment and evil is born from the rage we feel at the loss of our last vestige of hope.'

That night, before going back to his berth, William went and stood in the bow of the ship as it cleaved its way through the dark waters. He raised his arms to heaven and made a vow. Never would he let the injustices and cruelties of this world embitter his spirit. He would seek solace in the good things of this life – literature, theatre, art and the love of a good woman.

* * *

On June 20, 1864 William sailed into New York Harbour. On one side stretched Long Island Sound on the other the magnificent Hudson River. He was an anonymous figure among the hundreds of immigrants who crowded the deck of the steamship. Alone and filled with a timid hope he stepped ashore unregarded, and ventured into an uncertain future.

On that same day Maximilian, Archduke of Austria and a puppet of Napoleon III, entered Mexico City to be proclaimed Emperor of Mexico. The Emperor and his wife Carlota passed through the city gates in a state coach and were showered with coloured strips of paper bearing verses of welcome. They rode through streets carpeted with flowers and lined with cheering citizens. In the great hall of the National Palace the Emperor addressed his people:

'*People of Mexico! You have chosen me, by an overwhelming majority, to be your leader and to safeguard the future of this great nation. I respond with joy and a deep sense of the responsibility. I shall hold the sceptre with pride and the sword of honour with courage.*'

The crowd roared its approval. Maximilian, the young chivalrous knight-errant, and the beautiful Carlota were the focus of a great wave of adoration.

CHAPTER 8

William passed through the immigration shed and climbed the steep stairs that led into New York. Walking up Fifth Avenue, he was overawed by the crowds that buffeted him and drove him off the pavement. On one street corner, he was puzzled to see a set of long wooden stairs covered by a canvas awning where men sat reading newspapers. When he got closer he was amused to see that they were waiting to have their shoes polished by a young Negro. He came to Madison Square and, as he walked past the Fifth Avenue Hotel, he felt the urge to book in, regardless of the expense. But, aware that he must husband his resources, he pressed on in search of Mrs Mulligan and her worthy establishment. Nearing Central Park he came upon a large timbered house painted green and there on a sign hanging over the porch was the legend 'THE SHAMROCK – A Boarding House For Persons Of Discrimination.' A pretty woman in her mid forties was weeding the small garden in front of the house.

'Excuse me, but are you Mrs Mulligan?' William asked.

The women stood up and brushed a fringe of auburn hair from her eyes.

'Indeed I am and who is it be asking that question?'

'Allow me to introduce myself. I'm William Dawson from England. Dr Frank Howard gave me your name.'

'I see. Just come over the water have you, young man?'

'Yes indeed. Landed this morning.'

'Looking for lodgings, I don't doubt?'

'Yes indeed.'

'Come on in. You could do with a drink and bite after being a great while walking the streets with those two great bags burdening your shoulders'

Over a glass of milk and a slice of apple pie, they agreed terms – bed and board for three dollars a week. His bedroom was small and sparsely furnished but boasted a gigantic wooden crucifix on the wall behind his bed. To William's jaundiced eye the figure of Christ appeared to be life-sized and the crudely painted gouts of blood seemed ready to drop onto the bed beneath.

Seeing him staring, Mrs Mulligan said proudly, 'I see you're admiring my crucifix. And who was it fashioned that but my poor husband Tom. Sure it's destroyed I was and him after dying on me. Many men leave but an old shirt and trousers when they're after dying but not my Tom.'

William wondered why, if she loved the abomination so much, she had chosen to inflict it on one of her lodgers rather than hang it in her own room.

'Yes, a very fine piece of work Mrs Mulligan. Your husband was a sculptor of some sort?'

'God bless you, boy, he was nothing the like of that. Nothing so grand, only a plain carpenter but surely he was filled with the love of God and the fear of Hell's fire.'

'Well, Mrs Mulligan I think I'll take a stroll around the town before dinner.'

A look of concern clouded Mrs Mulligan's face and she grasped his arm.

'A fine young gentleman such as yourself should take care when he walks the streets of this sinful place. For are they not crowded with criminals and loose women? Surely, it's destroyed you'll be if you mix with the likes of them.'

That evening, as they sat eating around a large oak table, William was introduced to Mrs Mulligan's guests, one of whom, a large fresh-faced individual, interested William. The man's name was Peter Rowan and he was a member of a civil engineering team that had come to New York to test the feasibility of building a suspension bridge over the East River from Brooklyn to Manhattan Island. After the meal, Peter sat in a corner of the parlour with a small table at his elbow on which stood a glass and a bottle of whisky. William drew up a chair and sat facing him.

'Excuse me, sir,' William said tentatively, 'but the nature of your work interests me greatly.'

'Have a drop of the good stuff, my lad,' Peter said.

'Oh no. Thank you, but no. I rarely touch alcohol.'

'Then it's time you started. Mrs Mulligan, bring a glass for the lad.'

When Mrs Mulligan bustled over with the glass, Peter poured a large measure and handed it to William.

'Ah, it's leading the boy astray, you are, Mr Rowan,' Mrs Mulligan protested.

'Nonsense. You go and carry on with your womanly duties and leave us men to our affairs.'

Mrs Mulligan laughed and tapped him affectionately on the shoulder.

'Ah, go on with you now. It's the very devil you are,' she said as she bustled away.

William took a cautious sip from his glass and placed it on the table.

'I had a keen interest in mathematics at school,' William said. 'I was especially interested in the practical applications. And where could they be more complex than in throwing vast structures over raging torrents?'

'You certainly have a poetic turn of phrase, I'll say that for you,' said Peter. 'Do you actually know anything about bridge building?'

William took another sip of whisky and pronounced boldly, 'Not a damn thing.'

'I work for John Roebling, the finest bridge-builder in the world today.'

'What about Brunel?'

'Kingdom Brunel? He died five years ago and anyway, he spread his interests to railways and ships. I once worked over in England with Brunel and believe me, Roebling is the better man.'

Peter went on to explain the different types of bridge design, 'You have the simplest form, the beam bridge, made up of beams spanning between supports. The supports carry the loads from the beam by compression vertically to the foundations. The other forms are the truss, the arch, the suspension and the cantilever. But my favourite, and the bridge of the future, is the suspension bridge. A suspension bridge carries vertical loads through curved cables in tension. These loads are transferred both to the massive towers, which carry them by vertical compression to the ground, and to the anchorages that must resist the inward and vertical pull of the cables.'

Peter's open face lit up as he exclaimed, 'To see the majesty of those great towers and the graceful catenary of the lace-like cables silhouetted against the sky. To see the deck hanging delicately in the air as if by magic.'

'Is that going to be the design of the one you're hoping to build here?'

'You bet. And it will be the first bridge to use steel for the cable wire. One of the drawbacks of iron wire was corrosion. But first the bed of the river must be tested to see if it can support the massive foundations needed.'

'How are you going to do that?'

'Ever heard of a caisson?'

'Can't say I have'

'It's a large box-like structure, either rectangular or circular in cross-section. We use it in construction work underwater. It's open top and bottom with a cutting edge fitted at the bottom to facilitate sinking through mud and soft soil while excavation work is carried on inside through a honeycomb of large pipes. As excavation proceeds and the caisson sinks, new sections are added. We'll be using a pneumatic caisson where an airtight bulkhead is fitted near the top. The space between the bulkhead and the cutting edge is pressurised to control the inflow of soil and water so that men can work at the bottom of the caisson.'

'Are you recruiting labourers?' William asked eagerly. 'I'm in need of employment and the work sounds exciting.'

Peter looked hard at William and shook his head.

'No, lad. You haven't the physique for that type of work.'

'I'm very strong for my size and was boxing champion at school.'

'No. The work is too dangerous for a boy. You'll be working in compressed air and there's always the risk of the bends.'

'The bends?'

'Before you enter the working section of the caisson you have to pass through an airlock where the air is compressed to the level of that in the caisson. When you leave you have to be decompressed. If these operations are carried out too swiftly it could result in a convulsive fit. Deep-sea divers face the same danger.'

Undeterred, William persisted, 'Give me a trial for just one day. If I find it too strenuous, I promise to let you know.'

'You're a likely lad, there's no mistake. Come down with me to the site in the morning and we'll see. I set off at eight o'clock sharp. Pick up your glass and let's drink a toast.'

They both stood up and clashed their glasses together.

'Here's to Roebling and his next great bridge,' Peter said.

'And to the men who are going to build it,' William added.

Carried away with enthusiasm, he took a great gulp of whisky and nearly choked.

The following morning when they reached the site it became obvious that Peter was the man in charge of the operation. He was addressed as Mr Rowan or Chief and his orders were obeyed with alacrity. Peter entrusted William to the care of Ted, the foreman in charge of the gang of men about to start the first shift.

'See you keep an eye on him, Ted,' Peter said. 'He's a good friend of mine and I'd hate anything untoward to happen to him. The spirit is willing but the flesh may be weak.'

Ted was no taller than William but his compact body bulged with muscle.

He cast an amused glance over William and said, 'Don't be fretting yourself, Mr Rowan. Surely his own mother wouldn't take greater care of him.'

Peter smiled and marched off to his office located further along the bank. Ted took William into a long shed to join the rest of the gang. At the far end, arranged in neat stacks, were high wellington boots, picks and shovels.'

'Kit yourself out; grab a pick and shovel and follow the men,' Ted commanded. 'It'll get damn hot in that hell-hole, so strip to the waist.'

William donned a pair of wellingtons several sizes too large for him. Then, with a pick over one shoulder and a shovel over the other, he staggered into the airlock with the rest of the men.

Ted came up and sat beside William on the bench.

'When they turn on the air-cocks and the pressure rises, be sure to put your hands to your ears,' Ted whispered.

As more and more compressed air entered the chamber William felt as if the blood in his veins was about to boil. He experienced acute pain in his ears as if his eardrums were on the point of bursting. Gradually, as the tension of the gases in his blood and the air outside reached equilibrium, the pain eased. During this time Ted had been keeping an eye on William and now he gave him a slap on the back.

'Well done lad,' he said. 'It's many would be destroyed by the pain of it.'

The hatch swung open and they stepped down to the bed of the river. They stood in ice cold water that was only prevented from rising above the top of their wellingtons by the terrific air pressure. The heat was overpowering and as the shift wore on the air became foul. They worked in short bursts, taking a few minutes' rest at regular intervals. The sweat poured down William's naked back and the acute discomfort he had experienced in the airlock returned.

When the whistle sounded for the end of the first shift, he was near collapse. They re-entered the airlock where they remained for an hour being decompressed before being released into the shed where a makeshift canteen had been set up to serve soup and hot drinks. William, cold and wet, kicked off his wellingtons and put on his clothing. He had never felt so ill in his life and wondered how he was going to go back into that infernal pit, but such is the resilience of youth that, after spooning down some hot soup and taking a swig from the bottle of whisky the men were passing around, he was ready to enter the airlock for the afternoon shift. This time the work did not seem quite as arduous but when William returned to the shed at the end of the day the pain in his head was as if someone had embedded an axe in his brain. Ted helped him to a bench and he sat down holding his head.

'To be sure you're feeling bad now, lad, but after a few days you'll think nothing of it,' Ted said. 'And the pay is grand. Five dollars a day.'

'How is the boy, Ted?'

William looked up and there was Peter bending anxiously over them.

'Ah it's fine he is,' Ted answered. 'Did the work of two men.'

'William, are you all right?' Peter persisted.

William smiled through his pain and said, 'Yes indeed, sir. Today was bound to be the worst. But this afternoon was better than the morning, so give me a few more days and I'll be completely acclimatised.'

'Well if you're sure,' Peter said dubiously. 'Get out in the fresh air between shifts and don't over-indulge in alcohol.'

William gradually became accustomed to the conditions and might have continued in the job if it had not been for the accident. He had been working on the site for five weeks and they were well into the afternoon shift. William was busy digging out the muck that would be transported to the material room at the top of the caisson. Gradually he noticed that the air in the chamber was getting fouler by the minute. He felt icy water slip down inside his wellingtons. The water level was rising and that could only mean one thing – the air pressure was falling. Ted shouted a warning and they all made a dash for the airlock. At that instant, the loss of pressure became catastrophic and the water made a great leap up the sides of the caisson. William, with a few others, managed to scramble into the airlock but, looking back, he saw the rest struggle frantically in the water before being sucked under and drowned. Ted managed to reach the entrance but one of the men, in panic, tried to close the hatch and Ted was trapped with only his head and shoulders in the airlock. William tried to reopen the hatch and free Ted but the water flooding in forced him to retreat with his companions and escape from the airlock. The anguish on Ted's face as the water closed over him formed an image of a silent scream that would remain with William for the rest of his life.

Their hurried flight meant that they had not gone through the decompression process. The results were horrendous. William, like his fellow victims, lay writhing on the floor of the shed. He felt piercing pains shoot through his head while blood streamed from his mouth and ears. Every bone in his body ached and his limbs twisted and shuddered in grotesque spasms. They were taken to hospital but many of them were pronounced dead on arrival. William, however, was one of the fortunate few and he was released several days later – recovered but not unaffected. The experience gave him a lifelong horror of manual labour and he vowed that he would seek his living in a less arduous profession.

He made his intentions clear to Mrs Mulligan when he returned to the Shamrock.

'I have concluded that I'm not of the stuff from which heroes of labour are made, Mrs Mulligan,' he declared. 'I shall seek employment in a field where my more subtle attributes will be appreciated.'

'And didn't I say that too fine a gentleman you were for all that old digging in the dirt of the river?' Mrs Mulligan said. 'And what, if I may ask, is the profession that is to be honoured with your honour's participation?' she added, without a trace of irony.

'Dr Howard spoke of a fine hotel in Washington City called the National Hotel. I intend to enter the hotel trade. Start perhaps as a humble receptionist and ultimately attain the dignity of manager. Who knows?'

Peter, who had been listening to the conversation with interest, asked, 'Do you know a decent place to lodge in Washington?'

'Yes, most definitely. Dr Howard recommended a Mrs Surratt of 541 H Street. She is a widow like yourself, Mrs Mulligan.'

'I think you're making the right decision,' Peter said. 'If you're a trained civil engineer, bridge building is the finest profession in the world. But being an unskilled labourer is no life for a man. You have the appearance and intelligence to rise high in the hotel business. I wish you well.'

'Thank you, sir. Has work resumed at the river?'

'No. I've closed the operation down for the present while we study the results of the survey. It will be several years before we start to actually build the bridge. But build it we will, I assure you.'

The following morning William and his two kit-bags caught the train to Washington.

Mary Surratt was born near Waterloo, Maryland, in 1823. At the age of seventeen she married John Surratt who was eleven years her senior. They established a tavern and post office in the area and, when Mr Surratt was appointed postmaster, the district became known as Surrattsville. They had three children – Isaac, Anna and John Junior. When her husband died, Mary and Anna moved to Washington DC to a property on H Street, which John Surratt had bought some years earlier. She rented the tavern at Surrattsville to a Mr John Lloyd and started to run her Washington residence as a boarding house.

The house was a three-storey timbered structure with a stairway leading to the entrance on the first floor. The woman who opened the door to William had the slim, hard build of a boy. Her black hair was parted down the centre and pulled back severely. Dark, penetrating eyes stared out from a bloodless face and her thin lips formed a bitter line beneath a long pointed nose. On hearing William's request her manner was brisk but not unfriendly.

'Dr Howard, you say?' she queried. 'Yes, he was a frequent visitor to our tavern in Surrattsville. When we last met, I told him of our intended move here. Well, I do have a spare room and, since you're a friend of Dr Howard, the room is yours. Bed and board will be four dollars a week.'

That evening William met his fellow boarders: Elisha Reed, a bright-eyed little man who walked with a slight limp; Louis Weichmann, who sported a red bow tie, and David Herold, a large man of sullen aspect. Mrs Surratt's son, John, and daughter, Anna, completed the household.

Elisha had fought at the battle of Gettysburg and was always on the lookout for someone who had not heard the tale of his experiences.

He quickly cornered William and, with an ingratiating smile, asked, 'Noticed my limp?'

Disconcerted, William replied, 'Well, not really.'

'Shot through both thighs at Gettysburg,' Elisha said triumphantly.

'That must have been rather painful,' William said and then felt foolish.

'I was with Company H of the 2nd Wisconsin Infantry. The rebel army under General Lee was approaching Gettysburg from the west. Our army, under General Meade was scattered in a wide defensive arc. On the afternoon of that first day Lee mounted an overwhelming attack on the position held by our regiment and drove us from the field. We had not fallen back far before I was shot in both legs. No bones were broken so I was able to limber back rapidly to the rear and take refuge in the Lutheran Theological Seminary. But Lee drove on past the Seminary and right through the town to the foot of Cemetery Ridge, leaving me a prisoner of war. That's how I came to be, together with a dozen other Yanks, in the cupola of the Seminary and had a grandstand view of Pickett's Charge.'

Elisha paused and closed his eyes as if reliving the event, then continued: 'It was the third day, Meade had gathered together all the Union forces and placed them along Cemetery Ridge that curled like a fishhook around the Confederate army. Lee decided to storm the centre of the Union lines. It was General Pickett and his Virginia division that lead the charge. Oh, I can see and hear it now. Pickett cried, "Forward" and advanced, waving his sword in the air. Behind him marched the standard bearer, the flag rippling slowly on the hot air. Then came the men, their muskets pointing forward. They cheered and called out, "We'll follow you, Marse George. We'll follow you, we'll follow you." They looked as if they were going for a damn fool walk in the sun.

'At first nothing happened then our cannon opened fire. One solid shot hit the standard bearer in the right leg and tore it off. The poor fellow jumped up from the ground and hopped up and down on the leg he had left, blood gushing from the stump of the other. Another took a shot in his belly, it went straight through him. He lay bloody and flopping with his guts spillin' out – but already dead, like a chicken with its head cut off. Then the shells started exploding among them, wiping out whole lines. Jesus, I can smell the cordite and blood now. It became a massacre and even those who broke through Meade's line were killed or captured.'

John Surratt, who had been listening to Elisha with mounting agitation, crossed the room and, grasping Elisha's arm, said, 'For God's sake, stop boring Mr Dawson. Lee should never have sent Pickett on that charge. He sent Pickett and his men into a rat-trap. The bloody repulse of that charge was the turning point of the war. May God never forgive him.'

William was bewildered at this outburst from someone residing in a supposedly Union household.

David Herold sidled up to John Surratt and, putting an arm over his shoulders, gently moved him away.

Turning to William, he said, 'Please forgive John this outburst. He detests wanton loss of life, be it friend or foe.'

Elisha hurriedly wished William goodnight and left the room. William stayed on for a while making polite conversation but, sensing an air of disquiet among the others, he went to bed early.

William's main concern was to find suitable employment and the next day he went to the National Hotel. He succeeded in obtaining an interview with the manager, Mr Dixon, who expressed himself pleased with William's appearance and general demeanour. When William enquired if this would translate to the offer of a job, Mr Dixon informed him that he could start a week's trial as a trainee desk clerk.

In his room that night, William's elation at obtaining the position of night clerk slowly drained away with the realisation that he had no loved one to share his joy. Overwhelmed by a crushing loneliness, he resolved to write to his family. His first instinct was to address the letter to his mother but he knew that the Reverend Charles Dawson opened all the mail. Difficult though it might be, he would have to write to his father.

'*Dear and Honoured Father,*' he began and paused as he sought suitable sentiments and the appropriate words with which to clothe them.

'*I know you will be surprised to receive a letter from your banished son. You made it* quite clear at our last meeting that you never wished to see or hear from me again. But, Father, I have suffered vicissitudes and encountered all manner of unfortunate and desperate people. The son you thrust from your house no longer exists. A chastened and wiser son now writes to you in hope of reconciliation. A son who misses the love of father, mother and sister, and who needs to share with them his fears and hopes for the future. This day I secured employment as a reception clerk at the National Hotel here in Washington. Please write giving news of the family.'

He signed the letter, 'Your contrite son, William'.

CHAPTER 9

John Wilkes Booth strode into the lobby of the National Hotel, his black cape lined with scarlet silk billowing behind him. Though of average height, he was lean and athletic. His hair was jet black and his skin the colour of ivory. His appearance and manner proclaimed in blazing capitals: ACTOR.

Born in 1838, he was the ninth child of Junius Booth, who had been one of the most renowned actors on the American stage. From an early age, John Booth harboured a passionate desire to become as famous an actor as his father. He was seventeen when he made his stage debut as the Earl of Richmond in *Richard III*. At first he missed cues and forgot his lines; but he persevered and, during a season at the theatre in Richmond, Virginia, he perfected his art and became a competent actor. Now aged twenty-six, he had starred in several other Shakespeare plays and the critics rated him a good actor, though not up to the standard of his father and older brother, Edwin.

William had been employed as a desk clerk at the National for ten months and was still lodging in Mary Surratt's establishment. After the awkwardness of that first evening, he had settled in and found the place convivial, though he was rather perplexed by a number of mysterious looking individuals who visited the house and spent hours in a back room engaged in whispered discussions with Mary and John Surratt, David Herold and Louis Weichmann.

On reaching the desk Booth transfixed William with a fierce stare and announced, 'John Wilkes Booth, actor. You have a room reserved for me, I believe.'

'Yes indeed,' William said. 'Room 228.'

'I know, the large room with double windows at the front of the hotel.'

'You've stayed here before?'

'You're new here, boy. I appeared in the role of Raphael in *The Marble Heart* at Ford's Theatre here in Washington, two years ago. The President himself was in the audience.'

'I was still in England at that time,'

'So you have never seen me act? That is an omission you must remedy.'

Taking the proffered key with an elegant flourish, Booth swept away, leaving his baggage in the lobby to be brought up by the bellboy.

That evening William was very surprised when Booth appeared at the Surratt house. It soon became apparent that this was not the first time he had visited there. He was received as a friend and was soon reminiscing extravagantly about the life and times of John Wilkes Booth.

'Who would think, looking at me now, that I once worked as a farmhand?' he asked, surveying them all with a contented smile. 'To be sure, the farm was my father's and we had slaves but for a few years I was little more than a common farm labourer. My father had been a great actor and my brother Edwin was making a name for himself on the stage, so I was burning with the desire to become famous. My sister will tell you that I would cry out – "I must have fame, fame".'

'Well, Mr Booth, you certainly have that now,' Mary Surratt said dryly.

Looking at her inscrutable face, William could not decide if she was being genuine or ironic.

Booth acknowledged her remark with a satisfied nod and continued, 'It was a long hard road but I made it. My finest moment was when I appeared with my brothers Edwin and Junius in Julius Caesar before a standing-room-only crowd. I played Mark Anthony, Edwin played Brutus and Junius played Cassius.'

'I'd have thought acting before President Lincoln would be your finest moment,' William ventured.

Booth looked at William as if he had never seen him before and then his face cleared.

'Why, it's the bellboy at the National!' he said.

'Desk clerk, Mr Booth, not bellboy. William Dawson, formerly of England.'

'I beg your pardon, young man. Many might consider appearing before the President a singular honour but I do not. I believe slaves should remain slaves and the country should be preserved for native-born white citizens.'

David Herold intervened, 'I'm sure young Dawson here is not interested in our politics, after all he's an Englishman.'

There was a burst of uneasy laughter.

Booth, however persisted, 'Nonsense. I know I'm among friends here. Any true-blooded

Englishman believes in the supremacy of the white man. They built an empire on it.'

More laughter followed but, before William could reply, Booth was in full flow again, 'While I was in Richmond I was a member of the local militia and had the honour to stand in uniform at the foot of the scaffold with other armed men to guard against any rescue attempt as we hanged that nigger-loving bastard John Brown.'

At this point there was a knock on the door and Mrs Surratt went to answer it. She returned accompanied by two men whom William had seen at the house before.

Herold rose to his feet and said with some relief, 'Ah! We're all here now. Time to adjourn to the back room and start the meeting.'

He led the way, followed by Weichmann, John and Mary Surratt, the two newcomers and Booth. Anna said she had some work to do in the kitchen. Only William and Elisha were left in the parlour.

'They always seem to be having clandestine meetings in this household,' William said. 'Are they a drama appreciation class or what?' he added with a grin.

Elisha gave a furtive glance towards the door and said quietly, 'Better not enquire to closely. Ignorance is bliss, as far as we're concerned. But I'll tell you this – I don't trust that actor fellow.'

'Oh?' William exclaimed, inviting further comment.

'Notice him always talking about Richmond? It was there that he became enamoured of the Southern people and their way of life. I hear it said that he was arrested in 1862 and taken before a provost marshal in St Louis for making anti-government remarks. Some say he's a spy for the Confederates. He hates Lincoln because of the devastation the war has wrought in the South.'

'But the gossip at the hotel is that he's engaged to Lucy Hale, the daughter of John Parker Hale, who's a colleague of Lincoln. The family are staying at the hotel before going to Spain, where Hale is to be the American ambassador.'

'What better cover for a spy?'

While William and Elisha talked surreptitiously, the subject of their speculation was chairing the meeting in the small back room.

'I have it on good authority that, on March 17, Lincoln is to attend a performance of *Still Waters Run Deep* at the Campbell Hospital just outside Washington,' he announced.

'What do you suggest we do?' asked Herold. 'Storm the place and kill him?'

'No. He's more use to us alive than dead. We can intercept his carriage and kidnap him. Then exchange him for Confederate troops in Union prison camps.'

'But where the hell would we hold him?' John Surratt protested. 'Nowhere around here would be safe. Those blue bellies would look under every blade of grass.'

'Nowhere here. We'll take him to Richmond. I have friends there.'

'I'm not happy about this,' Weichmann said. 'His carriage will have an escort. We're too few.'

'I'm in contact with O'Laughlen, Arnold, Paine and Atzerodt. They're game for it. With them we'll be more than a match for the superannuated cripples they'll have guarding him. After all they'll not be expecting an attack on Lincoln in his own backyard.'

Booth swept an imperious eye over the company.

'Are you with me?' he demanded.

Each man raised an arm in affirmation. Weichmann's arm was the last and his face expressed serious misgivings.

'Right,' Booth said triumphantly. 'We'll meet with the others at Gautier's restaurant on Pennsylvania Avenue at six o'clock on the fifteenth to finalise the abduction.'

That meeting proved to be an anticlimax when Booth arrived in a foul humour and informed the assembled would-be abductors that Lincoln had decided not to attend the performance.

It must be said that this news was received by a few of the conspirators with guilty feelings of relief – although all faces registered acute disappointment.

'Would you believe it?' Booth cried in disgust. 'The philistine has chosen instead to address the 140th Indiana Regiment and present them with a captured flag. I could understand if the play had been one of Tom Taylor's historical pieces in blank verse. I've always considered them to be a load of pretentious rubbish, but *Still Waters Run Deep*, like *Our American Cousin*, is a well constructed play ideal for performance in the theatre.'

Booth's comments on the relative merits of Taylor's plays passed unheeded over the heads of his comrades. After a short discussion, they decided to hold themselves in readiness until another opportunity arose.

On April 9, General Lee surrendered to General Grant at Appomattox and ended the Civil War. Two days later William stood, with thousands of Americans, to hear Lincoln address his people from the north portico of the White House. The white-grey sandstone of the White House contrasted strikingly with the red brick of the nearby buildings, and the tall graceful columns of the portico dwarfed even Lincoln's gangling frame. With his long arms and legs, he was a figure to be easily ridiculed but the man exuded such honesty, resolution and insight that William could sense why he had become an icon of human decency for so many of his people.

Among the crowd William spotted Booth, an ugly scowl distorting his face, muttering to Herold and John Surratt. Obviously Lincoln's message of hope and reconciliation was not to his taste. Unable to decipher Booth's comments, he moved nearer.

It was then that Lincoln said, 'Die when I may, I want it said of me by those who know me best, that I have always plucked a thistle and planted a flower where I thought a flower would grow.'

Lincoln went on to suggest that he was considering conferring voting rights on the black soldiers who had fought for the Union cause.

This was too much for Booth, who hissed in fury, 'Now, by God! I'll finish him. This is the last speech he will ever make.'

Activity at H Street intensified and William, troubled by Booth's remarks in front of the White House, eyed his fellow lodgers and their visitors with increasing suspicion. The only one he was able to confide in was Elisha but he, on hearing William's fears, advised him not to stick his nose where it would not be welcome.

'Suppose you informed the authorities and it all turned out to be moonshine?' he said. 'Where would that leave you?'

'Out on the street,' William quipped.

'Exactly.'

'But what if I'm right?'

'If you're right, they'd probably kill you before you had a chance to report them, and if you did we'd probably all get implicated and hanged alongside them. Best keep your mouth shut and hope it's all hot air.'

Reluctantly, William accepted Elisha's advice but, had he been able to witness in detail Booth's behaviour on April 14, any hope he might have harboured that it all was indeed simply hot air would have been brutally shattered.

Booth's initial movements appeared innocent enough. After calling on his fiancée, who occupied a room on the floor beneath his, Booth left the National Hotel. He gave William, who was working the day shift, a flamboyant wave as he passed the reception desk. He proceeded to Booker and Stewart's barber shop on E Street where he had his hair trimmed and read the morning papers. He then returned to his room at the hotel. Michael O'Laughlen, a person whom William recognised as a regular visitor to the Surratt house, enquired at the desk if Booth was in and, on being told by William that he had just returned, he went up to Booth's room where he stayed for a short time. At around eleven o'clock Booth again passed through the lobby. He had changed into more formal clothes. He wore a tall silk hat and kid gloves. He had a light overcoat slung over his shoulder and carried a silver-topped cane. William guessed he was going to Ford's Theatre to pick up his mail.

At the theatre Booth learned that Lincoln was to attend a performance of *Our American Cousin* that evening. He walked around the Theatre in a state of suppressed excitement before going to a stable on C Street, where he rented a fast roan mare, saying he would pick the animal up at four o'clock that afternoon. He then, in quick succession, visited fellow conspirators Lewis Paine at Herdon House and George Atzerodt at Kirkwood House. Returning to his hotel he picked up a parcel, which he took to the Surratt residence. Weichmann drew up in front of the house in a hired buggy and, alighting, hurried up the steps into the house. Later he and Mary Surratt emerged carrying several bulky packages and boarded the buggy. They drove off in the direction of Surrattsville. Booth stood at the top the steps and raised his arm in salutation.

At eight o'clock William, who had finished his spell of duty at the hotel, was back at the house and preparing to go to the theatre when he heard an imperious knocking at the front door. Mary Surratt was out and Anna was busy elsewhere in the house, so he went and opened the door. Booth, accompanied by Paine and Atzerodt, stood impatiently on the doorstep. He wore calf-length boots, spurs, a dark cloak and a large black hat. He and his entourage swept past William and went to the back room where John Surratt and Herold were waiting. William smiled contemptuously. Elisha was right – they were such a ludicrously conspicuous band of traitors, it must all be a load of codswallop. Laughing quietly to himself, he picked up his coat and left early for the theatre, hoping for a good seat.

Dusk was approaching and the lamps had been lit in the room. Booth stood before his co-conspirators and, his eyes bright with fanaticism, outlined his master plan.

'For six months we have worked at plans to capture Lincoln,' he said, waving his arms and sending gigantic shadows dancing along the walls. 'But, our cause being almost lost, something decisive and great must be done. I know every line of that play and the biggest burst of laughter will occur fifteen minutes after ten o'clock, That will be the moment when I'll enter his state box and kill him.'

He pulled from his pocket a snub-nosed, single-shot derringer and brandished it menacingly. The trigger and mountings were made of silver and flashed in the lamplight.

'I'll shoot him at point-blank range in the back of the head and, if that doesn't kill him, I'll finish the job with this,' he continued.

Smiling broadly, he produced a vicious knife with a seven-inch blade of razor sharpness.

'I expect you all to carry out the tasks we have planned. Atzerodt!' He turned and stared at Atzerodt. 'You will go to Kirkwood House and assassinate Vice-President Johnson.'

Atzerodt nodded grimly.

Booth turned to Paine and said, 'Paine! Secretary Seward is your target. Herold will guide you to Seward's home and help you escape from Washington. All these attacks will take place at the same time. John, you will stay in reserve. Should we fail, you will have to organise the next attempt.'

Atzerodt rose reluctantly to his feet and said, 'I feel I'm speaking for the others when I say that three assassinations on the same night at the same time is a trifle ambitious.'

There were muffled sounds of approval.

Booth, sensing reluctance among his men, attempted to reason with them, 'But it has to be so. To be effective we must remove the President, Vice-President and Secretary all in one fell swoop. We must cut off the head with one sweep of the blade. Think of the confusion that will result.'

Atzerodt persisted, 'This is too hurried. We need more time to plan.'

'To plan! Our escape route is ready. Today Weichmann drove Mary Surratt to Lloyd's tavern in Surrattsville with field binoculars, rifles and other escape equipment. If a woman is prepared to risk her life for the cause, don't let us shame our manhood. This afternoon I wrote a letter to the editor of the National Intelligencer in which I gave the reasons for our triple assassinations. I not only signed the letter William Wilkes Booth but also Lewis Paine, David Herold and George Atzerodt.'

Booth paused, then said dramatically, 'Gentlemen. The die is cast. This country was formed for the white, not for the black man. So help me holy God! My possessions, my life, my very soul are for the South.'

Herold and John Surratt were talking quietly after the others had left.

Herold laughed bitterly and said, 'With that letter he's certainly condemned me, Paine and Atzerodt to the gallows whether we take part or not.'

'All of us,' John Surratt exclaimed. 'Once they pick up you and the others named in that damn letter, they'll soon round up the whole gang. What could have possessed him?'

'He's become a monomaniac, consumed by only one thought – the success of the Confederacy.'

William had been seated in the stalls for some time before the Presidential Party entered the state box. Mr and Mrs Lincoln were accompanied by two friends, Clara Harris and Major Henry Rathbone. Lincoln's bodyguard, John Parker, preceded them into the box and took up a position near the door. The audience rose and gave Lincoln a rousing ovation. He looked embarrassed and gave a clumsy wave of the hand while Mrs Lincoln, stoop-shouldered and thin, acknowledged the applause with a gentle smile. The audience resumed their seats and an expectant silence filled the theatre as the curtain rose.

At thirty minutes past nine o'clock, Booth rode into the alley at the back of the theatre and called one of the stagehands to take care of the mare while he went into the tavern next to the theatre. He sat at the bar and ordered a bottle of whisky and a jug of water. He had an hour to wait and this seemed as good a way as any to spend it. He half filled the glass, topped it up carefully with water from the jug and tossed it back in one gulp. He took more time over the next few glasses, allowing himself to savour the suggestion of sweetness and the gentle glow induced in his throat and gut. Completely oblivious of his surroundings, he allowed his mind to reel slowly back to the time when he was a boarder at a private school run by Quakers at Cockeysville. He and some of his fellow pupils had gone to visit an old gypsy living in the woods near the school to have their palms read. He could still see the interior of her shack and hear her croaking voice as she opened his palm with her dry and wizened hands.

'Ah, you've a bad hand; the lines all criss-cross! It's full enough of sorrow. Full of trouble. Trouble in plenty, everywhere you look. You're born under an unlucky star. You've got in your hand a thundering crowd of enemies and you'll make a bad end. You'll have a fast life but a short one. Now, young sir, I've never seen a worse hand, and I wish I hadn't seen it, but every word I've told you is true by the signs. You'd best turn a missionary or a priest and try to escape it.'

Booth had joked and boasted about it afterwards but deep within himself he had been frightened.

His reverie was disturbed when a customer, who had been eyeing him from the moment he entered the tavern, sidled up and, giving him a slight nudge, asked, 'John Wilkes Booth, the actor?'

'I have that honour, sir,' Booth answered. 'And who might you be?'

'A nobody, Mr Booth. Just someone who loves the theatre and has followed the careers of your illustrious family. I saw your brother Edwin play Tressel to your father's Richard III at Boston in 1849. A fine actor your father, a pity about his drinking. Killed him off in the end, I believe. Your own Richard was no mean achievement and your Mark Anthony last year, though a trifle bombastic, had its good points.'

'At this moment in my life I give not a fig for your miserable opinions, sir.'

'Indeed,' the stranger said indignantly. 'Well, let me tell you this, you arrogant bastard – you'll never be the actor your father was.'

Booth gave a short laugh and rose from his stool. He glanced contemptuously around the room and cried out, 'When I leave the stage, I will be the most famous man in America.'

He strode to the door and stepped quickly into the alley, where he made for the theatre lobby. As he expected, the play was still in progress and the lobby was deserted. He quietly ascended the stairs to the dress circle. Outside the white door that gave access to the state box he saw Forbes, the President's footman. He had prepared for this eventuality and, presenting Forbes with a forged card of identity, said he had an urgent message for the President. On gaining access to the dark area at the rear of the box, he propped the door shut with the leg of a music stand, which he had placed there on his earlier visit to the theatre.

He now stood outside the inner door behind which Lincoln and his party were sitting. Unknown to Booth, Parker had left the box a few minutes earlier. Booth waited tensely for the burst of laughter and when it came he pushed open the door and, rushing up to Lincoln, he pressed the derringer behind Lincoln's left ear and fired. Lincoln toppled from his chair and crashed to the floor at Mrs Lincoln's feet. She screamed and, falling to her knees, cradled Lincoln's bleeding head in her arms. Rathbone sprang from his seat and attempted to wrestle Booth to the ground. Booth pulled out his knife and stabbed Rathbone in the left arm. He then climbed onto the banister of the box.

William, like the rest of the audience, had not heard the shot due to the loud laughter. He only became aware that something terrible had happened when Booth with a bloodcurdling cry of 'Sic semper tyrannis' ('Thus always to tyrants') leaped from the box onto the stage. He caught the spur of his right foot in one of the decorative flags draped on the balustrade and this caused him to land awkwardly on the stage. He got to his feet and shouted in triumph, 'The South is avenged.'

Realising that Lincoln had been attacked, the audience rose to their feet and those in the front rows, William among them, rushed forward and clambered onto the stage. Booth stumbled through the wings to the back of the theatre and out into the alley, pursued by the angry crowd. Flashing his knife threateningly at the stagehand who was holding his mare, he pushed him aside and mounted. When his pursuers burst into the alley they could only watch in furious frustration as he sped away, clinging to the neck of his mare. A short time later Booth was galloping over the Navy Yard Bridge and heading for Maryland.

William went round to the front of the theatre, where he learnt that Lincoln was not dead. He watched as they brought Lincoln, his head cocooned in cotton wool, out of the theatre and carried him across the street to the Peterson House. He saw a grim-faced Parker assiduously superintending the operation, trying to atone for what he evidently saw as his dereliction of duty. He was assisted by Major Rathbone, his arm heavily bandaged and his face drained of blood. A large silent crowd formed in front of the house and waited for news of their President. With his head bowed and his mind in turmoil, William stood with them.

When Booth reached Soper's Hill he stopped and dismounted. This was the place where the conspirators had planned to meet after the assassinations. His left leg was causing him considerable pain and he realised that he must have broken it when he leaped onto the stage. He sat on the ground and nursed his injured leg as best he could. After a while he heard the sound of a horseman approaching at great speed.

'Pray God it's one of my men,' he muttered. 'For if it's the first of my pursuers, there's little I can do to defend myself now.'

The horseman drew to a shuddering halt and called shrilly, 'Booth?'

Booth wept with relief as he recognised the voice.

'Herold!' he gasped. 'Thank God. But where's Paine?'

'They were hot on our heels and we got separated. I don't know what happened to him.'

'Your mission?'

'Paine stabbed Seward. But fatally? I don't know.'

'If Lincoln survives my bullet, then he is indeed the devil incarnate,' Booth snarled.

The two waited for an hour in the confident hope that Atzerodt would join them with the news that he had killed Johnson. Their wait was in vain, for Atzerodt had left their last meeting determined to have nothing to do with what he had come to consider an insane operation. While they loyally waited at Soper's Hill, he was fleeing in the opposite direction.

The time came when they could wait no longer and rode off to the tavern in Surrattsville, arriving there just after midnight. They collected the equipment Mary Surratt had left earlier. Booth had an acquaintance named Mudd who was a doctor in Bryantown, thirty miles from Washington. The pain in Booth's leg had become intolerable, so they set out for Dr Mudd's farm. It was four o'clock in the morning when they reached their destination. There they were able to rest and Mudd set Booth's leg in a splint.

Dawn had broken before William returned from his vigil to the house in H Street. Elisha was waiting anxiously at the foot of the steps. On seeing William approach, he ran to him excitedly.

'What news?' he asked. 'Is he dead?'

William nodded and said wearily, 'He'll no longer pluck a weed and plant a flower.'

'God, I shouldn't have stopped you reporting them!'

'None of them in the house, I'll warrant?'

'Well, that's the strange part. Mrs Surratt and Weichmann returned around midnight. As cool as brass, they were. As if nothing had happened. Weichmann went to bed and Mrs Surratt is washing the kitchen floor.'

'The others?'

'John Surratt fled on horseback as soon as we heard of the attempt on Lincoln. Is it true that Seward has been slain?

'No. Wounded only. Rumour has it that Herold was involved but escaped.'

On entering the house, William went to the door of the kitchen and looked in. Mrs Surratt was on her knees scrubbing the floor. Sensing his presence, she raised her head and stared at him. Her face was devoid of all expression.

William went to Elisha's room and they talked anxiously of what they should do in the light of all that had occurred.

'We must go to the authorities and tell them all we have seen in this house,' Elisha said. 'If I hadn't dissuaded you from speaking out, this horror would have been prevented.'

William looked uncertain and said carefully, 'Think for a moment, Elisha. The deed is done and nothing can undo that. Booth was recognised. The police will soon be here and, whatever we do, justice will prevail. These people will pay dearly for their crimes.'

'It will help salve my conscience.'

'If we testify against them, what's to stop them saying we were part of the conspiracy too?'

Elisha turned pale and William pressed home his advantage. He grabbed Elisha by the shoulders and shook him.

'We say we saw nothing suspicious in this house. That way they'd not want to discredit us.'

'But I could never go into the witness box in their defence.'

'The police would only call us if we helped the prosecution. This way the authorities will be only too glad to send us packing. We'll be off into anonymity before the week's out.'

That afternoon Booth and Herold left Mudd's farm and headed South.

It took two days before the metropolitan police stormed into 541 H Street. During that time, Weichmann and Mary Surratt had not attempted to flee. William had made it clear to them that he and Elisha would swear to the police that they had seen nothing to arouse their suspicions. To which Mary Surratt answered that she too had been unaware of the conspiracy hatched under her roof.

'Mr Dawson,' she said. 'I'm a simple widow earning her living by running a boarding house. All my actions have a perfectly innocent explanation. As to Mr Weichmann driving me to the tavern in Surrattsville on the night of the assassination, I often have occasion to visit the place on business since I rent that property to Mr John Lloyd. Mr Weichmann and I are grateful for your support at this trying time.'

William and Elisha kept their word under intense questioning by the police. Mary Surratt and Weichmann indignantly denied involvement but were betrayed when the fugitive Paine, unaware that the police were in the house, scrambled up the steps and beat frantically on the door seeking shelter. William and Elisha watched from a window at the front of the house as the three were led away into custody, Mary Surratt still protesting her innocence.

Anna, her face as inscrutable as that of her mother, entered the room and said calmly, 'I wish to inform you that this establishment will continue to run as normal and I hope you will remain as residents.'

William, taken aback by her composed demeanour, stammered, 'Well … Yes indeed, Miss Surratt … We will, as the authorities are sure to want to question us further.'

Elisha nodded his head in agreement, at which Anna gave a bleak smile and left the room.

Booth and Herold had been on the run for ten days while the Union Cavalry scoured the countryside for them. A closed carriage containing two men and driven by a Confederate officer, Captain Jett, reached the ferry across the Potomac near Port Royal. It was a wild night and the waters were turbulent. When Captain Jett demanded to be taken across the river, the ferryman refused, claiming it would be unsafe. Jett produced a pistol and forced him to comply.

As they were crossing, Jett opened the door of the carriage to speak to the men inside. Through the open door, the ferryman caught a glimpse of one of the men. Wanted posters of Booth had been distributed throughout the region and the ferryman had no difficulty in recognising him. On reaching the other side, the carriage sped off in the direction of Port Royal.

They had travelled about three miles when they came in sight of the house of Richard Garrett. It stood some distance from the road and had a number of outbuildings. Garrett, who was a staunch confederate and a friend of Jett, lived here with his two teenage sons. Garrett was unwilling to shelter the fugitives in the house but agreed that they could hide in the barn. In this way, if they were discovered, he could claim that they had sneaked in there without his knowledge. Booth's leg was still giving him trouble and he could only move with the help of a crutch that Mudd had given him.

The barn was dilapidated, riddled with cracks and empty knotholes. The smell told them that the place had once been used to store tobacco but all it contained now was hay. Booth dropped the crutch and sank thankfully into the dry bales, Herold flung himself down beside him. Captain Jett left but assured them that he would return in a few days, when the pursuit had moved on, and escort them to a place of permanent safety. He said he would be staying close by in the hotel at Bowling Green.

They were sixty miles from Washington. During their flight, they had heard that Seward had survived Paine's knife attack and that no attempt had been made on Johnson's life. Now that they had found a safe haven, however temporary, it was time for recriminations.

'Atzerodt,' Booth muttered. 'He must have run the instant he left the meeting.'

'Still, your letter will be the death of him,' Herold said, bitterly. 'It will hang us all yet. Why did you do it?'

'Simple, my dear boy. I knew that you were all getting cold feet. So I thought, if they know they're for the high jump whether they take part or not, they'll fall into line.'

'Didn't work for Atzerodt.'

'No, I grant you. But it did for you and Paine.'

Herold rolled away in disgust.

Booth smiled and said to Herold's back, 'You might think that I coerced my friends by trickery and have forfeited their trust. But since childhood, I have been an ardent lover of the South and all it stands for. My devotion is so unswerving that I would yield up everything for the cause I espouse.'

'You're not on the stage now, Booth. Keep those words for when you stand with a noose around your neck.'

Silence followed as both men tried to sleep and gather strength to face the coming day.

Two days later Lieutenant Luther Baker and his troop of cavalrymen picked up the fugitives' trail at the ferry crossing. The ferryman told them about the closed carriage and offered to guide them to where Captain Jett was staying. It was near midnight when Baker threw a cordon around the hotel at Bowling Green and captured Captain Jett. At first Jett denied all knowledge of the carriage and its two occupants. However a trooper, Boston Corbett, requested permission to question the man alone.

Baker had heard a disturbing tale about Trooper Corbett, that he had, as a young man, castrated himself with a pair of scissors. He had carried on working for a whole day before seeking medical help. When asked why he had carried out this self-mutilation, he was said to have replied that he wished to save himself from the wiles of prostitutes. In the conversations Baker had with him during the hunt, Corbett had revealed a fanatical hatred of the South.

However, Baker was desperate to capture Lincoln's assassin and so, with considerable misgivings, he consented. Two muffled screams later, an ashen-faced Jett emerged and agreed to lead them to where Booth and Herold were in hiding.

It was in the early hours of the morning when, led by Jett, they stole silently up to the Garrett house. Baker hammered on the door and Garrett, in his nightclothes, answered.

'We know they're here,' Baker said firmly.

'Know who are here?' Garrett replied, pretending bewilderment.

'Trooper Corbett!' Baker commanded. 'Untie your picket rope. We'll hang this old man and see if it refreshes his memory.'

One of Garrett's sons pushed in front of his father and asked, 'What do you men want?'

'We want the two men who are hiding here and we want them at once,' Baker said.

'They're in the barn,' the young man answered.

Placing Garrett and his two sons under arrest, Baker threw a cordon of troopers around the barn and waited. Although it was still pitch black, the clouds were beginning to disperse, allowing occasional brief shafts of moonlight to illuminate the landscape.

Baker summoned Corbett to his side and said, 'I want a man to crawl up to the barn and see if the fugitives are in fact in there.'

'I'll go myself, Lieutenant,' Corbett promptly answered.

'Right, but remember Trooper, our orders are to capture them alive.'

On his hands and knees Corbett reached the side of the barn and peered in. Booth and Herold had spend a restless night and were already up and talking quietly. It was obvious to Corbett that they were unaware of the encircling soldiers. He carefully backed off and reported to Baker.

'The traitors are in there, Lieutenant,' he said eagerly. 'It will be easy to drop them both with two shots.'

'No. I want them alive.'

The fugitives only became aware that they were trapped when they heard a voice calling loudly from outside.

'Surrender, we have you surrounded,' yelled Baker. 'Come out at once.'

Booth placed his mouth to a gap in the side of the barn and shouted, 'Who are you?'

'It doesn't make any difference who we are. We know who you are. You'd better come out at once.'

'Well, my brave boys, you can wait until doomsday for me to come out. Prepare a stretcher for me. I will never surrender.'

Baker tried again, 'Surrender, or we'll fire the barn and smoke you out like rats.'

'If you withdraw your men thirty rods, I'll come out and we'll shoot it out – just you and me, Captain.'

188

'It's Lieutenant. I repeat, surrender or we'll fire the barn. I'll give you five minutes.'

Inside the barn, Herold said to Booth, 'I don't need five minutes. Tell them I'm coming out.'

'They'll shoot you as soon as you step out of the door.'

'I'll take that risk. It isn't as if we've the means to fight back. To hell with what you do, I want out.'

'You're a coward to desert me.'

'I owe you nothing.'

Booth shrugged his shoulders and called to Baker, 'Oh, Lieutenant, there's a man in here who wants to surrender awfully badly.'

Herold shook the barn door and screamed, 'I'm David Herold. I don't want to burn. I'm coming out. Please don't shoot.'

'Herold, pass your arms out first and then step through the door,' Baker commanded.

'He hasn't any arms,' Booth sneered. 'They belong to me.'

Herold opened the door slightly and slipped out through the narrow gap. Immediately he was thrown to the ground by the soldiers and dragged to a nearby tree where they trussed him up with rope.

'The man left in the barn is Booth, isn't he? Baker asked.

'Yes it is Booth,' Herold replied.

The Lieutenant gave orders to set the barn on fire. They rushed up with blazing straw and soon the barn was ablaze. The soldiers could see Booth scuttling around the barn on his crutch, like a frantic spider, trying to evade the encroaching flames. Baker waited confidently for him to emerge from that inferno and be captured. He had, however, not taken account of Corbett's paranoia. The trooper, having got Booth in his gun sight, could not resist the temptation and shot him in the neck. The soldiers rushed in and carried Booth to a locust tree where they laid him on the grass. He was paralysed and barely conscious. In an effort to ease his pain they moved him to the front porch of the Garrett home.

Distressed by the man's suffering, Baker knelt down and asked him if he had a message for anyone.

With difficulty, Booth said, 'Tell my mother I died for my country.'

A local doctor examined Booth and said that the bullet had punctured the spinal cord and that the wound was fatal.

Booth looked at his hands and moaned, 'Useless, useless.'

His head fell back and the doctor pronounced him dead.

Corbett stepped forward and said, 'Permission to search the body, Lieutenant.'

The thought of Booth's body being mauled by the man who had murdered him was too much for Baker.

'No. I'll do it,' he snapped.

Reverentially, he started to remove Booth's possessions — first a pair of revolvers and a few cartridges.

'See!' cried Corbett triumphantly. 'He would have made a fight of it if I hadn't shot him first.'

'The revolvers were unloaded and in his belt,' Baker said coldly. 'You virtually shot an unarmed man. He'd had his triumph, he'd killed Lincoln. He didn't need to add a few miserable soldiers to claim his place in history.'

The rest of the search produced a knife; a war map of the Southern States; a spur; a pipe; a file; a Canadian bill of exchange; a compass in a leather case; a signal whistle; pictures of four actresses and of his fiancée Lucy Hall; a diary and, symbolically, an almost burnt-out candle. Baker had finished laying these items out on the grass alongside the corpse, when Corbett bent down and picked up the diary.

A large grin spread across his face and he said, 'This should make interesting reading.'

Baker, his face red with anger, snatched it back and declared, 'This will be read by the proper authorities and no one else.'

Booth's body was sewn up in a horse blanket and placed on a wide plank which served as a stretcher. An old market wagon was obtained nearby and the body placed in it for the first stage of the journey to Washington. The wagon lumbered off the field with an escort of cavalry as Booth made his last exit from the stage.

Two days later a Sergeant from the Metropolitan Police called at the house in H Street and told William and Elisha that, since their only use would be as witnesses for the defence, the authorities felt that it would be in their interest to leave Washington and get permanently lost.

They complied instantly with such a compelling invitation. Elisha set out for Wisconsin where he had family and friends who would assist him on his journey to anonymity. William, after sticking a pin in a map, headed for Chicago.

CHAPTER 10

That first night in Mexico City, Maximilian and Carlota stood on the balcony and waved to the cheering multitude packed into the Zocalo in front of the National Palace. The whole city was bedecked with flags and the night sky bejewelled with fireworks. Maximilian felt his heart swell with emotion. What need had he of French troops? He would be the Great Conciliator. Mexico was rich in mineral resources but was a land of obscene contrasts – private wealth set in the midst of public squalor. In his journey from Vera Cruz he had seen the beggars dressed in rags, crying for alms in the filthy streets, their women carrying starving babies in their arms. He would devise a compromise between the liberal and conservative factions that would result in a prosperous and equitable nation.

A week later, while driving out of the city, he came to Chapultepec Castle. A guide informed him that the castle was built on the site of the summer palace of the Aztec emperors. Maximilian's sense of history took over and he pictured Montezuma seated on his throne receiving the news of the approach of Cortés, with his iron heel and iron will. He resolved to make Chapultepec his official residence and ordered that the castle be renovated and refurbished, since it had fallen into disrepair.

Carlota smiled indulgently and said, 'No doubt, you'll supervise the work. You've found another Miramar.'

'Yes, we'll move in immediately. That way I'll be able to keep a close eye on the restoration.'

As soon as Maximilian moved into Chapultepec Castle, he met his first big obstacle on his road to becoming the 'great conciliator'. He was in the grounds of the castle organising his vast army of labourers and tradesmen when Schertzenlechner, his private secretary, came running out of the castle and told Maximilian that Archbishop Labastida had arrived and was seeking an audience with the Emperor. The visit was not unexpected and Maximilian knew exactly what the Archbishop had come to demand.

Antonia Pelagio Labastida was a tall, lean man, embittered by many years of exile. When Maximilian entered the room, Labastida stepped forward and, in a gesture that dared the Emperor not to kiss it, held out his right hand bearing the heavy gold ring of his episcopacy. Maximilian, determined to keep all factions sweet, bent slightly forward and raised the hand to his lips. Gratified, Labastida bowed low.

Maximilian seated himself behind the desk and with a cordial wave of his hand said, 'Dear Archbishop, please take a seat.'

'Your Majesty, I would rather stand while I deliver a message from his Holiness Pope Pius IX.'

Maximilian nodded his head in acknowledgement and waited for Labastida to continue.

'His Holiness requests that the Emperor immediately restore to the Church all the wealth and property that was confiscated during the rule of Juárez – that Satan.'

'This demand was made of the French before I arrived here and I understand that they refused,' Maximilian said slowly.

'Indeed that is correct, your Majesty. But the reason you were chosen and made Emperor by the Conservatives was in order to right the infamous wrong that was done the Church.'

'My dear Archbishop, guerrilla bands roam the countryside outside Mexico City and while that situation continues we will need Marshal Bazaine and his French soldiers. I plan with God's help to reconcile the conflicting forces that are tearing Mexico apart, to bring fairness and modern civilisation to this land. It would be a horrendous mistake to return to the Church the properties she has lost. It would cause terrible upheaval and alienate all those with liberal sympathies. I'm sure that the Pope will realise that I must stand above the battle and be a compromiser.'

Labastida was scandalised and his body shook with anger as he stormed, 'The Pontiff can never compromise with the evils of progress, liberalism and modern civilisation.'

Maximilian decided that it would be better to give the Archbishop the full dose now rather than keep the next news for a later time.

'I must inform you that I have this day written to Benito Juárez inviting him to a conference here in Mexico City that could lead to peace and felicity, and offering him an honoured position in the administration.'

Labastida found it difficult to remain civil, so outraged was he by Maximilian's words. His voice was barely audible as he said, 'It was not for this that Hidalgo and de Estrada brought you here as Emperor. His Holiness will hear of this and he will send a Papal Nuncio to make clear his demands. You may dismiss the request of a humble Archbishop but you will accede to the demands of the Pope's emissary.'

He gave a short bow and swept from the room.

'A difficult encounter,' Schertzenlechner said, entering from another door.

'You were listening?' Maximilian enquired.

Schertzenlechner laughed and said, 'I thought if he got violent and tried to strangle you, I could come to your rescue.'

'If the Pope knew of the conditions here, he would understand what I'm trying to do.'

'What! Old Pius IX? He was as liberal as they come when he was a young cleric but when he became Pope the Italians drove him into exile, for betraying the revolution, and Napoleon had to use French troops to put him back in the Vatican. They say he dare not stick his nose outside the gates of the Vatican in case the people of Rome stamp on it.'

'We have a difficult task, Schertzenlechner, to be the champions of the poor indigenous Mexicans and at the same time reassure the privileged, who after all made me Emperor, that I will preserve their hegemony.'

'Keep throwing magnificent functions at the National Palace, with Count Bombelles and his Palatine Guards, resplendent in their shining silver and blue uniforms and black plumed helmets, strutting back and fore in front of the entrance. At the same time let the Empress be seen knitting shirts for the naked poor.'

Maximilian frowned but then gave a wry smile and said, ' Ah! If only it was that simple, my friend.'

Defeated and driven north, Benito Juárez, deposed President of Mexico, took refuge in the border town of Paso del Norte. It did not warrant the dignity of the designation 'town', since it was no more than a collection of crude adobe huts. Adobe huts, prevalent in the more primitive parts of Mexico, used bricks made by mixing straw with clay and allowing them to dry in the sun.

Juárez was born in the village of San Pabola Guelato in the state of Oaxaca, situated in the Sierra Madre del Sur mountain range in central Mexico. His parents, who were Zapotec Indian peasants, died when he was three years old. The Zapotec Indians were the survivors of an ancient Mesoameric civilisation that declined under pressure from the Mixtecs from AD 900 until the Spanish conquest in the 1530s.

He was raised by his paternal grandparents and worked in the fields until the age of twelve. In his village there was no school and one rarely heard Spanish spoken, the main language being one of the primitive Zapotec dialects. Determined to gain himself an education, he walked the forty miles to Oaxaca City and was befriended by a bookseller, Antonio Salanueva, who arranged for him to study at the Royal School in the city. Juárez became very unhappy at the inequality practised in the school, where the children of wealthy parents were taught with care by a qualified teacher while the poorer youngsters, such as Juárez, were left to the care of an assistant who was almost as ignorant as the children themselves. Every day he saw groups of young men going to and coming from the Seminary College, where they were studying for careers in the church, and he remembered his uncle saying that the only learned profession a poor person could aspire to was being a priest. He grasped at this one escape route from his repressive ignorance and asked Salanueva to enrol him in the Seminary.

After two years at the Seminary, Juárez realised that he did not want to become a priest and his patron allowed him to study law at the newly established Institute of Sciences and Arts, where he received his degree in 1834. He was now able to practise as a lawyer and that same year he was elected to the state legislature. That was the start of his long climb up the political ladder which culminated in 1861, after many vicissitudes, in his being installed in the capital as the President of Mexico.

Now he was back where he had started, sitting in an adobe hut among an ignorant and primitive people. He was isolated from his family, he had sent his wife and children to sanctuary in America, and his defeated supporters were scattered in small guerrilla bands across the land. It was still possible to see in this lonely figure the young boy who had set out from his native village all those years ago in search of an education. He walked with the same spring in his step and his soft black hair hung about a face made remarkable by penetrating dark eyes.

The letter from Maximilian had finally reached his humble refuge and Juárez sat, hunched forward on his chair, reading Maximilian's portentous words:

> *'I have forsaken friends, fortune and, what is most dear to a man, country, to come, with my wife Dona Carlota, to this distant and unknown land to satisfy a call made by a people that rest their hope for the future in me.*
>
> *'I invite you to Mexico City for a conference from which will flow peace and prosperity. I pledge my word of honour that sufficient forces will be made available to guarantee your safety. Should you agree to place your talents and patriotism at the service of the Empire, I can assure you that I will find you a position of great distinction within the administration.'*

Juárez laid the letter down on the table and called for paper and ink. An old peasant woman shuffled into the room and placed by his elbow some sheets of paper and an ink pot, out of which protruded a quill pen.

He smiled at her and said, 'I must reply to the Chosen One.'

'So be it, Señor,' she replied, retreating through the door. 'God's will be done. I'm sure.'

Juárez picked up the pen and started to write, speaking the words slowly as he did.

'To Archduke Maximilian. I find it strange that you should class as a call from the people what was in fact no more than a group of traitors calling at Miramar and offering you the Mexican Crown. You attempt to bribe me with the offer of a distinguished position in your government. I tell you that the President of the Republic will never betray the obscure mass of the people who have placed their hopes in him. If I fail, at least I will have satisfied the promptings of my own conscience.'

Although Maximilian and Carlota had moved into Chapultepec, they continued to hold state banquets in the lavishly furnished National Palace. Faces set in the bright, synthetic smiles worn for official functions, they stepped determinedly into the first of a long line of drawing rooms, connected by folding doors, and greeted their guests. The usual mixture, thought Maximilian wearily, of French officers, Austrian aristocrats and Conservative politicians – all accompanied by their elegantly attired wives. To further his aim of reconciliation, Maximilian tried, on these occasions, to leaven the mixture with a sprinkling of Liberals.

Tonight was going to be particularly tiring, he feared, because after the banquet there was to be a concert in which an orchestra would play a seemingly endless succession of tediously similar Strauss waltzes.

During the banquet, Maximilian cast a satisfied eye around the table with its crystal glasses, fine Meissen porcelain and silver cutlery.

He leaned across the table and said quietly to Carlota, 'Our Indian servants look startlingly handsome in their Imperial livery.'

At that moment one of the servants with great deliberation picked his nose and, after inspecting the result, rolled it between thumb and forefinger, before dropping it on the floor. Maximilian flushed angrily and Carlota suppressed a giggle.

After the concert Maximilian tapped Schertzenlechner on the shoulder and said, 'A word before you retire for the night.'

'Yes, Majesty?'

'Our Indian servants are handsome fellows but at the meal tonight I saw one of them pick his nose in full view of the guests.'

'Oh, that's nothing. I've seen one scratch his head with a fork.'

'They may be peasants but surely they can be taught correct etiquette. Have a word with the comptroller of the household.'

'As you say, Majesty. They are handsome peasants, but their behaviour is far from handsome. One scratches his head with a fork, another picks his nose and I heard one of them break wind as he bent to serve soup to Marshal Bazaine. The poor old Marshal thought for a moment Juárista guerrillas had invaded the Palace and he was under fire!'

'They can be trained.'

'No, I'm afraid not. They steal the cutlery, linen, plates and food. In fact, anything they come across that's not tied down. I was going to bring these matters to your attention but was hesitating because I know how anxious you are to employ the indigenous people. But, if we are to attain the excellence that prevails in the Courts of Europe, they must be replaced by Austrians.'

'See to it.'

Maximilian had made a habit of venturing out into the surrounding countryside to see how the Mexican and French forces were succeeding in pacifying the country. On one occasion Carlota, despite his warnings of the danger involved, insisted on accompanying him. Riding in the heavily guarded coach with them was Marshal Bazaine. The escort was made up of French cavalry, supported by units of the Mexican Imperial Army under the command of Colonel Miguel Lopez. Carlota recognised Lopez as the officer who had commanded the Mexican troops escorting Maximilian and herself from Vera Cruz to Mexico City. The appearance and discipline of the Mexicans shocked her.

Turning to Marshal Bazaine, she said, 'Surely, Marshal, those soldiers are not the men who escorted us from Vera Cruz to the Capital.'

'They are the same units, Your Majesty.'

'But they've become so ragged and undisciplined.'

Bazaine laughed and said, 'The authorities made a special effort then to impress your Imperial Highnesses. Bought them new uniforms and promised cash rewards for good discipline. Now they've lapsed into their natural state. It is no secret that we French view our Mexican comrades with the utmost contempt.'

Maximilian stirred uncomfortably and said sharply, 'Marshal! These men have the necessary

201

courage and, with training, will become as efficient a force as your vaunted Imperial Guard.'

'Majesty,' Bazaine replied. 'You know that Emperor Napoleon is waiting impatiently for the day when the Mexican Army can take over control of the country and he can withdraw his troops. But, at the present rate of progress, that day is a long way in the future. You talk of the courage of the Mexican soldier, well you have some brave officers. Colonel Lopez for one, whom I've seen waving his sword in fury as he attempted to drive his men back to battle as they fled, a disordered rabble.

'Then there's General Marquez, a man of immense determination and valour, and General Mejia, though I find him a little too pious, always on his knees. But as for the rest – the Liberal irregulars would eat them for breakfast if it were not for the French troops.'

'General Marquez employs methods that alienate the peasants,' Maximilian answered stiffly. 'I believe the man has a blood lust. I did not come to Mexico with a sword in my hand. That is not the way to win over the people.'

Bazaine flushed angrily and retorted, 'I can't fight this war with one hand tied behind my back. Unless we crush the opposition soon, Napoleon will withdraw his support and all that will be left between you and your enemies will be a bunch of cowering, corrupt cowards. God help your Majesty then.'

Realising that he had gone too far, Bazaine smiled apologetically at Carlota and an uneasy silence prevailed as the coach continued on its journey.

Some time later the cavalcade reached a small village and halted. Colonel Lopez appeared at the coach door and informed the Emperor that earlier that day General Marquez at the head of a unit of Mexican troops had cleared the village of a band of Liberal guerrillas. Maximilian and Bazaine alighted but when Carlota attempted to follow them Lopez placed an arm across the open door of the carriage.

'Your Majesty,' he said, 'I would respectfully advise you not to enter the village. The ravages of war should not be seen by a lady such as you.'

Carlota brushed his arm aside and said, 'I, sir, am first an Empress.'

She had witnessed scenes of violence during her time in Italy but nothing had prepared her for the carnage she saw as she walked through the village. The primitive dwellings had been ransacked and smashed to pathetic mounds of adobe bricks. The mutilated bodies of men and boys lay scattered on ground stained with blood, drying in the sun. The full horror was not revealed until they reached the small wood at the end of the village and saw that every branch held a gruesome fruit. The women of the village had been stripped; hung by their hair from the trees and whipped mercilessly. Some were still alive and Colonel Lopez was frantically supervising his men as they cut through the women's hair with their bayonets and gently lowered the violated bodies. Carlota turned her face away from this abomination and vomited into a handkerchief. She then stumbled back to the carriage, waving away all attempts to assist her.

Bazaine quickly recovered his composure and said to a white-faced Maximilian, 'The villagers were obviously sheltering guerrillas. General Marquez was simply making an example of them.'

Maximilian spoke in a shocked whisper, 'I came here to win the people's love, not to slaughter them. This is unbearable.'

'Oh come, your Majesty. We are all strong enough to bear the misfortunes of others.'

'You are the commander of the forces in Mexico, both French and native. I charge you to curb the excesses of the men under your command. Remember, you are answerable to me.'

Maximilian stalked back to the carriage.

Bazaine saluted and murmured under his breath, 'I am answerable only to Napoleon, as you will find out one fine day, my squeamish friend.'

That night Carlota lay beside Maximilian, her body rigid with shock. He placed his arm gently around her waist and tried to pull her close to him but she angrily pushed him away and rose from the bed.

'Please, Max, don't come near me,' she pleaded.

'But Carlota, I realise your hurt and I want to comfort you.'

'Nothing you can do will wipe my mind clean of the scenes I witnessed today.'

'You should have listened to Lopez and stayed in the carriage.'

'So I would have gone on living in this fool's paradise, surrounded by sycophantic courtiers. Those peasants were mutilated and killed to keep you on the throne. Why, oh why, does everything we touch turn to disaster? We are not wanted here, Max.'

'Listen, Carlota. I've given Bazaine orders to curb Marquez. I can yet win these people by my actions. The Papal Nuncio will be arriving soon demanding I return the confiscated lands back to the Church. Whatever his threats, I'll remain firm and refuse. I'll enact laws to mitigate the plight of the poor. Believe me, I will win them all over and then there'll be no need for brute force. Napoleon can recall his soldiers and we'll rule this land with kindness and justice.'

'Oh Max, you're an impossible dreamer. An empire founded on war has to maintain itself by war. This is a man's world and what I've learnt today is that man is a heartless rapacious beast.'

'Come to bed, my love. Sleep will soothe your anguish.'

Carlota gave a sad laugh and said, 'Sleep is good, death is better but the best thing would be never to have been born.'

Maximilian sprang out of bed and tried to gather her in his arms but she stepped back and pushed him away.

'No, Max!' she cried. 'Don't touch me. God knows I love you, but at this moment I couldn't bear to be touched by you. Please go to another room.'

She had never spoken to him in such a manner before and Maximilian, though badly shaken, attempted to placate her, 'I understand how you must feel and I share your repugnance for what happened today. I'll leave you now and in the morning we'll both set about seeing that such things will never happen again in a country where we rule.'

As he left, Maximilian glanced back at his wife and saw that she was standing with her hands covering her face and sobbing quietly.

Maximilian's hope that time would heal Carlota's pain proved misplaced. While affirming her love for him and a determination to stand with him in his fight to bring peace and justice to Mexico, she insisted that she now found it abhorrent to lie with a man. Maximilian ordered his valet to set up a small bed in their room and from then on he and Carlota slept apart. To the world outside their bedroom nothing appeared to have changed and it would be true to say that their love for each other still burnt brightly, but the sight of those naked, bleeding women hanging from the branches of the trees in that small Mexican village had crushed Carlota's sexual desire.

Carlota was seated at Maximilian's side when the Papal Nuncio, Monsignor Pedro Francisco Meglia, was ushered into the throne room at the National Palace. Ostensibly he had come to Mexico to officiate at the religious services connected with the coming Christmas celebrations, but Maximilian knew that he came with a demand from the Pope that Mexico once again became a vassal of Rome.

Monsignor Meglia, dressed impressively in full ecclesiastical trappings, offered the Pope's felicitations and then immediately got down to the business in hand.

'Your Majesty, now that Mexico is once more ruled by a Catholic Monarch, I deliver a message from his Holiness Pope Pius IX. He demands that every jot of property stolen from the Church must be returned. Furthermore, there must be no compromise in the matter of religious tolerance. The only faith allowed will be Catholicism and the state shall have no jurisdiction over Church officials.'

'You may assure the Holy Father that Mexico will be a Catholic state in every sense of the word,' Maximilian replied.

'I take it this means you accede to the demands I have presented,' Meglia said, firmly.

Maximilian smiled and, leaning towards Meglia, said, 'A Catholic state but a modern one. Catholicism will be the religion of the state but, to promote harmony and gain the trust of the people, I must allow other faiths the freedom to operate. I am sure his Holiness will understand.'

The Nuncio's face turned a bright red and he spat out, 'Understand! Never! Understand why you tolerate heretics. Not just tolerate them, positively encourage them. And what of the matter of returning the Church's property and of the status of Church officials? Are you going to refuse the Holy Father's demands in these matters too?'

'I dare not turn back the clock and restore the Church to its former position of supreme power. The people would never accept it. The government will pay the salaries of the priests and will maintain all their religious buildings and institutions.'

Carlota intervened in an attempt to assuage the affronted Nuncio, 'Monsignor, what leads you to believe that Mexico is a truly Catholic country?'

Meglia looked startled and said, ' Why Majesty! In every hamlet of this land one sees the simple peasants thronging the streets on holy days bearing the images of Jesus and his saints. They fill the churches with lighted candles and revere the relics of the martyrs.'

Carlota answered gently, 'But are we not making a mistake when we take these outward signs of

207

reverence as an expression of deep religious beliefs when they are no more than the manifestations of ignorant superstition?'

'What you call ignorant superstition the Church calls faith,' Meglia retorted. 'How else can poor uneducated peasants learn to love their God but through blind faith? Can they read the word of God written in the Bible? Can they discourse with scholars? They reach God through the teaching of the Church and their love of wax statues, candles and relics. What do you have against the veneration of relics? Does it not redound to the honour of the saint? Did not the Church at the Council of Trent in 1563 approve the veneration of relics and lay down strict rules to assure their authenticity? Take those things away from them and they will be lost and condemned to everlasting hell.'

'No,' Carlota cried. 'Maximilian and I will build a Catholic Church securely founded in a society where justice and tolerance reigns. The Church will grow in strength when we show our confidence by allowing other religions to exist alongside it. Go back to Rome and plead our case. Tell His Holiness that the Emperor and Empress of Mexico are devout catholics and should be allowed to build a Church suited to the conditions of a modern society.'

These words proved too much for the Papal Nuncio. He rose to his feet and, bowing stiffly towards Maximilian said, 'I will convey your intentions to His Holiness Pope Pius IX but I will in no way endorse them. You have heard the Pope's word and remember that he is the infallible interpreter of divine revelation and the Vicar of Christ.'

With a curt nod in Carlota's direction, he turned and swept from the room without waiting for the customary permission to depart.

Maximilian lifted his hands in despair and said, 'Oh the curse of the supremacy of Rome. The irony is that it rests on two historical accidents: the primacy of Peter among Christ's Apostles and the identification of Peter with the church in Rome.'

Carlota smiled and said, 'Don't despair, Max. We'll save the Church despite that old curmudgeon in Rome.'

'They say he's insane but does have his lucid moments when he's only stupid.'

They both laughed and for a brief moment the cares of office slipped from them. They appeared young and radiant again as when they stood on the balcony and waved to the cheering multitude packed into the Zocalo in front of the National Palace on the day of their coronation.

They would however need more than a sense of humour to deal with the problems that crowded in on them. Maximilian's attempts to modernise and discipline the Mexican army were making little progress. The letter from Juárez, rejecting his peace offer, arrived on the same day that Archbishop Labastida called and with great relish informed him that he had lost the support of the Church. Napoleon, who was becoming increasingly alarmed at the growth of Prussian power, started to question when the country would be pacified and so allow the French troops to be repatriated.

To add to Maximilian's woes, Carlota was still unable to tolerate sexual contact and continued to deny him access to her bed. For a man of Maximilian's healthy sexual appetite, this was proving intolerable. He was loath to avail himself of the services of the ladies at court, fearing that the inevitable gossip would tarnish the image of the monarchy.

Help was at hand in the ample form of Juana, the wife of the gardener at Chapultepec. Maximilian first saw her one morning as he was wandering in the garden nursing a huge frustration. She was bending down tending a clump of bright blue delphiniums. Stealing up unobserved, he gave her a friendly slap on her generous behind. Juana gave a startled cry and spun around to see who was taking such liberties with her person. On seeing Maximilian, whatever words she had intended to utter stuck in her throat and she was reduced to a strangulated, 'Majesty.'

After such a robust approach it did not take long before Juana was fully appraised of Maximilian's problem and, honoured to be of service to their Emperor, she and her husband agreed to a discreet arrangement whereby Maximilian and Juana met secretly in the gardener's small house which was situated in the grounds at a safe distance from the Castle. Carlota, feeling guilty that she was unable to satisfy Maximilian's physical needs, acquiesced in the arrangement.

It did not take long before Maximilian discovered that Juana had a flower fetish. One afternoon he arrived at the cottage for their regular rendezvous to find the room festooned with flowers. Before they consummated their lovemaking she insisted on threading long-stemmed, blue-petalled larkspurs through his hair and garlanding his naked thighs with two small bunches of pink campions. Maximilian, although disconcerted at first, grew to accept this and he would occasionally respond in kind by placing a slipper flower, with its pouchlike yellow petals, on her shining brown belly.

Maximilian and Carlota were caught in a time warp in which nothing changed. They tried to alleviate the lot of the poor by issuing scores of edicts on education, welfare and agricultural reform but, with little money to implement them, they proved to be no more than pious hopes. The population continued to be alienated by the repressive and brutal excesses of the French and Mexican soldiers. Napoleon fretted and grumbled at Maximilian's inability to impose peace in Mexico. At the start of 1865, in an attempt to mollify him, Maximilian awarded him the Grand Cross with Collar, of the Order of the Mexican Eagle.

When the insignia arrived in Paris, Napoleon was incensed and, flinging it on the floor in front of a startled Eugene, declared, 'What does an Emperor of France need such a bauble as this? I've a good mind to recall my troops immediately and see how he fares then.'

But Napoleon had invested too much blood and money into the Mexican adventure to pull out. He had no alternative but to continue supporting Maximilian. French honour and greatness demanded that the enterprise end in triumph. On April 9, 1865, General Robert E Lee surrendered to General S Grant at Appomattox and ended the

American civil war. Four days later John Wilkes Booth entered the State box at Ford's theatre and, pressing his derringer pistol against Lincoln's left ear, squeezed the trigger. These two events marked the turning point in Maximilian's fortunes.

America had always been concerned about French intervention in Mexico but, while their own civil war raged, they were not in a position to do anything about it. Lincoln, while resolutely refusing to recognise Maximilian's regime, had adopted a policy of non-intervention. The triumph of the Unionists and Lincoln's assassination significantly changed the situation. His successor, Andrew Johnson, was no longer under the same constraint and saw an opportunity to unite the country in a crusade to drive the French from Mexico.

CHAPTER 11

William's journey to Chicago was through a landscape that seemed to him bare, harsh and unfinished, and yet exuded a promise of future prosperity. Chicago had started out as a minor trading post at a swampy river mouth near the south-western tip of Lake Michigan. The opening of the Erie Canal in 1825, joining the Atlantic states and the Great Lakes, shifted to the north the great westward migration and made Chicago the principal western terminus. Retail stores opened to serve the newcomers and great blast furnaces were built to smelt the iron ore brought from Upper Michigan by lake vessels. The coming of the railroads made Chicago the centre of the commodities market.

Alighting at the depot on Michigan Street he made for Kendrick's hotel which was situated nearby. William inquired at the desk if there were any staff vacancies and to his surprise was sent immediately to Mr Kendrick's office. Kendrick was a large cheerful man with a red face and a friendly manner. As soon as William entered the room Kendrick rushed forward and dragged him to a chair facing the desk.

'Want a job with us do you, young man?' he boomed. 'Well I must say you look a presentable young fellow.'

'I've only just arrived in Chicago and was hoping you might have something suitable,' William answered.

'Something in the kitchens, perhaps?' Kendrick suggested with a laugh.

'Well no, not exactly. I was hoping for something more on the management side. I worked for a year on the reception desk at the National Hotel in Washington.'

'You were in Washington when the President was murdered by that villain Booth?'

William nodded solemnly and thought it better not to volunteer the information that he had lodged in the house at the centre of the conspiracy.

Kendrick continued, 'We here in Chicago supported the Union throughout the war. Unlike those damn Downstaters in southern Illinois, always pressing for an alliance with the Confederacy. We were a major supplier of goods and men to the Union. Washington might give itself airs as the capital of America but, young man, Chicago is one of the world's richest industrial and commercial centres.'

William's attention must have wandered for a moment, because Kendrick suddenly frowned and said sharply, 'Am I boring you, sir?'

William sat up in his chair and said, 'No indeed, Mr Kendrick. I was thinking how my sentiments match yours. I left Washington for Chicago because I knew that here lay the best opportunities for a young man who wished to make something of himself.'

Kendrick's face cleared and he beamed. 'Yes sirree. We are the nation's major lumber-distributing centre.' He thumped the desk. 'But the coming of the railroads has ensured our future. The railroads haul cattle, hogs and sheep here to Chicago for slaughtering and packing in our stockyards. So you see, young man, you certainly made the right choice coming to Chicago. Furthermore, the climate here is kinder than in the surrounding area. Lake Michigan mitigates the extremes – lowers the temperatures in the summer and raises them in the winter. Though, I must admit, we do occasionally get some almighty awesome snowstorms. A job in management, you said?'

'Yes, sir,' William said, eagerly.

'Well it so happens that we are looking for a personable young man to work at the reception desk. You know the routine, welcoming incoming guests and seeing they go to the correct rooms; speeding departing ones on their way and ensuring they pay their bills.'

'The very same duties I undertook at the National,' William said, triumphantly.

'You would be on the night shift, eight in the evening to six in the morning. Your duties would also involve assisting our book-keeper. You have some experience in that area?'

'Most certainly,' William lied. 'I was in charge of accounts at the National.'

He decided to further impress Kendrick with another untruth.

'At school I was just pipped at the post for a closed mathematics scholarship to Cambridge.'

Kendrick was impressed. 'Not *the* Cambridge?' he said. 'Your ancient university?'

'Yes indeed, sir.'

'Well! To think that Kendrick's hotel will have a live pipped Cambridge scholar as its night clerk.'

Kendrick rose and extended his hand to William. 'Welcome aboard, young fellow.'

William was pleased to learn that the job entitled him to a room in the hotel and free board. The hotel had a hundred rooms and, when William opened the door and stepped into the one allocated to him, he concluded that it must be the worst. At least, he hoped that it was the worst because, if the others were like this, he was wasting his time working there. The floor space was little more that the size of a large bath towel and lacked a carpet; a truckle bed, with no pillow and a stained torn mattress the colour of mud, occupied the whole length of one side of the room. A plywood chest, missing half its drawers, completed the furnishings. It turned out that his room was typical of the servant quarters in most hotels. When he was taken on a tour of the guest-rooms, since the nature of his job demanded that he knew their good and bad points, William discovered that they were well furnished and comfortable. The hotel had obviously been in the second class category but now, as Chicago grew in importance and wealth, the hotel was striving to improve its image.

Chicago was home to a mixed population of three hundred thousand Americans and northern European immigrants. Care had to be taken, when walking along its bustling streets to avoid confrontation with the many aggressive hobos who loitered there looking for the vulnerable newcomer. William had quickly settled in and was feeling particularly pleased with himself one sunny afternoon as he sauntered along Michigan Street. He had refurbished his room with two pillowcases; a blue mattress, complete with matching sheets and blankets; a red carpet; a wall mirror and a small chest of drawers. Mr Kendrick had told him that he had heard glowing praise from guests about the night clerk who they said was the epitome of courtesy – 'friendly manner', 'knows everything', 'spares no pains' and 'a clerk in a million' were among the phrases used.

'Yes, sir,' William murmured, 'life in Chicago is sure the tops.'

Suddenly a tall, unkempt man with a straggling beard grabbed his arm and said, in a hoarse voice, 'Spare a dollar for a starving man. A gent like you could surely spare a dollar.'

William hesitated for a moment and then pulled a small bundle of notes out of his pocket. These few dollars were all that remained of his previous week's wages. He was about to peel off one of the bills when the tramp attempted to snatch the bundle. William hung on to his money and pushed the fellow away. The man staggered and fell, striking his head on the ground. William started to walk away but compassion for a fellow human being tugged at his conscience and he returned to the spot. The man had risen to his feet and was ruefully rubbing a large lump that was forming on his forehead. William had noticed how easy it had been to repulse the stranger's attack and now, studying the man more closely, he observed the threadbare clothes and the half-starved body.

'I didn't mean to knock you down,' William said. 'Come to Kendrick's Hotel and I'll buy you a meal.'

In an attempt to give the man a certain dignity, he asked, 'What's your name?'

'Miller,' he replied.

'Mine's Dawson. Come on Miller, let's go to Kendrick's.'

Miller laughed and said, 'No. Don't waste your money in a hotel. I know far cheaper places to eat. Follow me.'

He led William down a mean side street and into a dingy eating-house. Bare wooden tables stood on a sawdust-strewn floor, but the place was clean and the waiter who served them was polite and attentive. Miller ordered a goulash and a cup of coffee and when they arrived, William was agreeably surprised at the quality of the food and the price, thirty cents.

Miller eyed him over the bowl of steaming beef and vegetables and said with a grin, 'Only millionaires or fools would waste their money in hotels.'

'Don't say that,' William said. 'I make my living working in a hotel. The people you call millionaires or fools give me my livelihood. The rich make it possible for the likes of me to have a decent life.'

Miller became agitated and cried, 'Bah! All rich men are nothing but thieves. The workmen slave and create the wealth, then the rich steal it from under their noses and they're too damn dumb to realise it. Stupid sheep, the lot of them. You won't catch me helping to line any rich bastard's pocket.'

'How do you earn a living, then?'

'I'm a tramp. I live by begging and I'm my own boss. I go where I like and when I want to.'

'But how do you travel, if you have no money?'

'I steal rides in freight cars and boxcars and on the top of coal wagons. When I'm caught and thrown off, I wait for the next one.'

When he stood up to leave, William slipped him two dollars. Miller pocketed the money and said, 'So long, pal. Life is full of happenings and some of them are painful.'

Here, he rubbed the lump on his forehead and continued, 'But no fat bastard is getting rich on my efforts.'

He sidled through the door and was gone. Walking back to the hotel William thought about the significance of the encounter. It had resonances of his meeting with the prostitute on the streets of Liverpool. Then, the girl's squalor and depravity had made him vow chastity until he met a woman he could make his wife. The confrontation with Miller had induced in William a horror of poverty and a determination that he would never allow himself to fall to such a degraded state.

'From now on,' he resolved, 'I will husband my resources and save a little each week from my wages until I have a sum of money sufficient to invest in some sound capital venture. This is the land of opportunity and William Dawson is the man to seize the shining hour. Sorry Miller, but I'm with the rich bastards.'

Since leaving Washington, William had read in the lurid pages of the *Chicago Times* sensational accounts of the trial of those involved in Lincoln's assassination. Among those arraigned before the military tribunal, William recognised the names of Mary Surratt, Herold, Weichmann, Paine and Atzerodt. One prominent conspirator was missing:

John Surratt. He had evaded capture and the paper said that the police believed he had escaped to Canada. Throughout the trial, Mary Surratt, dressed in black with her head covered in a black bonnet and her face hidden by a black veil, claimed total innocence. She said that she knew nothing of Booth's plans and that her trips to Surrattsville were to collect money she was owed. Her credibility suffered when she insisted that she had never set eyes on Paine when it had been clearly established that he was a frequent visitor to the boarding house.

William's last task each day before he finished his shift was to receive the bulky bundle of newspapers and allocate them to the rooms of guests who had ordered them. One morning the front page of the Chicago Times bore a heading two inches high:

CONSPIRATORS TO HANG
All found guilty. Mary Surratt, Paine, Atzerodt and Herold sentenced to death. Dr Mudd, O'Laughlen and Arnold sentenced to life imprisonment.

BLACK WIDOW COULD
ESCAPE THE NOOSE.
Tribunal adds a recommendation: the undersigned members of the Military Commission detailed to try Mary E Surratt and others for the conspiracy and murder of Abraham Lincoln, the late President of the United States, do respectively pray the President, in consideration of the sex and

age of the said Mary E Surratt, if he can upon
the facts in the case, find it consistent with
his sense of duty to the country to commute
the sentence of death to imprisonment in the
penitentiary for life.

Throughout all the excitement and ill-informed gossip that the trial had provoked, William had been careful never to reveal that he had lived right in the heart of the conspiracy. He shuddered as he imagined the horrified reactions of Mr Kendrick, the chambermaids and bellhops if he had informed them that he had sat at table with the main conspirators and had opened the door of 541 H Street to Booth, Paine and Atzerodt on the night of Lincoln's murder.

On July 7, 1865, the hangings took place. President Andrew Johnson ignored the plea for mercy and Mrs Surratt took her place with the others on the scaffold. William read in the *Chicago Times* that as Mary Surratt, still shrouded in black, was guided towards the noose she stumbled and cried aloud, 'Pray God, don't let me fall.'

Reading that, a wave of compassion for that inscrutable woman swept over him. He recalled Mrs Surratt on her knees scrubbing the floor and how, on sensing his presence, she had raised her head and stared at him – her face devoid of all expression. He saw again John Wilkes Booth striding into the lobby of the National Hotel, his black cape, lined with scarlet silk, billowing behind him. Images of the others passed before him: Herold, Weichmann, Atzerodt, John Surratt and poor Anna. He knew that these people would remain with him for the rest of his life and that he would never be able to draw a line under the frightening affair.

The noise of their altercation preceded the two guests and startled William out of his reverie. When the revolving door jettisoned them into the lobby, they stood for a moment and gazed around defiantly before the younger woman marched up to the desk.

Fixing William with a gimlet eye, she announced in a loud cut-glass English accent, 'Miss De-ath and Mrs De-ath. I believe you have a room booked for us.'

William studied the register and said triumphantly, 'Ah yes. Here it is, Miss and Mrs Death.'

'No, no. De-ath, young man. De-ath. Are you deaf?'

'Of course, De-ath. Pardon me.'

The older woman, in her late sixties, had now hobbled up to the desk.

'Ask him about the size of the room,' she demanded, in a shrill squeak.

A look of extreme annoyance flashed across the face of Miss De'ath and she snapped, 'Mother, give me time. You're so impatient.'

Mrs De'ath bridled, opened her mouth but then thought better of it.

Miss De'ath smiled coldly at William and said, 'When I booked, I specifically asked for a room of spacious dimensions.'

'All our rooms are spacious,' William answered.

'Yes, yes, yes. But have you allocated us one that is more spacious than the general run of rooms?'

'Would you like me to go up and measure it for you?'

'No need to be facetious, young man,' Mrs De'ath snapped.

'Mother, stop interfering and allow me to deal with this.'

William decided it was time to be firm and said, 'I can assure you that the dimensions of the room are perfectly adequate for whatever you plan to do there. Why don't you let the bellboy take you up? If it doesn't measure up to your specifications, I will place you in another room.'

This appeared to mollify the pair and they registered without further controversy. The bellboy gathered up the luggage and led the way up the stairs to their room. As soon as they disappeared from sight round the turn in the stairway, an argument broke out between them again. William was unable to decipher the words but the duet of piping flute and strident horn was unmistakable.

During the next week, William became better acquainted with the two ladies. Going out or coming in their approach was always heralded by their voices, sent out like a party of skirmishers in front of the main force. What life must have been like in their room, William trembled to think. Never once, during William's shift, did they pass the desk without registering some complaint, however trivial. Yet he grew to like them.

Miss De'ath, in her early forties was obviously a spinster who felt a pitying contempt for all men.

She once told William, when he had failed yet again to deal satisfactorily with one of her grumbles, 'You're no better than my brother-in-law, about as useful as a wooden leg in a forest fire. Men! Who needs them?'

There was something splendid in her upright stance and complete faith in her own infallibility.

Mrs De'ath was a formidable old lady who more than held her own in the war with her daughter and William detected a sparkle in her eyes as battle waged, showing that she was secretly enjoying the fray.

Their stay was nearing its end when the old lady fell ill and was confined to her bed. A doctor was called and after examining Mrs De'ath, he left at the desk a list of medicines to be procured. William went out to the apothecary's shop in Michigan Street and on returning he took the palliatives up to the De'aths' room. He knocked gently on the door and entered. The curtains were partly drawn and in the half-light he was able to see Mrs De'ath lying on the bed with the quilt drawn up to her chin. Her face looked pathetically small and wizened against the vast expanse of pillow. Her eyes were closed and her breathing was laboured. Her daughter was bent solicitously over her, moistening her lips with a damp cloth. It was then that William learnt another lesson - love can be manifested in many ways. The tender care with which Miss De'ath nursed her mother back to health revealed a bond between the pair that outsiders, such as William, would never comprehend. He smiled contentedly on the day of their departure as he listened to the furious altercation that erupted outside the hotel as they boarded their carriage.

'Mrs De-ath is herself again,' he said to a startled guest as he handed him his key.

William's conditions of service allowed him one night off every week and he soon discovered that the streets of Chicago at night were as full of vice and promiscuity as those of Liverpool. There were dark, smoke-filled drinking dens where men played faro – one of the oldest gambling games played with cards, supposedly named from the picture of a pharaoh on the back of the cards imported from France.

In the game facsimiles of the thirteen cards of the spade suit, representing the ranks of all suits, are enamelled on a layout on which the bets are placed against the house. A bet may be placed on any rank to win or to lose; or, by the manner in which the chips are placed on the layout, a bet may cover several ranks. A shuffled pack of playing cards is placed face up in a dealing box. The top card is removed and not used. The next card taken from the box loses and the house pays out on the bets placed to lose and takes in the bets placed on the card to win. The card left showing in the box wins, and the house pays the amount of any bet placed on that rank to win. The two cards constitute a turn.

The dealer then removes the exposed card from the box, puts aside another card, which loses, and leaves exposed another card, which wins. The game continues in this fashion through the pack. The last card in the box does not count. When cards of the same rank appear in the same turn and so both win and lose, the house takes half of each bet on that rank, whether to win or to lose. This is called a split.

At the very time that William was wandering the streets of Chicago peering into these sleazy gaming-rooms, Leo Tolstoy was writing *War and Peace* in which the young Count Rostov loses a fortune at the faro table. Gambling had no class barriers.

William had remained true to the vow of chastity he had made after his alarming encounter in Liverpool. At the National Hotel and Kendrick's he had not lacked the opportunity to lose his virginity but, although a number of the chambermaids were pretty, he had not wished to compromise his status by having a liaison with a member of staff in a subordinate grade. Viewing the lines of brazen prostitutes who lifted their skirts and shouted their prices only served to strengthen his resolve. He decided to seek the sanctuary of the modest diner that Miller had taken him to. He was about to enter when he felt a tentative tug on his coat and, turning around, he found staring up at him a young girl whose childlike, open face radiated innocence.

Imagine his surprise when she whispered, 'One dollar to five dollars, depending on what you want.'

He carefully perused her, noting the poor but clean clothes and the face devoid of rouge and lipstick. She looked nothing like a whore. He felt a compulsion to find out more about her.

'Have you a place to go?' he asked.

'Oh yes!' she said eagerly. 'Just round the corner. A nice place.'

It turned out to be a narrow poorly furnished room, ill lit and smelling of stale cooking.

She started to undress in a rather clumsy fashion and said, with assumed nonchalance, 'Take your clothes off, dear. Make yourself comfortable.'

It was obvious from her gauche behaviour that she was inexperienced.

'We haven't decided the price yet,' William said.

At that moment, a faint wailing noise rose from a dark corner of the room. The girl gave a cry of alarm and rushed over. She bent down and picked up what appeared to be a small bundle of rags but which on closer inspection turned out to be a baby. A more pitiable little scrap of humanity would have been hard to find.

Shocked, William blurted out, 'You have a child?'

The girl answered defiantly, 'Yes and what's wrong with that? Aren't the likes of me allowed to have children?'

'Of course. Please forgive me but I thought a woman with a child would have a husband to support her.'

'I had a husband till the war took him. Head blown off by cannon in the siege of Petersburg. Grant may have won the war for Lincoln but he sacrificed me and my baby's future in doing it.'

She gave a short, harsh laugh and asked, 'Want to see the fatherless little cherub then?'

Before William could answer, she thrust the wretched bundle towards him. All that William could see was a pair of tiny flailing arms and a small round face that suddenly creased into an impish smile.

'Is it a boy or a girl,' he asked.

'A girl. Rebecca.'

'And your name?'

'Rachael.'

She clasped the baby back to her body and said bitterly, 'My Tom worked in the stockyards here, earning good money, before he went off to fight for the Union. What is it about men that they can go off to fight for some great idea, leaving their loved ones to the mercy of cruel fate? A woman has more sense. What do I care if the southern states seceded?'

William answered rather pompously, 'It's in man's nature to care deeply about abstract notions such as ethics, justice, honour and democracy. Women take a more pragmatic view of life.'

'I don't understand one half of what you've said, but I suppose you mean that's it all right for Tom to go and fight for the Union while his wife becomes a prostitute to stop his baby from starving.'

Her desperate plight now got through to William and he wanted to get out of that squalid room, away from a situation he was unable to deal with. He produced a dollar bill and thrust it into her hand.

'I don't want anything,' he said as he hurried out and shut the door behind him.

In the street there came into William's mind the lines from Lovelace's poem 'To Lucasta, Going to the Wars':

'I could not love thee, Dear, half so much, Loved I not honour more.'

'Try telling that to Rachael, you glib bastard,' he thought scornfully.

Cattle bought in South Texas for a dollar a head would fetch twenty dollars each in the Chicago cattle market. When the cattlemen, or cowpunchers as they were known, hit town they behaved like feudal lords. They took the best rooms in the hotels and, after washing away the smell, grime and sweat of weeks in the saddle under a burning sun, they would set about slaking a thirst matured by the all pervasive dust of the trail, and satisfying a lust nurtured by long nights of tingling frustration. Whisky slopped down the stairways and no female was safe.

William became friendly with Dobson, the boss of one of these gangs. He was nicknamed Stiletto because of his prowess with a short-bladed knife that he always carried concealed in his right boot. Dobson owned a ranch near Kansas City. He was saturnine in appearance with jet-black hair and a short, muscular body. In the evenings Dobson would sit drinking in the bar with his three companions: Jones, Haig and Taylor. Every evening there would always be a time when those guests due to depart had all booked out and all incoming guests had booked in. Dobson and his men occupied a table that had a clear view of the reception desk so, during this period, William was able to join them, while still being able to deal with any unexpected event. One evening after a few drinks Dobson started to boast about his success as a cattleman.

'I couldn't count the number of times I've gone down to the Rio Grande to buy cattle and driven them back to my ranch,' he said, slapping his whisky glass on the table. 'Of course, you don't get through unscathed, the Indians of the Great Plains see to that. But enough get through to pay real big'

William's grasp of the geography of America was still sketchy and when he asked what exactly these Great Plains were, Dobson's eyes lit up.

'The Great Plains!' he exclaimed. 'A vast high plateau that covers one-third the area of this United States of ours. It stretches from the Mexican border in the south to the Arctic Ocean in the north and from Canada in the east to the Rocky Mountains in the west. And, my boy, it's where the Cherokees, Blackfoot and Sioux roam. I've had many a skirmish with those red devils.'

Jones, whose lilting accent marked him as a Welshman, said, 'Don't ask him about the Indians, boyo, or we'll be here till hell freezes over. Proper expert he is on them. Isn't it?'

'Savages but of a noble ancestry,' said Dobson. 'Magnificent horsemen and hunters of the buffalo. You know there are no hereditary social classes. Wealth and standing are won only through prowess in battle. They don't all speak the same language, you know. Sioux, Blackfoot whatever, they're designated by the different languages they speak.'

'But what if one tribe wishes to talk with another?' William asked.

'If communication is needed between different tribes, they resort to a sign language of fixed hand and finger positions symbolising ideas common to all tribes.'

Jones, seeming to want to egg Dobson on, said, 'Tell him about the sun dance, then. Stilleto is the only white man to have seen one. Isn't it? Or so he says.'

Dobson needed no second bidding, 'Some tribes believe in a supreme deity and others do not but they all have tribal ceremonies and the sun dance is the supreme rite – held by each tribe once every year in early summer to reaffirm their beliefs about the universe and the supernatural. A great camp circle is formed with a central pole to symbolise the source of mystical power which radiates from the sun. Then the dance begins and lasts for several days and nights non-stop.'

Dobson looked proudly round the table and said solemnly, 'I was privileged to witness one of these dances and I assure you it was a spectacle I'll never forget. The half naked warriors, their bodies highlighted by the flickering light from the many bonfires circling the clearing, danced round and round the pole, their movements becoming more and more frenzied.'

'Probably pissed as newts,' Jones interjected.

Dobson was outraged. 'No! No!' he shouted. Neither before nor during the long days and nights of that dance did they eat or drink. To end the rite, the young men of the tribe would undergo self-torture and mutilation.'

Haig, a blonde giant, smiled grimly and said, 'Tell our friend the nature of these tortures. I'm sure he'd be interested.'

Dobson looked uncomfortable and said, 'Oh, I think we can leave that to his imagination.'

William laughed and said, 'Please go on. I'm sure there is nothing you can say that would be more horrific than the tortures of hell as described by my father every Sunday from his pulpit.'

'Well, if you insist,' Dobson said. 'A warrior would slash his arms, legs and chest and fill the wounds with burning ash. Another would pierce his nipples with hooks and suspend himself from the branch of a tree, where he would hang until the hooks tore loose from his body. Some danced naked on a bed of hot coals, while the squaws of the tribe scourged them with knotted ropes.'

'Now that sounds like one hell of a square dance,' quipped Jones.

Taylor, who had been silent until now, leapt from his chair and, stamping his feet rhythmically on the floor, started to sing:

> 'John Brown's bo-dy lies a-mould-'ring in
>   the grave,
> 'John Brown's bo-dy lies a-mould-'ring in
>   the grave,
> 'John Brown's bo-dy lies a-mould-'ring in
>   the grave,
> But his soul goes march-ing on.
> Glo-ry, glo-ry, Hal-le-lu-jah!
> Glo-ry, glo-ry, Hal-le-lu-jah!
> Glo-ry, glo-ry, Hal-le-lu-jah!
> His soul goes march-ing on.'

He was a small neat man with a lugubrious face that flashed a sarcastic leer as he finished his performance with a curtsey, his arms posed Nijinsky-like above his head.

The others laughed but Dobson scowled and called for another whisky.

'Laugh at them at your peril,' he said. 'Look at the Spirit Lake Massacre. A band of Sioux led by Chief Inkpaduta attacked a settlement of five cabins in Iowa near the Okoboji lakes and killed more than thirty white people including women and children. A relief expedition sent from Fort Dodge arrived only in time to bury the dead. Have they been avenged? Have they hell. Inkpaduta and his men outsmarted the army and escaped to the west. The army had better watch out, these Sioux are particularly incensed by the government's attempt to build a road across their favourite hunting grounds in the Bighorn Mountains. I've heard that Red Cloud is gathering thousands of warriors to stop the road's construction. There could be a blood bath.'

William looked thoughtful and asked, 'What is it in the Indian warrior psyche that makes him such a killer?'

'His belief, and this is especially true of the Apache, that when he kills a foe he takes into himself the strength of that man.'

'But that doesn't explain why he inflicts such prolonged mutilations and torture on his victim?'

Dobson's reply was brief and chilling, 'The more he prolongs the man's death agony, the more strength he imbibes.'

William, who was rather disconcerted by Dobson's erudition, ventured, 'I'm told, that their burial rituals are rather strange.'

'The North American Indians believe that a corpse is so unclean that to bury it or cremate it would contaminate the elements of earth, fire and water. So they robe the dead body in the finest clothing and sew it up into a deerskin or buffalo hide. They then place the corpse on a high platform together with gifts and various possessions. The body is left for a year at which time it is considered to be cleansed of all impurities and can be buried.'

Talk degenerated into tales of womanising and gunfights until Dobson fell into a drunken stupor and was carried to his room.

Only her head and shoulders appeared above the top of the reception desk. The face was young, the lips full, the complexion innocent of make-up, the eyes bright blue and the shining auburn hair cascaded over her shoulders in a profusion of tight curls.

'I have an appointment to see Mr Kendrick,' she said, enunciating her words carefully.

'Name?' William asked.

'Miss Martha Hooper.'

William officiously consulted the appointments book and said, 'Ah. Here it is. Miss Hooper, interview for position of chambermaid.'

Relieved, she said, 'That's all right then.'

'I'll take you there myself,' William said, coming from behind the desk.

He was now able to inspect the whole of Miss Hooper and he was not disappointed. Her figure was slim and he detected beneath the folds of her cloak the swell of two generous breasts.

He took her by the arm and led her to Kendrick's office where he knocked.

'Enter,' called Kendrick.

William opened the door and pushed Martha gently into the room

'A Miss Hooper to see you, sir,' he announced.

'Thank you, William. Wait outside. I'll want you to take Miss Hooper to the housekeeper, should she be successful, so that she may be briefed in her duties.'

William gave Martha a whispered, 'Good luck,' before he closed the door.

He did not have to wait long before he heard a call, 'William, come on in.'

When he entered, Kendrick said, 'William, Miss Hooper is the right kind of employee for a first class hotel such as ours.'

Martha flashed a smile of happy triumph at William.

Turning to Martha, Kendrick said, 'Mr Dawson will take you to Miss Ward, the housekeeper, she will allocate you a space in the female dormitory and inform you of your duties.'

Miss Hooper had made quite an impression on William and, under the pretence of monitoring her progress, he made numerous visits to the female staff quarters. Miss Hooper received him with kindness, being flattered that he was taking such an interest in her progress. The time came when, feeling sufficiently confident of her response, he asked her to take tea and cakes with him in the hotel lounge.

William glanced across the table at his guest. She had put on a very pretty dress that emphasised the gentle curves of her neat figure and her blue eyes sparkled with delight as she gazed around at the sumptuous surroundings.

'Oh! Mr Dawson, here I am in my Sunday best taking tea with the cream of Chicago society in the place where I work as a chambermaid,' she said.

'I think you'll find the so-called cream of this society are no better than your dear self,' William countered. 'In fact, probably inferior.'

'Oh! Mr Dawson, you're so gallant.'

'I think we know each other well enough now for you to call me William.'

Martha blushed and said, 'If you call me Martha.'

'Consider it done.'

From that moment on the romance developed rapidly. They would spend their off-duty time walking hand in hand along the banks of the Chicago River to the shores of Lake Michigan. There they would sit on the beach or stroll through beautiful parkland. Although each meeting ended with a kiss, that was as far as their physical intimacy went.

Martha had told William little concerning her past, just the stark facts that her mother had died when Martha was a baby and that she had been brought up by her father, who had been a schoolmaster in the town of Chambersburg. He had enlisted in the Union army at the start of the conflict and had been killed resisting Lee's drive towards Gettysburg.

At first William too had been circumspect in disclosing the events that had brought him to Chicago but, as their friendship grew, he gradually laid bare all the wretched incidents of his young life: his banishment from the family home by his bigot of a father; his involvement with Lincoln's assassins; the scuffle with the hobo Miller and his encounters with prostitutes. He told her how he had written to his father seeking reconciliation but, after many months, had received no reply. One thing he found difficult to reveal – the reason why he had been expelled from Fetters. Fear that Martha would fail to understand the emotion that had gripped him as he clasped Oliver's naked body prevented him from articulating the words.

They were sitting on the beach one hot summer's afternoon when there suddenly came to him the certainty that she would not be repelled. Tentatively at first then with increasing boldness he revealed his shameful secret.

Martha smiled, took his hand, and said softly, 'I understand. You were expressing your love for all that is clean and beautiful. You felt you wanted to protect something that was unique and precious.'

The next time they met, Martha spoke of the day the Confederate army occupied Chambersburg.

'Rumours were rife for days that the Greybacks were approaching the town.

Early one morning our local militia pulled out. I was washing some clothes when I heard the sound of horses in the street and I went to the window. A bunch of Confederate cavalry clattered past the house and then I heard gunfire and they came streaming back as fast as their horses could carry them. My heart leapt for joy. They're retreating, I thought. But no. Soon the main body marched into the town, hands on the gun triggers ready to fire. They called out that they would lay the town to ashes if anyone fired on them again. Then they started rounding up the contrabands.'

William interrupted, 'Contrabands?'

'Refugee slaves. Slaves who had escaped and come north. It was a pitiful sight as they were herded along the street. All were women and children since the men had fled thinking that their families would not be harassed. I could see many of our own coloured people among them. They offered no resistance and shuffled along, with their heads hanging down. When our men recaptured the town, we never discovered what happened to them. But I learnt that my father had been killed at the battle of Gettysburg.'

Martha pulled a letter out of her pocket and handed it to William.

'Here is the last letter I received from him,' she said.

It was written in a long elegant hand.

William read the letter aloud in a voice tinged with sadness:

'My darling daughter Martha,

'I must write these lines knowing that when you read them I might be dead. If I should fall on the battlefield tomorrow for my country, I am ready. I have no regrets and my courage does not falter, for I am convinced of the justice of our cause.

'On this calm summer night, two thousand men sleep around me, many of them enjoying the last sleep before that of death. Memories of the blissful moments I have spent with you ensnare me and it is cruelly hard for me to destroy the hopes of future years together. Martha, my love for you is deathless but my love of Country comes over me and sweeps me to the battlefield.

'Oh Martha, look not for me in some dank grave. If the dead can come back to earth, I shall always be near you in the happiest day

and the darkest night. I will be the wind on
your cheek and the sunlight in your hair.'

William raised his eyes and looked at Martha.
Tears streamed down her cheeks and her hands
trembled.

He gathered her in his arms and whispered,
'We both have suffered the savage pain of living.
Martha, will you marry me?'

CHAPTER 12

President Andrew Johnson sat behind the large mahogany desk in his office. Born in Tennessee of working class parents, he lacked any formal education but his homespun qualities appealed to the American people and now, at the age of fifty-eight, here he was ensconced in the White House as a result of the assassination of Abraham Lincoln. He looked with affection at the two men sitting facing him.

William Henry Seward, the Secretary of State, now in his sixties, was one of the world's great survivors. While lying severely injured in bed after a carriage accident, he had been stabbed in the throat by Paine, as part of John Booth's conspiracy.

'Look at him,' thought Johnson. 'He's as sprightly as a bantam cock. Why, you can't even see the scar!'

General Ulysses Grant, at forty-four, was the youngest of the three. The son of a tanner, he had escaped following his father's trade by accepting a place at West Point, although he had no interest in military life. He had distinguished himself in the Civil War and been the only commander to take full advantage of the Union's numerical superiority. He had returned from a tour of the South, undertaken at Johnson's request and was here to give his report.

'Mr President,' he began. 'I know that when you sent me on this mission you already felt that in order to achieve reconciliation with the Confederates it would be necessary to deal leniently with them.'

'That's dead right, Ulysses,' Johnson said.

'Well, Mr President, I've been all over the South and I was amazed at the friendliness with which I was received by most of the ordinary people there. Of course you've got your dyed-in-the-wool slavers but the majority are looking for rapprochement. I will recommend that we avoid the mistake of imposing heavy reparations and instead help them with the task of reconstruction.'

'My thoughts exactly,' Johnson said delightedly. 'I'll call it the Lenient Reconstruction Policy. The more radical republicans will be mightily upset but I'll see them off.'

'I've a further suggestion, Mr President.'

'Let's hear it.'

'You know General Schofield, Mr President?'

'Isn't he the one who beat hell out of Hood's troops at Franklin?'

'That's the man. Well he's approached me with the idea of forming a combined force of Union and Confederate veterans to invade Mexico and kick the French out. This would go a long way to heal the wounds inflicted by the war. It would unite the whole nation in a common purpose.'

Johnson looked thoughtful and said, 'That Maximilian fellow wrote to Abe, you know. Some bullshit about how the French had helped us during the war for independence and that it was now our turn to help the French establish him in Mexico.'

Grant said decisively, 'It's as important to drive the French out of Mexico as it was to crush the Confederates. Let me send Schofield, with a combined army of a hundred thousand men, down to the Mexican border. He's straining at the leash.'

Secretary of State Seward intervened, 'I have a better plan. Let's send that young cavalry officer Sheridan, with fifty thousand men, to patrol the Mexican border. Give him orders to find Juárez, who's hiding in some miserable hamlet near the border, and offer him money and arms in exchange for a guaranty that when he is restored to power there will be good relations between his government and the United States. Then send Schofield to Paris to tell Napoleon to get the hell out of Mexico.'

Johnson smiled approvingly and said, 'Sounds good to me. With well armed Juárista bands harassing the French troops and an army of fifty thousand battle hardened soldiers hovering on the border, he'll soon get the hell out of it.'

Grant sounded dubious, 'Schofield sure is going to be one frustrated guy. He's the type that likes to get in there and kick ass. Can't see him taking kindly to the role of diplomat at Napoleon's court.'

'Send him to me. I'll put him straight,' Seward answered.

'What are we going to call Sheridan's army?' Grant asked.

Johnson thought for a moment and said, 'I know, the Army of Observation.'

They all laughed.

Major General Phillip Henry Sheridan was a flamboyant cavalry officer whose driving military leadership contributed significantly to the Union victory. He was to the American Civil War what Rupert of the Rhine had been to the English Civil War, only Sheridan had been far more successful. The purpose of his presence on the Mexican Border with the Army of Observation was to play the part of the Sword of Damocles above Napoleon's head. Seward could not have chosen a better man for the task. Sheridan held extensive military exercises at strategic points along the border, and ensured that the French were fully cognisant of them. He now had to carry out the other part of his mission. Locating the Liberal leader had been easy, Juárez had many agents in Washington. A meeting had been arranged and now Sheridan was standing outside an adobe hut in the border town of Paso del Norte, accompanied by one of his lieutenants.

An old peasant women came out of the hut and beckoned them in. Inside, Sheridan was faced with three native Mexicans, sitting behind a rickety table. Sheridan had never met Juárez and had no idea of his appearance. He thought it likely that the leader would be in the centre of the group and his judgement was vindicated when this person, seeing his hesitation, rose and smiled. Juárez cut a striking figure, in a black broadcloth coat, white linen vest and highly polished boots. On the table lay a pair of spotless white gloves.

'Please, gentlemen, be seated,' Juárez said, indicating with a wave of the hand two chairs that been placed in front of the table.

'President Benito Juárez,' he continued. Gesturing to his left he said, 'General Refugio

Gonzales.' Gesturing to his right he said, 'General Marino Escobedo.'

The men nodded curtly as their names were announced, then stared suspiciously at the Americans.

Sheridan cleared his throat nervously and said, 'General Phillip Henry Sheridan, commander of the Army of Observation and Lieutenant John Hosgood.'

Despite being dwarfed by the men on either side of him, Juárez radiated a quiet dignity.

'I understand your government wishes to lay certain propositions before me,' he said.

Sheridan launched into a carefully prepared speech, 'The government of the United States of America has long been concerned at the presence of French forces on the soil of Mexico. While the civil war raged the government was too preoccupied to contemplate any action but, now that the conflict has been resolved, the United States is determined to end French hegemony over the Mexican Nation.'

'What action is your government proposing?' Juárez asked.

'We will supply you with money and rifles...'

Escobedo interrupted, 'Uniforms... Bright new uniforms, very important for the men's morale.'

'Well yes, that can be arranged,' Sheridan answered.

'Money, rifles and bright new uniforms,' Juárez said. 'Anything else?'

'You are aware of the military manoeuvres my army is conducting on the border?'

Juárez nodded.

'Well, so are the French.'

'What does your government want in return?'

'Very little, sir. Only the assurance that, when you are returned to power, relationships between our two countries will be one of mutual respect.'

Negotiations on the details continued late into the evening until agreement was reached. As Sheridan and Hosgood were leaving, Juárez called Sheridan back.

'General, am I right in assuming that the name of your army has some significance?' he asked.

Sheridan grinned and replied, 'Army of Observation, yes I think the name has a certain significance.'

Juárez grasped his hand and said, 'Good. I would not want to get rid of one form of hegemony only to have it replaced by another.'

Achille-Francois Bazaine had come to Mexico in 1863 as a major general in the French expeditionary force. After the capture of Puebla he was made commander and promoted to the illustrious rank of Marshal, so redolent with memories of France's earlier glory. Now this pipsqueak of a secretary was subjecting him to the indignity of being barred access to Maximilian.

'I'm afraid the Emperor is too busy to see you,' Schertzenlechner said firmly.

Bazaine exploded, 'Too busy to see the commander of an army that is the one thing standing between him and oblivion. What is it today? Let me guess, perhaps he's drafting another unenforceable law to eradicate poverty. No? Well, perhaps he's drawing up plans for a

National Museum or was it Observatory? or Theatre? No? I've heard that he's thinking of introducing philosophy into the curriculum of the state schools or is he perfecting the minutia of court ceremonial?'

'I must ask you to show the respect due to the Emperor you serve,' Schertzenlechner answered angrily.

'The Emperor I serve is in Paris and he does not retreat into a fantasy world and leave his poor wife to deal with the nation's problems. Especially at this time when she has received the news of her father's death.'

'Empress Carlota loved her father dearly. His death has hit her hard but she stifles her emotions. Maximilian was in tears when he told her.'

'Yes, no doubt, but he should be at her side offering comfort and support. Do you know the latest joke going round the court? If you can't find Maximilian then he's raking the gardens at Chapultepec or the gardener's wife.'

Bazaine knew he had struck home when he saw Schertzenlechner's face turn bright red.

'What matter is so urgent that you must see his Majesty?' the secretary asked.

'The delegation from Belgium that brought the news of Leopold's death and the accession of his son are due to leave tomorrow. I am informed that no arrangements have been made for an escort. This is dangerous folly. Should anything happen to Baron d'Huart and his party the repercussions would be disastrous.'

Schertzenlechner hesitated and then said, 'I'll announce you. Wait here a moment.'

'No need for such protocol,' Bazaine cried and, sweeping past the startled secretary, he burst into Maximilian's presence.

He had not seen Maximilian for a number of weeks and he was disconcerted by the change in the Emperor. For a man who had always taken a pride in his immaculate appearance, Maximilian looked slovenly. His tunic was unbuttoned, his hair unkempt and shirt crumpled. He was bent forward studying a number of brightly coloured drawings depicting soldiers' uniforms. On hearing the clatter of Bazaine's precipitate entry into the room, he looked up.

'Sire,' Bazaine said, giving a curt bow. 'Forgive my intrusion but…'

Maximilian interrupted him, 'No no, my dear fellow you have arrived at a most opportune moment. I would value your opinion on the modifications I'm making to the uniforms of my Imperial Austrian Guard. Here, take a look. What do you think?'

He pushed the drawings across the desk towards Bazaine who ignored them and addressed Maximilian as if he was a spoilt child.

'Sire, I have something of far greater importance to discuss with you.'

Maximilian smiled sadly and said, 'Bazaine why won't you understand that I am concerned to enhance the status of Mexico in the eyes of Europe by improving our ceremonial and building great national institutions.'

'You must provide an escort for Baron d'Huart and his party when they leave tomorrow,' Bazaine blurted out.

'I have. An armed Mexican officer will sit with the driver of the carriage.'

'But, sire!' Bazaine exclaimed. 'Contingents of rebel soldiers have penetrated well into the south and the pass at Rio Frio is particularly vulnerable to attack.'

'Marshal, tonight we are holding a magnificent ball to show the delegation from Belgium that Mexico is a happy and stable country. What sort of an impression will they take back to Belgium if we have to escort them to Vera Cruz with a heavy body of cavalry?'

'A far better impression than if the majority of them are slaughtered. Also you know that young d'Huart is a close friend, and I use the term advisedly, of the Empress Carlota's brother Philippe.'

'You exaggerate the danger. One armed officer will be sufficient. Now tell me what you think of these new uniforms.'

'Your Majesty must forgive me. Many urgent matters require my attention.'

Bazaine bowed and hurried out of the room. Maximilian gave a resigned shrug and turned his attention back to the drawings.

That night, a very different Maximilian led a radiant Carlota onto the dance floor for the first waltz. He was dressed in the uniform of Admiral of the Fleet decorated with the orders of the Golden Fleece and the Grand Cross of Saint Stephen, while Carlota was resplendent in a gown of crimson silk with the black ribbon of the Order of Malta. Those who had been present at Miramar when Gutierrez and Hidalgo had presented Maximilian with the petition begging him to take the Mexican throne, would have had a sense of *déjà vu*. It was as if Maximilian and Carlota were trying to recapture the splendour and hope of that moment.

French, Austrian and Mexican officers in dress uniform and their gorgeously gowned wives danced and drank champagne under hundreds of brightly painted lanterns. Baron d'Huart and his party were suitably impressed and remarked how the Mexican Court outshone the monarchies of Europe. A more observant guest might have detected the weariness in Maximilian's smile and the growing panic in Carlota's eyes.

Mountain passes have played an important part in history and legend.

The Khyber Pass, connecting Kabul and Peshawar, has been the gateway for invasions of the Indian subcontinent from Afghanistan. In the fifth century BC Darius I of Persia marched through the pass to the Indus River. The years when the British controlled it gave rise to many tales of derring-do.

The pass at Thermopylae was the stage for an act of selfless bravery that still holds the world in thrall. In 480 BC, Leonidas, King of Sparta, commanded a small Greek force that resisted the advance through Thermopylae of the vast army of the Persian king Xerxes. Leonidas' troops held the pass for two days until the Persians, guided along another mountain pass by a Greek traitor, outflanked them. Sending the majority of his troops to safety, Leonidas with three hundred of his royal guard remained to delay the Persians. That night the Spartans washed and combed their shoulder-length hair and prepared for battle. The next day they fought until the last man lay dead. A monument now marks the spot and bears the epitaph:

'Go tell the Spartans, thou that passest by,
That here obedient to their laws, we lie.'

The cardinal law was: conquer or die. A Spartan mother, bidding farewell to her son as he set out for battle, would hand him his shield with the words, 'Carry this shield home in triumph or be borne home dead upon it.'

Such an act of heroism would be repeated centuries later when at the battle of Hastings King Harold's house-carls were hacked to pieces as they stood defending their stricken king.

In myth, we have the pass that the ill-fated Oedipus entered as he journeyed to Thebes. Daylight was verging on dusk when he rode into that pass cut through the high mountains. Storm dark clouds swept in cohorts across the sky. Menacing sounds of thunder filled the air; lightning flashed its forked tongue among the crags. It was there he met in combat and slew the noble stranger robed in cloth of gold, who wore upon his head a kingly crown – a deed from which such savage consequences flowed.

The pass at Rio Frio is remembered not for some deed of heroism but for an act of political murder. When the carriage containing the Belgian mission entered the defile, they found the road blocked by a number of large boulders and, before they could turn and head back to Mexico City, a large contingent of rebels swarmed down the steep side of the defile and overwhelmed them with a merciless barrage of rifle fire. The officer, charged by Maximilian to guard the party, fled from the scene without removing his revolver from its holster. The ground around the carriage was strewn with the bodies of the dead and wounded.

The next day, Maximilian and Carlota stood in mourning at the side of the bier on which lay the body of Baron d'Huart. Carlota, for the first time since her father's death, showed signs of grief. Tears glistened in her eyes and her body shook with stifled sobs as she whispered, 'My poor brother will be distraught at the death of d'Huart, coming so soon after the death of my beloved father.'

Maximilian raised his arms in a gesture of helplessness and said, 'God's will be done.'

'God's will! Never! If Marshal Bazaine had done his duty this would not have happened.'

Maximilian ignored the remark and, turning to Bazaine who stood a few feet behind him, said, 'I have tried leniency with these people and look at the result. From this time on, anyone bearing arms illegally will be executed on the spot and there will be no appeals.'

'An excellent decision, sire, but made too late,' Bazaine replied drily.

CHAPTER 13

The deteriorating situation in Mexico was causing Napoleon considerable trouble in Paris. He was having to face angry questions in the Assembly as its members saw vast resources in men and money being expended without any tangible results. It was also souring his relations with Eugenie. The slightest hint that he was contemplating withdrawal from Mexico and she would fly into an uncontrollable rage. Now he was faced with a visit from an American general who would undoubtedly be the bearer of more unwelcome news.

General John Schofield was still trying to come to terms with his disappointment at not being given command of the army on the Mexican border. His fat, heavily bearded face was set in a grimace of defiance as he was ushered into the presence of the French monarch. A staunch republican, he had decided not to use the accepted form of words when addressing royalty.

'Sir,' he said. 'I have the honour of representing the government of the United States of America.'

Napoleon flushed angrily at the obvious snub and retaliated by not inviting Schofield to sit down.

'You are?' he asked.

'General John Schofield, representative of…'

'Yes, yes. I know that bit. Tell me the purpose of your visit.'

Schofield glanced meaningfully at one of the many chairs festooning the room. Napoleon began to regret his initial reaction to the general's slight and thought that a more courteous approach might produce a more favourable outcome to their meeting.

Forcing himself to smile, he said, 'Please, General be seated.'

Schofield moved to obey but his sword became tangled in the legs of the chair and he had to spend some time extracting himself, his embarrassment affording Napoleon considerable amusement.

When he had regained his composure, Schofield addressed the Emperor, 'Sir, my government has been severely dismayed by the intervention of France in Mexico. They request that this interference in the internal affairs of a sovereign state cease immediately and that you withdraw all French forces from Mexico.'

Napoleon adopted a conciliatory if not downright wheedling tone. 'We are merely attempting to keep on the throne a man whom the Mexican people chose to be their sovereign.'

'Maximilian was never chosen by a democratic vote of the people but by a bunch of rich landowners and conservative politicians.'

'General, did not France assist you in your hour of greatest need, when you fought Britain for your independence? Do the names Marquis de Lafayette and Count Rochambeau mean nothing to your leaders? Did not these two brave officers and the six thousand strong French expeditionary force that they led play a vital part in the siege of York Town, a battle that sealed your victory in the war of independence? The time has come for America to repay that debt by helping France to establish Maximilian on the throne of Mexico.'

Schofield shook his head emphatically and said, 'No! While the United States has been preoccupied with her civil war, the nations of Europe have tried to take advantage by attempting to return to the American continent. Now America is able to deal with that threat. We are providing aid to the forces of the legitimate ruler President Benito Juárez and we have stationed an army of fifty thousand battle-hardened soldiers on the border. A number that can be increased to one hundred thousand in a matter of days. Sir, withdraw your troops and his Imperial Highness with them.'

Stung, Napoleon answered, 'I understand that Austria is planning to send a force of four thousand men to the aid of their Archduke.'

'I fear your intelligence is at fault. Our ambassador has informed Emperor Joseph that, should they do any such thing, America will declare war on Austria. He has been given the assurance that Austria no longer considers Maximilian to be an Archduke since he abrogated that title when he took the Mexican throne. Therefore there is no question of them sending him assistance.'

'You would go to war with Austria over this matter?'

'Yes and any other nation that insists on meddling in the internal affairs of Mexico.'

That night Napoleon broke the news to Eugenie that the time had come for him to withdraw his forces from Mexico. He reasoned with her until the early hours of the morning and finally a broken-hearted Eugenie agreed that he was left with no other alternative. Despite her acceptance of the situation, relations between them were never the same again. From that night on she treated him with contempt, even upbraiding him in front of the court.

Unable to sleep, he decided to write to Maximilian that night. It proved to be the most difficult letter he had ever had to compose. Sitting alone in his study dressed in a night shirt with floppy slippers on his feet and a hair net protecting his magnificent moustache, he began by telling Maximilian of the great pain he felt in having to send him such a communication. He outlined all the pressures that had been brought to bear on him, not least the brutal belligerence of the American government, then he broke the news that he was going to have to get out of Mexico. In an attempt to prevent everything falling into chaos after they left, he would phase the withdrawal over a period of one year. This would give Maximilian time to stabilise the situation. The letter ended with profuse protestations of affection and regard.

Laying down his pen, Napoleon gave vent to his feelings, 'God damn it! It's his own fault. If he'd shown a bit of backbone this would never have happened. I never believed the rumours that he was Reichstadt's son. He, Napoleon's grandson – never!'

Carlota sidled up to Maximilian, as he worked at his desk, and whispered in his ear, 'Dear Max, be careful what you eat.'

She then slipped away through the open French window into the garden. The strange message and the hint of hysteria in her voice turned Maximilian's blood cold. He rose and hurried after her. Spring had come early and the blue-flowered jacaranda and the diminutive larkspurs were in full bloom. He caught up with her and touched her gently on her shoulder. She turned and he was shocked by the glint of madness in her eyes.

'He wishes to poison us both!' she cried.

'Who?' Maximilian asked quietly. 'Who would wish to poison us?'

Carlota looked furtively around and hissed, 'Bazaine.'

'But beloved, what reason could Marshal Bazaine have for killing us?'

'He killed d'Huart.'

Maximilian was on the point of telling her that his obstinacy was to blame for D'Huart's death, when the thought of her possible reaction stilled his tongue.

Carlota took his silence for agreement and said, 'After removing us, the path will be clear for him.'

'What path?'

'The path that leads to Mexico becoming a French province with him as Governor General.'

She then ran swiftly away to disappear into the castle, leaving Maximilian with the worrying thought that she might be right.

At their next meeting, Carlota showed no signs of her previous paranoia, as she chatted animatedly about a visit she had made to a charity caring for destitute children. It was during this conversation that Schertzenlechner entered and announced that Marshal Bazaine was in the anteroom with an important letter from his Imperial

Majesty Napoleon III. When Bazaine solemnly handed over the heavily sealed envelope, Maximilian felt a premonition of doom.

'Marshal, would you do me the courtesy of retiring while I read this communication,' he asked. 'If a reply is needed, you will be recalled.'

Maximilian read the letter and, making no comment, passed it over to Carlota, whose face paled as she studied the document. Without waiting for Carlota's comments, Maximilian went over to his writing desk and started to pen his reply, his hand shaking with fury. He had filled a page with harsh, bitter recriminations before he stopped and looked at Carlota. She sat rigid with shock, the letter lying on her lap and her hands gripping the arms of the chair. He went across and, kneeling, took her in his arms.

'There, my love,' he said gently. 'Remember that day in Miramar when we received Joseph's letter? We were in despair then, but we acted together and saved the day. We must do the same now.'

He felt Carlota stir and saw tears course down her cheeks.

She caught his face in her hands and said, 'Yes, Max. I must be brave and stand by your side. Together we will win the affection of our people. Who needs that doddering old fool Napoleon?'

Maximilian stood up and in mock heroics flung open his arms and declaimed,

'Come the three corners of the world in arms,
And we shall shock them. Nought shall make us rue
If Carlota to her Max remain but true.'

Maximilian was transformed. This was the Max who had wooed Carlota and stood with her on the balcony of the National Palace waving to the cheering crowds in the Zocalo below.

He hurried over to his writing desk and picked up the letter he had written to Napoleon. He read it carefully and shook his head.

'No!' he said. 'He would not think this worthy of a Habsburg and I do not consider it worthy of a Bonaparte. It is but the petulant outburst of a spoilt child.'

He crumpled it up and flung it to a far corner of the room. He sat at the desk and started writing. Carlota came over and stood behind him, her hands resting on his shoulder.

'*Dear Brother Monarch*,' he began.

'*I am your friend and do not wish to be the cause of the slightest inconvenience to your Majesty. I, therefore, with a solidarity that matches your own, give you permission to immediately withdraw your troops from Mexico. What will happen to me? I shall deal with the problems of my country in a manner that befits a Habsburg.*'

Maximilian signed with a flourish and said, 'The right touch of irony, I think.'

Troubled, Carlota asked, 'But are you wise to give him the opportunity to withdraw his troops immediately?'

Maximilian smiled and said, 'There's no danger of him doing that. He'll want a gradual and dignified withdrawal. We'll have at least a

258

year's grace. A time that must be exploited to the full.'

During the ensuing months Maximilian took charge of the Imperial Mexican army and attempted to instil discipline and courage into units that were prone to flee at the mere sight of the enemy. Carlota exhausted herself as she visited the impoverished regions of the country with promises of improved health care, education and employment opportunities. The pair worked ceaselessly but to no avail. Napoleon did not order the instant return of his forces but gave Marshal Bazaine orders that the French soldiers were only to fire at the rebels in self-defence and were to slowly retreat towards Mexico City. Only the Belgian and Austrian Legions fought with conviction while Maximilian's native army still proved incapable of offering serious resistance to the rebels. The inevitable consequence of the confluence of these circumstances was that the Juáristas advanced inexorably on the capital.

Strange though it may seem, this period was one in which the royal couple regained the rapture of the first years of their marriage. The gardener's wife was left to languish while Maximilian and Carlota became a team again. They gave each other comfort and support as they battled against an increasingly threatening world. Many of the carpetbaggers who had come over to Mexico with Maximilian decided it was time to return home. Even Schertzenlechner contrived a quarrel with one of Maximilian's staff and left for Austria. As the crisis worsened, Carlota became convinced that she was the only one who could save

Maximilian. She approached him in a highly excited state.

'Max, I must travel to Paris,' she said breathlessly. 'I know I can confront Napoleon with his treachery and shame him into changing his mind.'

Maximilian looked shocked and said emphatically, 'In no way will I allow you to humiliate yourself, or me, in this manner.'

'But Max, I know Eugenie is on our side.'

'No Carlota. The answer is no.'

Carlota persisted, 'If that fails, I can go on to Rome and plead our cause with the Pope.'

Maximilian adopted a patient tone, 'My love, do you remember the manner in which we dealt with the Pontiff's demands to have the Church's rights restored in Mexico?'

Carlota, her face registering apprehension, nodded and Maximilian continued, 'I hardly think he will be in a receptive mood for any pleas for help from us. Do you?'

That appeared to be the end of the matter but the situation continued to deteriorate. Posters, demanding the restoration of Juárez and the death of Maximilian, were appearing in the streets of the capital. Carlota renewed her pleas and an increasingly desperate Maximilian at last gave his consent.

Maximilian stood on the quayside at Vera Cruz and waved to Carlota standing forlornly on the deck of the lighter that was ferrying her to the French mail steamer, Empress Eugenie, lying in the bay. Curtains of heavy rain swept across the harbour and yet the heat was oppressive. He felt a sense of impending doom and the vulnerability of that diminutive figure tore at his heart. Carlota had been unnaturally animated when they parted and he had been alarmed when he noted again that glint of madness in her eyes that had turned his blood cold that day in the gardens of Chapultepec.

Carlota's party, consisting of four ladies-in-waiting and two aides-de-camp, spent a very miserable crossing having to cope with the tantrums of a seasick and unpredictable mistress. On arriving in Paris they took up residence in the Grand Hotel and Carlota immediately sent an aide-de-camp to Saint Cloud to inform Napoleon that Empress Carlota of Mexico requested an audience. Napoleon, worn down by the weight of world affairs, had spent the previous few days in bed being bled by leeches. The thought of having to face the wife of the man he had betrayed terrified him and he dispatched Eugenie to the Grand Hotel with instructions to avoid talking specifics and to inform Carlota that he was far too ill to see her. Carlota received the Empress with courtesy, because she knew that Eugenie's heart was with her and Maximilian. They talked pleasantly about the customs and ceremonies of the Mexican people but, when Eugenie explained that Napoleon would be too unwell to grant her an audience, Carlota's response brooked no denial.

'Nonsense! I'll visit him tomorrow. Send a carriage from the Imperial stable for me at eleven o'clock sharp.'

When Carlota's carriage pulled up outside the entrance to the palace at Saint Cloud a detachment of Napoleon's Imperial Guard, dressed in the full splendour of their First Empire uniforms, presented arms. She led her party up the staircase to where Napoleon and Eugenie, surrounded by their courtiers, waited to greet her. She noted bitterly that Napoleon was wearing the Order of the Mexican Eagle, awarded him by Maximilian. Carlota cut a strange figure; her black dress was crumpled and ill fitting; her white hat was skewed on her head and her face was flushed with an unnatural excitement. The formalities having been completed, Napoleon, Eugenie and Carlota retired to the Emperor's study. Carlota, her voice trembling, addressed Napoleon.

'Sire,' she said. 'I am here to represent my husband Maximilian – the man you made Emperor of Mexico.'

Napoleon demurred, 'Carlota, he accepted the invitation of the Mexican people. I did not make him Emperor.'

'Do you think he would have undertaken such a task if you had not encouraged him at every stage? Do I have to list all the promises you made? Your troops were already in Mexico and you used Maximilian to strengthen your position there. This cause is as much yours as it is Maximilian's.'

'Please understand. I don't wish to be unkind but Maximilian has allowed the situation to deteriorate to such an extent that I have no other alternative. He has failed to organise the systematic collection of taxes with the result that, while I keep pouring resources in, there is no compensating flow out. His attempt to train an effective native army that could take over from my troops has proved a farce.'

This enraged Carlota and, abandoning all pretence of dignified argument, she shouted, 'Where have you been getting these reports? Marshal Bazaine has been poisoning your mind. From the outset it has been his incompetence that has brought us to this. Dismiss him and give Max more time. Think of the honour of France. Think of the First Empire and of the man who founded it. He was your uncle, I believe.'

The venom in that last remark struck home and Napoleon buried his face in his hands. Eugenie felt that Carlota had gone too far and gestured to her that she should desist. It was at that moment that the butler entered with a tray bearing three glasses of lemonade. Glad of the respite, Napoleon and Eugenie gratefully accepted but Carlota declined. The butler placed the tray bearing the one remaining glass on a small table near Carlota. It was a very hot day and the sun was streaming in through the wide casement windows. Eugenie pressed Carlota to take a sip from the glass, saying how it would refresh her.

At first Carlota refused, eyeing the glass with obvious suspicion, but then reluctantly she drank a little. Eugenie smiled kindly but to Carlota it appeared as if the Empress was leering at her in a most obscene manner. Glancing at Napoleon she was horrified to see him slowly transmogrify into a monstrous, obnoxious toad. She closed her eyes and on opening them found that he was now a devil replete with horns and tail. She gave a cry of relief as the image faded to reveal Napoleon's prosaic form. Her behaviour puzzled the French monarchs and they exchanged bewildered glances.

Napoleon had recovered his composure and he spoke calmly, 'Carlota, try to understand the pressures I am under. Circumstances change. The United States has stationed an army on the border and is threatening to invade unless I move out. Now another complication has arisen – Austria and Prussia are at war.'

Carlota answered curtly, 'Yes, and that should suit the interests of France. The two of them weakening each other.'

Napoleon continued, 'While the German states fought among themselves France was content. Yesterday I received news that the Prussians have inflicted a massive defeat on the Austrians at Sadowa and Vienna lies at their mercy. This means that Prussia has become the dominant power in Europe and threatens France. It is imperative that I recall my soldiers. They are needed for the defence of France itself.'

Carlota was contemptuous, 'France, a nation of over forty million people with vast resources and untold wealth, afraid of a petty princedom like Prussia!'

In vain, Napoleon went through all the reasons why he could not revoke his decision. Finally he had to admit that he feared the reaction of the Paris mob who had driven other French rulers from their thrones. Carlota refused to accept that the decision was final. The only way Napoleon was able to end the audience was to promise that he would call a meeting of the Ministerial Council the next day to review the matter.

Exhausted, Carlota returned to the hotel where she collapsed and was put to bed by her ladies-in-waiting. On waking, she found Maria sitting at the bedside. Although Señora del Barrio was the most senior of Carlota's suite, Maria was her favourite. Carlota sat up in panic and grasped Maria's hand.

'Maria,' she cried, 'they want me dead!'

'Majesty, what do you mean?' Maria asked. 'Who wants you dead?'

'Those two devils incarnate, Napoleon and Eugenie.'

'No, you are mistaken. They are your friends.'

Carlota became hysterical, 'Friends! Friends! They tried to poison me. I saw what they did. Left the poisoned drink for me. Oh Maria, you should have seen their faces when I refused to drink it. They kept pestering me until I drank a drop. You saw how ill I was when I returned. Thank God I took only a sip. Think what would have happened if I had drunk more.'

Maria tried to calm her, 'No, it was the hot weather. Their majesties would not wish to harm you.'

'Believe me Maria, I know them. They gave orders to Bazaine to poison us in our own home.'

She gave a mad smile of triumph and said, 'But I warned Max and we thwarted them.'

Despite Maria's efforts to pacify her, Carlota began to thrash about on the bed, babbling incoherently about toads and devils. Alarmed, Maria alerted Señora del Barrio, who took one look at Carlota and summoned the doctor. He gave Carlota a sedative and she lapsed into a troubled sleep.

The next day the Ministerial Council met and confirmed the decision to withdraw from Mexico.

The Ministers of War and Finance were given the task of conveying the news to Carlota in her hotel room. She was sitting stiffly on an upright chair, her face pale and tense. As soon as the unfortunate men informed her that the decision to end France's involvement in Mexico was irrevocable, she rose to her feet and pointed an accusing finger at them.

'There are the persons whose pockets are filled with Mexico's gold!' she screamed.

When they protested indignantly, she shouted back, 'Ingrates, all of you! I will not accept this from Napoleon's lackeys. I do not believe it is true. Napoleon must come here himself and tell me to my face that he has betrayed the noblest of men.'

Napoleon stood tense and defiant before a stone-faced Carlota.

'Tell me, is it true?' Carlota demanded.

'Yes. This is the only way I can remain on the throne of France. I have done my best for Maximilian. We must extricate him safely from Mexico.'

'You do not know my husband, if you think he will abandon Mexico in its hour of need. He is no charlatan, no parvenu, no hypocrite.'

'It is over, Carlota. Harbour no more illusions,' Napoleon answered and walked swiftly from the room.

That night Carlota wrote Maximilian a letter which, when he read it, made him fearful for her sanity. She informed Maximilian that they could expect no further help from France and gave a lurid account of how Napoleon had, before her eyes, turned into a hideous toad and then the devil. She recounted how the French royal couple had attempted to poison her and warned Maximilian to be on his guard. The letter continued with a statement of her belief that Napoleon was a Satan, who wished to wipe from the face of the earth the last vestige of goodness, and that she and Maximilian were the only people who could thwart him. The letter ended with the words, '*I embrace you with all my heart, your ever loving Charlotte.*'

Carlota wished to travel directly to Rome but Maria and Señora del Barrio, alarmed at her fevered state, persuaded her to break her journey at Miramar. As her carriage approached Miramar, Carlota leaned out of the window and gazed again at the carved minarets of pure white marble, the medieval battlements and vaulted arches. Later she wandered in the gardens with their flowing fountains and cascading flowerbeds. In the castle she went from room to room, each one elegantly furnished and hung with magnificent paintings. Everywhere she saw the touch of Maximilian's hand. She thought only of the happy times and suppressed memories of the frustration they had felt, trapped there with no purpose to their lives. It was when she came to the library, stacked with the works of all the great writers from Aristotle to Goethe and embellished with their marble busts, that a memory of the past overwhelmed her.

She saw Maximilian seated at his desk while she stood at his side.

He was near tears and his mumbled words crept eerily into her ears: 'I should have given this more thought. To be responsible for the welfare of millions of people, the idea terrifies me. Charlotte

I know I am not capable of holding high office. Charlotte, please go and tell them that it has all been a mistake. Tell them I am not the man they think I am. Tell them I am not worthy.'

She heard her response ring confidently out, 'Not worthy! No man is more worthy of this crown or more fitted to administer the power it represents.'

The vision faded and the room was silent save for the sound of her frantically beating heart. Carlota sank into the chair and, collapsing across the desk, wept.

She spent two weeks at Miramar but if her ladies-in-waiting had hoped that the interlude would calm her, they were sadly wrong. Her condition worsened and they watched helplessly as she began her precipitate descent into the snake pit of insanity. Convinced that French agents had infiltrated the castle and were plotting to poison her, Carlota insisted that Maria or Señora del Barrio tasted every dish placed before her. She would then wait up to twenty minutes, anxiously scrutinising the taster, before she picked up a fork and hesitatingly placed a few morsels in her mouth.

Her madness fed an irrational belief that the salvation of Maximilian and herself lay in the gift of the Pope. Therefore, after two weeks and despite the pleas of her suite, Carlota boarded the train for Rome.

It could be taken as a mere coincidence or a bad omen, but the hotel in Rome where Carlota took up residence bore the same name as her hotel in Paris – the Grand Hotel. An audience with Pius IX was arranged for the morning of September 27.

Sitting bolt upright in the Papal coach, staring straight ahead with eyes clouded by madness, Carlota was driven through the oppressive heat to the Vatican. On entering the throne room, she ran and, throwing herself on the floor, kissed the Pontiff's foot. Pius IX lifted her up and led her over to a couch covered by a golden drape. Dismissing everyone else from the room, he went and sat beside her.

Pius IX had been infuriated when the Papal Nuncio had returned from Mexico with the news that Maximilian and Carlota had rejected his demands for the restoration of the Catholic Church's rights in Mexico. He had vowed that hell would freeze over before he would lift his little finger to assist the royal pair in any way whatsoever. One might therefore have expected him to derive great satisfaction in seeing Carlota's abject and pitiful state. Who could have blamed him if he saw it as divine retribution? But Pius IX, while he might have been a bigot, was also a human being and had a heart that was capable of being touched.

He took her hands in his own and said gently, 'What is it that troubles you, my child?'

Carlota stared wildly into his concerned face and cried, 'Oh Holy Father, only you can save Maximilian and me from the Evil One!'

Pius IX, while fully conversant with Napoleon's decision, chose to prevaricate, 'The evil one? I don't understand.'

'The Emperor of the French,' Carlota hissed. 'The Great Satan! He who has treacherously abandoned Maximilian. He who plans to rid the world of all goodness. You, as God's representative on earth, must assist Maximilian and me to thwart his evil intentions.'

'My child, you are mistaken. France is a good Catholic country. Napoleon intends no evil.'

Carlota flew into a frenzy, 'You are deceived. He is the Dark One that threatens the world.'

Realising that Carlota would never change her attitude to Napoleon, Pius IX tried a different approach, 'Even if you are right, what can I do? The Pope has no battalions.'

'You have the power of the Catholic Church and you are refusing to use it because you are in league with the powers of darkness.'

The Pontiff's patience snapped and he said, 'You and your husband thought little of the power of the church when you contemptuously dismissed my emissary.'

For a moment Carlota became lucid and she answered calmly, 'You were too bigoted to realise that we would have built a strong Catholic nation through consent, not coercion.'

Those were the last coherent words Carlota spoke during the audience. She sprang from the bench and, pointing a finger at the Pope, accused him of being in league with the devil. When he ordered that refreshments be brought in she screamed that he wanted to poison her. At this point the Pope discovered that he had a pressing engagement elsewhere and hurriedly left the room. Carlota was left standing in the middle of the throne room raving and gesticulating to the empty air until the Guardia Nobile escorted her out of the building to where Maria and Señora del Barrio were waiting with a carriage to take her back to the Grand Hotel.

Throughout the journey Carlota mumbled incoherently and resisted any attempts to comfort her.

The more Pius IX reflected on Carlota's behaviour the angrier he became. How dare she scream such blasphemies at him, Christ's representative on earth! The man who had declared the dogma of the Immaculate Conception and who was planning to call together all the bishops and cardinals in a great ecumenical council, an event the world had never witnessed. A council that he intended would endorse the doctrine of papal infallibility.

He summoned Cardinal Giacomo Antonelli and said, 'Never, on any account, let that woman set foot again in the Vatican.'

When Carlota's carriage drew up in front of the Grand Hotel, she refused to alight, crying that her attendants planned to murder her. Maria and Señora del Barrio, with the assistance of hotel staff, carried her struggling and screaming into the hotel. A doctor was summoned and he administered a sedative. This induced a period of sleep from which she woke refreshed and calm. Calling for writing materials, she sat at a desk in front of an open window with a view over the city and wrote what proved to be her last message to Maximilian:

'My most precious beloved

Death is my companion and it is time to bid you farewell. You have been my life and I give thanks for the happiness you have brought me. It breaks my heart that I have failed you but

271

I can do no more. The forces of darkness have defeated me and your fate now lies in the hands of God. May he bless you and give you eternal bliss.

Your ever loving Charlotte.'

The tenor of Carlota's letters and reports of her bizarre behaviour had been disturbing Maximilian but he was totally unprepared for her farewell message. He was at Chapultepec in a meeting with his generals when an aide-de-camp handed him the letter together with a short note from Señora del Barrio, expressing concern over Carlota's mental and physical state and saying that she was being taken to Miramar. Immediately he dismissed his officers and sent for Marshal Bazaine. When the Marshal entered the room Maximilian thrust the letters into his hands and commanded him to read them. He tapped his right foot impatiently on the floor as Bazaine carefully studied the documents. When Bazaine finished reading he raised his head and looked inquiringly at Maximilian.

'My place is by her side,' Maximilian said hoarsely. 'For too long I've been blind to the fact that she is the most important thing in my life.'

'What exactly does your Majesty intend to do?' Bazaine asked cautiously.

'Do! Why, leave tonight for Miramar, of course.'

'You would be leaving a very confused and dangerous situation behind you.'

'What would you have me do?'

'Abdicate the throne and end the strife. Then you can leave with the French army.'

Maximilian gave a short laugh and said, 'That would suit your master. No question then of Napoleon deserting a friend in his hour of need. I'm going to my wife's side but I will return.'

Bazaine gave a short bow and said, 'I only wish the best for you and Mexico.'

Late that night Maximilian, with an escort of Palatine Guards, left for Vera Cruz. A messenger had gone ahead to order that the Austrian frigate Dandolo be made ready to sail to Europe. He broke his journey at the town of Orizaba, it was there that Generals Marquez and Miramon caught up with him and persuaded him to spend some time reconsidering his decision. They spoke persuasively of the possibility, after the French had departed, of establishing the Empire on a purely Mexican base. Marshal Bazaine arrived and continued to urge abdication. Maximilian suffered the vacillation of a Hamlet. A telegram arrived on the new interoceanic cable from Miramar stating that Carlota was an incurable lunatic and would not be able to recognise Maximilian if he came.

In Vienna, Maximilian's mother, the Archduchess Sophia, was torn by two conflicting emotions – fear and pride. Maximilian was the child of her love affair with young Reichstadt and the thought of his death filled her with dread, but honour would not allow her to countenance her son returning to Europe a failure. She wrote to Maximilian and her letter settled the matter.

He summoned Marshal Bazaine and announced, 'I stay.'

'As your Majesty knows, I believe you should abdicate,' Bazaine replied.

273

'I'll not flee from the battle field.'

'The enemy is sweeping south and I have orders to withdraw my forces in the next few days. You will be left helpless.'

'I must face my destiny. Goodbye, Marshal.'

Maximilian set out for Mexico City in a carriage drawn by four white horses. He knew that he was journeying to certain death but this held no fear for him. Better to die on the battlefield fighting for a noble cause than live a coward like that pathetic creature in Paris.

When he reached Mexico City, he found the capital swept with rumours that he had fled the country. His first action was to appear on the balcony of the National Palace. The realisation that this was the first time he had stood there without Charlotte by his side hit him hard. A longing to recapture the past made him think of the Empress as Charlotte. A vision rose before him of Charlotte prowling like a caged animal around a locked room in the palace at Miramar and staring with bewildered, hurt-filled eyes through barred windows at a cruel sky. He knew it was an image that would haunt him until the day he died.

He fought to regain his composure, and raised his arms. The turbulent crowd in the Zocalo fell silent.

'Look,' he cried, 'I have not fled! I am your Emperor and I will never desert you. People of Mexico, on June 20, 1864, in the great hall of the National Palace I accepted the throne of Mexico and swore to hold the sceptre with pride and the sword of honour with courage. I renew that vow. I will make the Mexican Empire the most prosperous on the face of the earth and this city will be renowned for the prestige of its institutions and the beauty of its buildings '

He was rewarded by ragged cheering from some parts of the square but the rest of the crowd silently and sullenly dispersed. General Marquez stepped out onto the balcony and pulled Maximilian back into the palace.

Maximilian was holding a council of war and General Marquez, as usual, was laying down the law.

Stabbing his finger down on a map spread on the table, he said, 'Escobedo is advancing from the north and has forced the surrender of General Mejia. Diaz is coming from the south leaving death and destruction in his wake. They are both converging on the capital.'

'What's to be done?' Maximilian asked.

'The situation is desperate and calls for desperate measures. We must be ruthless. We must threaten every hamlet, village and town that does not submit to the rule of your Imperial Majesty with total annihilation.'

'What exactly do you mean by total annihilation?' Maximilian asked, his voice dangerously quiet.

'Every house burned to the ground and every man, woman and child killed.'

The words stung Maximilian into a frenzy and he shouted at Marquez, 'Charlotte and I have witnessed the results of your butchery. Never will I sanction such barbarity again. I came to this land to bring peace, not slaughter.'

Marquez flushed angrily but, realising that his future in Mexico depended on the Emperor, he answered deferentially, 'I am yours to command Majesty. I seek only to serve.'

An aide-de-camp entered the room and announced that Marshal Bazaine sought an audience. Maximilian asked his officers to leave and gave orders that the Marshal be admitted. The relationship between Maximilian and Bazaine had always been clouded by mutual suspicion. From the outset both had known that in their reports to Napoleon each had questioned the competence of the other. Now on the point of his departure Bazaine felt a grudging respect for the stand Maximilian was taking.

'Sire,' Bazaine said. 'Tomorrow the French forces march for Vera Cruz and embarkation. The majority of Austrian and Belgium troops are also leaving.'

Maximilian interrupted, 'Those Austrian and Belgium soldiers who choose to leave do so with my blessing. I'll not hold such men against their will'

'But you'll be left with a Mexican army, ill-equipped and undisciplined. Your situation is untenable. I beg you again to abdicate and leave with me.'

'Many placed their faith in me and I'll not abandon them. Go tell your master that I stay here obedient to the vows I made. Farewell, Bazaine. You'll never see my face again.'

The next day, February 5, 1887, Marshal Bazaine mounted his horse and, to the sound of drums and trumpets, rode at the head of his troops through streets lined with silent crowds. As he past the National Palace he turned and saluted a lone figure standing on the balcony. The French were leaving Mexico City.

A fierce debate ensued among the Mexican generals as to whether it would be better to wait in the capital and confront Escobedo when he arrived or move north to Queretaro and attempt to halt his advance there. Maximilian told them to stop squabbling, he was the commander-in-chief and the decision was his. They would march to Queretaro and give battle there. A great change had taken place in Maximilian since the French had left. Gone was the gentle dreamer and in his place was the legendary hero, foredoomed to meet his death on the battlefield. Maximilian rode at the head of his Imperial army as they marched the hundred miles north to Queretaro. Around him rode a small group of staff officers consisting of General Marquez, General Miramon, and Colonel Lopez. There was a startling contrast between the gorgeously arrayed officers and the ill-equipped raw recruits that straggled shambolically behind them.

Also riding at the head of the column was Prince Salm-Salm, who had recently joined the Emperor's staff after serving with the Prussian army. Queretaro lies in a valley surrounded by mountains and anyone wishing to defend the town would have to position men on the top of those mountains. As soon as Maximilian entered the town and looked up, he knew he did not have sufficient men to occupy them. Within a few days Escobedo, with a force four times the size of the Imperial army, took possession of those heights. The circle was closed and Maximilian was trapped in the centre.

CHAPTER 14

William and Martha decided that they would start married life in a home of their own. To achieve this, William would have to lay his hands on some real capital. He remembered Dobson's boasts of the huge profits cattlemen made. He approached Dobson and, after telling him of his intention to marry Martha, requested that he be allowed to join the next cattle drive.

'Well, we're off to El Paso in a few days and then across the Rio Grande into Mexico to buy cattle in the province of Chihuaha,' Dobson said. 'But as for taking you with us, I have my doubts. Can you ride a horse?'

'No, but I'm sure I could learn in time.'

'Tell you what. Come down to the stables and we'll put you on my horse, White Lightning.'

At this Dobson's men guffawed loudly and placed bets as to the length of time William would remain in the saddle. When the moment came to mount, William looked round at the grinning faces and his resolution almost failed him. Then, realising that going on the cattle drive depended on his being able to stay upright on a horse, he heaved himself into the saddle. White Lightning reared up on his hind legs and William was pitched backwards onto the cobbled floor of the yard. He lay stunned with every bone in his body aching, while all about him roared with laughter.

Dobson helped him to his feet and asked, 'Do you really want to ride a horse, lad?'

'Sir, if Martha and I are to have a home of our own, I must master this.'

Dobson sent his men away and brought from the stable a horse of more docile appearance.

'Meet Flash,' he said. 'A fine horse but not quite as mettlesome as White Lightning. I'm prepared to stay here all day and if at the end you can control Flash, I'll take you with us.'

There followed an ordeal that tested William's resolution to the full. Repeatedly he went crashing to the ground but each time, battered and bleeding, he climbed painfully back into the saddle. Dobson patiently corrected his mistakes and gave him useful tips. One of the secrets of controlling a horse is through the grip of your knees on the horse's flanks. Dobson therefore made William place coins between his knees and the saddle. By the end of the day, William was able to ride Flash out of the yard and take a canter round the neighbouring lanes. Dobson informed William that all he needed now were two pairs of cord breeches, a revolver, a rifle and a horse. When he saw the dismay on William's face he laughed and told William that he would give him an advance on his expected profits. The first thing William did when he received the advance was to persuade Dobson to sell him Flash.

Leaving Martha proved to be a far more searing experience than that morning in England when he had taken leave of his mother, sister and Gwener.

Two orphaned spirits had found, in each other's company, solace and the hope of future happiness. Now they were to be separated, not for a few weeks but for many months. William persuaded Martha that it would be less upsetting if they said goodbye on the steps of Kendrick's instead of at the railway station. Taking her in his arms, he vowed that within days of his return he would carry her over the threshold of their own home and they would never be apart again for the rest of their lives. Smiling through her tears, Martha begged him to take care and said she would pray that God would watch over him. William ran down the steps and carefully mounted Flash. Martha followed him down the steps and stood forlornly waving a handkerchief. William, not daring to look back, rode off.

After loading Flash, William boarded the train with Dobson and his men. They alighted at Kansas City, the end of the line, unloaded the horses and rode out to Dobson's ranch. The ranch proved to be a large wooden building with an adjoining stable, a splendid brick edifice containing twenty capacious loose boxes. When they arrived, they were greeted by a large genial Negro who immediately set about cooking them a feast of barbecued buffalo steaks.

'That's Abraham,' said Jones. 'Isn't it? Stiletto always leaves him in charge of the ranch when he's away.'

The walls of the sitting room were festooned with revolvers and rifles while the floor was covered with buffalo and bear hides. A small shelf of books stood out incongruously among all this machismo. This discovery increased William's respect for

Dobson. One leather bound tome bore the title *Letters and Notes on the Manners, Customs and Condition of the North American Indians.* Evidently, Dobson had an interest in anthropology.

They were to spend one night at the ranch before setting off for El Paso. That evening Abraham brought a keg of rye whisky into the sitting room and they all sprawled indolently, drinking and smoking cheroots. Jones questioned Dobson about the wisdom of venturing into Mexico while a civil war was raging there but Dobson dismissed his fears, saying that the action was now taking place far to the south where the forces of Juárez were laying siege to Queretaro, the last refuge of Emperor Maximilian and the tattered remains of the Imperial army.

William asked how they were able to control a large herd of cattle as they drove hundreds of miles across the plains.

Taylor spoke, 'It's simple really. Every wild herd has its own leader and follows him without question. Whenever we corral a number of different herds, all hell breaks out and only ends when we choose a new leader whom they can all follow. The secret of success in a cattle drive is to spot the leader and control him. That way you can drive a thousand head of cattle to the moon and back, no problem.'

'You must always keep an eye out for them Indians,' piped Jones. 'Isn't it? A small band is quite capable of stampeding the herd.'

'A small band!' said Haig. 'I remember one night on a drive, I was keeping watch when I saw something white moving towards the herd and they were on the point of stampeding. I took aim with my Winchester and brought it down with a shot. What do you think I found when I went over to it? A bloody white bed sheet with a great brute of an Indian under it. A small band? One is enough.'

'I've heard tell,' said Jones, 'of Indians that lived in what is now North Dakota who had blonde hair and blue eyes. Isn't it?'

This was greeted with cries of scepticism but Jones continued, 'And spoke Welsh.'

The room exploded with laughter.

'Oh yes, A very small peaceful tribe they were too... very warm and friendly. Isn't it? Never attacked first but if you attacked their village, God help you. It was the pipe of peace or have the shit beaten out of you. Isn't it?'

'God but you're a comedian,' Haig said.

'Jones is right, you know,' said Dobson. 'They were the Mandans, a distant branch of the Sioux.'

'But how could they have spoken Welsh?' William protested.

'There was a Welsh settlement on the Ohio River in the fourteenth century and that's the region that the Mandans originally came from,' Dobson answered. 'Though there's a legend that a Welsh Prince called Madoc discovered America three hundred years before Columbus and that the members of his expedition were the ancestors of the Mandans.'

'There! What did I tell you?' Jones said proudly. 'We Welsh get in anywhere. Isn't it?

'Doesn't explain the blonde hair and blue eyes,' Haig grumbled. 'Look at Jones!'

Dobson gave a wry smile and shrugged his shoulders.

The next morning they set out for El Paso and the Mexican border. Jones sat in the provision wagon and drove the four mules. By day they traversed the Great Plains. As far as the eye could see the ground was covered with buffalo grass and sagebrush. Rabbits, deer and buffalo abounded and, in the creeks, snakes swarmed among the cotton wood trees. At night a light breeze would spring up and they would sit around the campfire made from dried buffalo excrement. Taylor was the cook and made them coffee and biscuits in the morning and cooked sowbelly for supper. The air on the plains was so hot and arid that an animal, when killed, would dry up without stinking. As they rode down to Mexico they passed many an animal hide filled solely with dust.

It was five o'clock in the morning and William, having eaten his breakfast, was some distance from the camp with his rifle slung over his shoulder and his eyes peeled for grouse or deer. Suddenly, with a great flapping of wings, a large ruffed grouse rose cumbrously into the air. The poor bird was only a few yards in front of William and he had no difficulty in bringing it down with a single shot. He stepped forward and stooped down to pick up his booty, but a small rattlesnake that had been concealed in the long grass reared up and struck him on the back of his right hand. It then coiled up and began to rattle. Infuriated, William beat it to death with the stock of his rifle. He consoled himself with the fact that it was only a small prairie rattlesnake and so could not be very poisonous.

He still felt it would be wise to hurry back to the camp and seek help.

When he told them what had happened, Dobson cried out, 'God man, those little prairie rattlers are every bit as poisonous as their big cousins of the wood! Jones, get the whisky from the wagon.'

Dobson pulled his knife from his right boot and made a deep cut where the snake had struck; then he sucked hard at the bleeding wound. When his mouth was full of blood and snake venom, he spat it out and wiped his mouth with the back of his hand.

'Feel any pain in your hand?' he asked.

'Strangely, no. My arm and hand are numb.'

Jones had returned with the small keg of whisky, which they kept for emergencies such as this. He ran out a generous measure and Dobson poured it down William's throat.

'Do you feel drowsy?' he asked.

'Well now that you mention it, I do,' William answered.

'Taylor, Haig, keep him walking. On no account let him fall asleep,' Dobson ordered.

For the next hour William was forced to walk round in circles, supported on either side by Taylor and Haig.

William was now dragging his feet along the ground and begging, 'Just let me rest for a few minutes.'

'Fall asleep and you'll wake up dead!' Haig yelled in his ear.

'Here, I'll give him more whisky,' said Jones. 'Helps to burn up the poison.'

They halted while Jones forced another measure of whisky down his throat. William was now completely incoherent and hung limply between Taylor and Haig, babbling utter nonsense.

Dobson returned and barked, 'Keep him moving, you two. Jones, you walk behind prodding him with your rifle. Make him move those legs.'

Two hours later, William felt sensation returning to his hand and the wound began to sting.

He cried out, 'Damn, my hand is hurting abominably.'

'That's it,' said Dobson. 'Put him down, the danger's over.'

After a few days of rest William was fully fit again. The whisky they carried in the wagon was strictly for medicinal purpose and the men jokingly accused him of feigning the snakebite to get a drink.

They travelled for weeks under the burning sun without a sign of civilisation. Gazing at the horizon, they could see no boundary between earth and sky.

'There ain't a bottle of whisky or a town to spend a dollar in,' grumbled Taylor.

'It's better than pushing a plough,' Haig retorted.

One afternoon a large party of Indians started following them from a distance.

'They'll not attack us now,' growled Dobson. 'They'll wait until we return with the cattle.'

He appeared to be correct, for after a few hours the Indians turned tail and rode out of sight.

That night it was William's turn to stand guard and tend the fire. He patrolled nervously around the ring of sleeping men and stared vainly into the obscurity beyond the flickering orange glow cast by the fire. A hard day spent in the saddle began to take its toll and, feeling a desperate tiredness flood through his limbs, he decided to sit for a while. The heat from the fire and his own weariness caused him to fall into a comfortable stupor. He was startled into consciousness when something heavy crashed onto his back, pitching him forward. Springing to his feet, he saw Dobson kneeling with his right arm fully extended. An Indian lay spread-eagled on the ground with a stiletto buried up to the hilt in his throat. William caught a glimpse of another swiftly fleeing from the scene. In the excitement that followed, Dobson told the others that William, as alert as ever, had raised the alarm and that they both had seen the attackers off. Those words earned Dobson William's undying gratitude and loyalty.

When they made camp near the first of the southern towns in Texas, the men spruced themselves up and rode to the nearest saloon in search of whisky, women and gambling. Dobson and William stood at the bar and looked at the antics of Jones, Taylor and Haig. Although they had been in the saloon for under an hour they were already crazy drunk.

'Look at them,' Dobson said with disgust. 'Soon each of them will be off upstairs with some poxy tart. I warn them of the dangers, I've lost three men over the years to that damn disease, but will they listen?'

Dobson's weakness was gambling and he spent the rest of the night at the faro table. He prided himself on his expertise and luck. That night he came away with his pockets full of dollars and wearing a satisfied grin.

'I can spot the cards that will win and the ones that will lose,' he boasted. 'It's a God given gift.'

But when they reached El Paso his luck ran out and he lost badly to a banker. The next day they were due to cross into Mexico but Dobson told the gang that he was going back to El Paso. His losses clearly irked him and he suspected the banker of cheating. William insisted on accompanying him. The rest of the party moved off and forded the Rio Grande with the understanding that William and Dobson would catch up with them the following day.

On entering the saloon, the atmosphere heavy with the stench of dismally burning oil lamps, Dobson headed straight for the faro table while William went to the bar. After a few hours, it was clear from Dobson's demeanour that he was losing again. William walked over to the table and observed the banker's smirk as he brandished a card in Dobson's face.

'Three of clubs wins,' he called. 'Lost again, sir.'

'That card was not pulled from the top of the pack,' Dobson said. His voice was hard and menacing. 'You've been cheating all night.'

Both men rose to their feet, sending their chairs reeling. The people in the saloon quickly scattered and cowered against the walls. The banker, with a curse, produced a gun. Dobson crouched and, with his right hand, snatched the stiletto from his boot and deftly flicked it at the man's chest. As the knife penetrated between his ribs, the banker fired.

In the resulting confusion William and Dobson escaped through the swing doors and ran for their horses. As they rode furiously away, they heard the clamour of pursuit and bullets winged past them. White Lightning was hit and crashed to the ground. William pulled up, returned and, reaching down, helped Dobson up onto Flash. Dobson clutched convulsively around William's waist and gave a low moan.

The two resumed their headlong flight and after a time the sounds of pursuit grew fainter and eventually ceased. The darkness that had enabled them to elude the chasing pack now proved their undoing. Flash plunged into a creek and broke his neck in the fall. Picking himself up, William went over to where Dobson lay motionless on the ground. His duster coat was thrown open and, peering down, William could just discern that a great red flower had blossomed and spread over Dobson's silver waistcoat. He was dead – the banker's shot had found its mark. William covered Dobson's body with stones, the hardness of the ground and his lack of a spade making it impossible to bury him. He fashioned a simple cross from two pieces of wood and planted it at the head of the mound. As the sun rose above the eastern horizon, William stood with head bowed and mumbled a short prayer over the body of his friend.

William was faced with the frightening realisation that he was irredeemably lost. He decided to strike out in a south-easterly direction in the hope of finding the Rio Grande. A day's painful march and he reached its banks. He followed the course of the river until he found a place where the water was shallow enough for him to wade across. He was now in Mexico and, despite his hunger and weakened condition, he resolved to press on in the hope of finding Jones and the others. There followed desperate days of unavailing search in the wilderness until, overcome by starvation, dehydration and exhaustion, he sank to the ground. Kneeling there he saw a shimmering figure rise from the desert floor and glide towards him.

When it reached him he closed his eyes, fearing to look on its countenance. He experienced a sensation as if a gentle breeze had kissed his cheek and opening his eyes he saw Martha gazing down at him with a look of such sublime compassion that it almost stopped his heart. She smiled and with a wave of her hand invited him to follow her. Despite his desperate condition he crawled for hours, scrabbling with his bleeding fingers in the desert sand, following that ethereal figure, until he collapsed and a profound blackness overwhelmed him.

He was awakened by the shock of cold water on his face. Looking up he saw a ring of grinning Mexican faces.

'Lost, Gringo?' one of them enquired.

At this the rest of them roared with laughter and slapped each other on the back in high good humour. Lying there at their mercy, the first thought that came into William's mind was that these were a bunch of bloodthirsty marauding bandits. Terrified, he pictured them stripping him naked and burying him up to the neck – leaving him a helpless prey to the creatures that crawled on the burning desert floor. William was fortunate, these were no bandits but a disciplined contingent of the Liberal army of Juárez who – dressed in their brand new uniforms, courtesy of the American Government – were on their way to join their comrades at the siege of Queretaro. Being alone and destitute William took the one course open to him – he enlisted and was fitted out in a neat white uniform with two bandoleers criss-crossed on his chest.

CHAPTER 15

On entering Queretaro, Maximilian set up his headquarters in the Convent of the Cross, which was called La Cruz, and found Mejia lying seriously ill there. The general had managed to avoid capture after his defeat at the hands of Escobedo. Maximilian's first act was to call together his chief lieutenants. The room in which they gathered had a large window that gave a panoramic view of the mountains that encircled Queretaro. Clearly visible on their peaks were the gun emplacements of Escobedo's men.

Pointing through the window at the enemy positions Marquez said, 'We're trapped inside a ring of steel. They can shell us at will, destroy the aqueduct that brings water into the city and cut off our supply lines. They won't even have to attack us.'

'All the more reason why we should take the fight to them,' Miramon countered eagerly.

'But they outnumber us. We'll be overwhelmed,' Marquez protested.

'Not if we concentrate all our forces at one point in the circle,' Maximilian broke in excitedly. 'That was the secret of Napoleon Bonaparte's greatest victories.'

Lopez and Salm agreed enthusiastically but Marquez continued to express his doubts. Finally, it was agreed that the bulk of Maximilian's army would carry out an assault at one point while Marquez would remain in reserve with a small body of men.

Before they left, Maximilian made a personal statement. Speaking with great feeling he said, 'Gentlemen, this is the moment that I have long desired. The moment when I take command of the army and lead it in the battle for independence and internal peace. We will fight with valour and pride for our beloved Mexico. Our trust is in God.'

Miramon with Lopez and Salm led the attack, storming up the slope, through a hail of shells and bullets. They reached the emplacements but were forced back down and suffered severe causalities. Marquez watched with quiet satisfaction as the Imperial troops streamed back into the city.

He turned to his adjutant and said, 'Maybe his Majesty will pay more heed to my advice in the future.'

Escobedo, trying to take advantage of the enemy's disarray, launched a massive attack on the city. Maximilian leapt onto his horse and, with lance in hand, rallied his fleeing soldiers.

'Soldiers of the Imperial army of Mexico,' he cried, 'defend the honour of our glorious national banner!'

He lowered his lance and charged at the enemy. To a man his soldiers turned and followed him. They fought with pikes, hatchets, swords, ancient muskets and pistols against a foe armed with the latest American rifles. Such was the ferocity of their resistance that, after several hours of bloody conflict, Escobedo withdrew to the mountaintops and settled for a long siege.

Escobedo now deployed all the devices of attrition. He destroyed the aqueduct; polluted the river, flowing from the hills into the city, with dead bodies; imposed a tight blockade and kept up an incessant bombardment. At first the city had enough stocks of food, and the wells within its boundaries provided a stringent but adequate supply of water.

As the weeks passed, despite strict rationing, the food stocks dwindled and the people began to starve. The constant shelling was also having a demoralising effect and Maximilian realised that continued resistance would soon become untenable. When Marquez came to him with a plan, Maximilian was ready to grasp at anything that might save them. Marquez proposed that he, together with a thousand cavalry, break through the Liberal lines at night and make for Mexico City. There he could raise a large body of reinforcements and attack the besieging forces from the rear.

Despite reservations expressed by Miramon and Lopez, Maximilian accepted the plan enthusiastically. Marquez waited for a night when cloud cover diminished the light of the moon. Mounting his horse, he saluted Maximilian and his officers.

'Sire!' he announced. 'I will return with sufficient reinforcements to save you and the Empire.'

He rode to the front of the waiting column of horsemen and, drawing his sword, led them at a quick canter into the darkness.

Watching them disappear, Miramon exclaimed, 'That's the last we'll see of Marquez.'

'Courage, Miramon,' Maximilian said 'I think he has every chance of breaking through.'

'Oh yes,' answered Miramon. 'He'll break through but he won't return.'

Maximilian sighed and said, 'Miramon, I'm disappointed in you. Such cynicism. I have every faith in Marquez.'

Marquez and his cavalry caught Escobedo's men totally unprepared and cut cleanly through their lines. With a smile of triumph on his face, Marquez set off at a gallop for Mexico City.

Maximilian strained every sinew to hold Queretaro until Marquez arrived with reinforcements. He would spend his days visiting the soldiers at their posts and mingling with the ordinary people of the city. To all he would speak of his belief that help was at hand and that ultimate victory would be his. He promised that he would establish a country where justice and prosperity would reign supreme. One night, in an effort to find out what his soldiers really felt, he decided to visit them incognito. Wrapped in a long black cloak and with a large black sombrero pulled down low over his forehead he left La Cruz.

Approaching a sentry post he was challenged by a burly veteran, 'Who goes there?'

'A friend,' Maximilian answered.

'Under whose command?'

'Colonel Lopez.'

'A good soldier. What does he make of our situation?'

'As shipwrecked sailors waiting for the final wave.'

'And has he told the Emperor this?'

Maximilian was beginning to enjoy his subterfuge and said, 'No, I think not. For is the Emperor not a man as I am? What is different for a monarch but ceremony? Rob him of ceremony and is he not like you or me?'

'True, but if we lose this battle the likes of you and me will have our throats cut. But he'll be sent back to Austria and will end his days peaceably in bed. Where's the justice in that?'

'I have heard it said that he would die on the battlefield and not return to Austria.'

'Aye no doubt he said that to make us fight more cheerfully, but when our throats are cut and he's safely back home we'll be none the wiser.'

Maximilian laughed and said, 'In that case, I'd never trust his word again.'

'I'm a simple man and know not if his cause be just. But a great sin will lie on his soul for all the men he has sent to their deaths, if his cause be not worthy.'

'That's a burden all monarchs must bear. His cause is the Mexican nation and he believes it worthy.'

'Well, he's sacrificed his wife's sanity for it. No one can gainsay that. Pass, friend.'

The frantic activity of the past few weeks had driven the thought of Charlotte's plight to the back of Maximilian's mind, but the soldier's reference to her brought the pain flooding through him again. Raising an arm in farewell he hurried back to his room at La Cruz. He knelt down before a crucifix hanging on the wall and struck his breast three times.

'Mea culpa,' he cried. 'Mea culpa, mea culpa. I took a young spirited girl and broke her on the wheel of my venal ambition. I make this vow: I will strive with superhuman strength to overcome my enemies so that the sacrifice of her sanity will not have been in vain. Should I fail, then I will forfeit my own life.'

A Captain Gonzales commanded the contingent that William had joined. The captain took a proprietorial interest in William and questioned him closely on how he came to be alone and half-dead in the desert so far from his native England. When William narrated the section where he had crawled for miles following the image of his betrothed, Gonzales was deeply moved and made the sign of the cross.

'That was divine intervention,' he said. 'The vision of your loved-one led you to a place lying in our line of march. You'd be dead by now, fit only as meat for the buzzards, had you remained where she found you.'

During the march to Queretaro the soldiers gossiped about Maximilian and Carlota. He sensed a reluctant sympathy for Maximilian whom they considered an honourable but misguided man. They reserved their contempt for Napoleon, who was deserting him in his hour of need. They were aware of rumours that Carlota had visited Paris and Rome in a vain attempt to save her husband, and that her failure had made her mad. The fate of the royal couple did not concern them greatly. They were more interested in the progress of the siege they were about to join. One wit composed a little song about conditions in the city and it caused considerable merriment when he sang it, accompanying himself on the guitar.

'Gather ye acorns while ye may
For food there is no buying
And that small mouse half dead today
Tomorrow will be frying.'

They reached the heights above Queretaro on May 14 and found the Liberal army preparing to launch what Escobedo hoped would be the final assault on the city. William spent a troubled night haunted by dreams of the battle to come. He had encountered war in the dry, impersonal accounts given in school texts; in the overwritten romantic passages of historical novels and, more recently, in Elisha's eyewitness report of Pickett's charge at Gettysburg. In the morning he would meet the iron face of battle, and he did not know how he would behave.

As the first light of dawn surged over the mountaintop, the Supremos Poderes, the élite Liberal regiment, led the charge down the slope against the beleaguered city. Escobedo concentrated all his men at one point on the southern outskirts.

William was in the vanguard when they broke through and entered the city's cemetery. Fighting their way forward gravestone by gravestone they drove the enemy back towards La Cruz. William had been totally unprepared for the noise, blast, passage of missiles and the confusion of human movement that assailed him as he sheltered behind a particularly large headstone. Cowering there, he wondered what on earth had possessed him to get into this predicament. He had no burning zeal to see Juárez reinstated as President of Mexico. He knew nothing about the man. He had no desire to destroy Maximilian. What harm had the man done to him? The whole thing was a horrible mistake.

A shell exploded in front of the gravestone and sent pieces of masonry flying past his head. He wet his trousers and called out for his mother. The thing that astonished him was that when the men around him rose from behind their sheltering gravestones and charged forward screaming obscenities, he joined them. It was not bloodlust, he did not hate the enemy, it was simply that he was too afraid to stay behind on his own. He felt safer being part of the herd. He had discovered the secret of all the great heroic charges in the history of warfare. Men raced en masse into the most deadly situations because they felt there was safety in numbers and they were afraid of being alone in a hostile environment.

Having cleared the enemy from the cemetery, they burst through into the plaza in front of La Cruz. William saw three men standing on the steps of the convent looking down as the Liberals poured through a gap in the defences. The figure in the centre was dressed in the uniform of a general in the Imperial army; he held a revolver in each hand and a sabre hung at his side. What made the figure unmistakable was the black cloak slung carelessly over his shoulders and the large white sombrero on his head. William watched as the three men descended the steps and disappeared into the mêlée. This was the first time William had set eyes on Maximilian.

Escobedo's assault had taken Maximilian's forces completely by surprise and, by concentrating his attack at one point, he penetrated as far as La Cruz before the Emperor was alerted. Prince Salm-Salm ran into the room where Maximilian, fully clothed, was lying with his sabre and revolvers at his side.

'Wake, sire!' he shouted. 'The enemy is at the gate. General Miramon is wounded and taken prisoner.'

Maximilian received the news calmly and gave orders that all officers and men should regroup at the Hill of Bells in the centre of Queretaro. He strapped the sabre at his side, placed his sombrero on his head and picked up the revolvers. He stepped out into the corridor where Salm rejoined him. As they walked past Mejia's room, the sick general appeared in the doorway.

'Majesty, grant me the honour of accompanying you,' he said.

Maximilian doffed his sombrero and the three men stepped out to the head of the stairs.

'Well, gentlemen,' Maximilian said. 'We must obey our own orders and report to the Hill of Bells.'

They descended the steps not knowing if this was the last walk they would ever take. The fighting was so confused in the plaza that they were able to force a passage through and head for the Hill of Bells. If Maximilian had been hoping to find most of his army there to greet him, he was disappointed. When Salm, Mejia and

Maximilian stood on the top of the hill all they found was a small huddle of demoralised soldiers. Colonel Lopez rode up with the news that La Cruz had fallen and that the soldiers of the Imperial army were throwing down their rifles. In a short time the base of the hill was ringed with the massed ranks of the Liberal army.

Maximilian turned to Mejia and asked, 'Could a body of determined men on horseback break through and escape?'

Mejia replied, 'It cannot be done but if you ordered it, I would obey.'

'No, there has been too much blood spilled already.'

Maximilian pulled a white handkerchief from his pocket and tied it to the point of his sabre then, flanked by Salm and Mejia, he descended the hill to where Escobedo waited, astride his horse. Escobedo hurriedly dismounted and advanced to meet him.

When the two men stood face to face, Escobedo said, 'Your Majesty is my prisoner.'

Maximilian lowered his sword, removed the white handkerchief and handed the sword to Escobedo.

'I accept this sword on behalf of the people of Mexico,' Escobedo announced loudly. 'The Empire is over. Long live the Republic of Mexico.'

'General, let no more blood be split,' Maximilian said. 'Execute me if you must but spare the others.'

'Your Majesty, I admire your chivalry. You deserved better at the hands of Colonel Lopez.'

Maximilian looked puzzled and ask, 'What of Colonel Lopez?'

'He betrayed you. How do you think we broke so easily into the plaza?'

Maximilian was unable to mask the bitter disappointment this news caused him and he said, 'My dear wife and I placed great trust in Colonel Lopez. He commanded the Imperial Guard that escorted us into Mexico City on the day of our coronation, you know.'

Maximilian paused and then continued wistfully, 'I can see him now riding at the side of our state coach. And the crowds! Oh, you should have seen the crowds cheering and throwing flowers.'

'You never had the support of the true people of Mexico.'

'I was never given the time to earn it, my friend. What was Lopez's reward for betraying me?'

'Money, what else? But I would willingly have made it a rope around his neck. I have no time for traitors, although we have to use them.'

'Such men are to be pitied rather than reviled.'

Escobedo called forward Captain Gonzales and ordered him to escort Maximilian back to La Cruz. Guarded by a squad of ten men, William among them, Maximilian was marched back to the convent and imprisoned in the room he had occupied during the siege. That night William was stationed outside Maximilian's room when he heard a knocking on the door. He cautiously opened the door while a fellow soldier stood alert with rifle at the ready. Maximilian was standing by the door, his face thrown into relief by the light of the oil lamp suspended from the ceiling.

'Yes?' William asked nervously. This was the first time he had ever spoken to an archduke and ex-emperor. 'What do you want?'

Maximilian gestured towards the small table beside the truckle bed, and said, 'The water jug is empty.'

'You want it replenished?'

'Yes, if it's not too much trouble.'

William scurried out of the room with the water jug. He filled it from a tap in the yard and, returning, placed it back on the table.

'You're not a native Mexican, are you?' Maximilian asked. 'American, perhaps?'

'No, sir, I'm English.'

'English! And what would an Englishman be doing fighting for Juárez in Mexico?'

'It's a long story, sir.'

'I don't think I'll be going anywhere for a while, so maybe you'll tell me that story sometime.'

William glanced up and caught an expression on Maximilian's face of such weary affliction that he felt moved to pity. Until that moment Maximilian had been to William merely a symbol of oppression but now, having met him, he saw him as a human being. It is easy to countenance the killing of a man in the abstract but when you see the emotions flit across his face, the sanctity of life becomes real.

Maximilian made a request that, to relieve the cruelty of solitary confinement, William be allowed to spend one hour each day in the captive's room. Captain Gonzales – after instructing William that should the ex-emperor attempt to bribe him, he was to report it immediately – gave his consent. At first

William was petrified and sat stiffly on the edge of his chair as Maximilian questioned him, but the genuine interest exhibited by his questioner soon put him at ease. He carefully obscured the reason for his emigration to America, saying that a mutual antipathy between father and son and his own desire for adventure had sent him on his odyssey. He did, however, give a full and truthful account of his adventures in New York, Washington and Chicago. When he told how Captain Gonzales had rescued him from certain death in the desert, Maximilian smiled wryly.

'So it was not republican convictions that brought you here, just self-preservation,' he said quietly. Then, seeing William's hurt reaction, he added, 'Though of course I understand your reasons for wishing to live. You have your Martha waiting for you back in Chicago and I have come to realise that there is nothing more precious in the world than the love of two people for each other.'

Maximilian spoke of his first meeting with Charlotte, of how she had captivated him with her beauty, forthright manner and erudition. There in that dismal room he rejoiced in memories of their gilded life together in the castle at Miramar where Charlotte painted and read among the gleaming towers, the medieval battlements and flowing fountains. His eyes lit up when he told William of the triumphant entry into Mexico City on the day of his coronation.

'We rode, Charlotte and I, in the state coach through the city gates and were showered with coloured strips of paper bearing verses of welcome. We passed down streets carpeted with flowers and lined with cheering citizens. We stood side by side on the dais in the National Palace and the people roared their adoration.'

William shuffled uncomfortably on his chair and murmured, 'Yes indeed, sir. A day to be remembered.'

Maximilian gave a harsh laugh and said, 'Look at us now. I languish here, betrayed by adventurers like Hidalgo and Gutierrez who fed my ambition with false promises, while Charlotte is imprisoned in Miramar, her sanity destroyed because she believed in my destiny.'

CHAPTER 16

Juárez had moved south to the town of San Luis Potosi, a three-day journey across the desert from Queretaro. When an officer sent by Escobedo arrived at the new headquarters he was ushered into the presence of the President by the same old peasant woman who had served Juárez in Paso del Norte. The President was dressed in his accustomed uniform, a black broadcloth coat, white linen vest and highly polished boots. On the table in front of him lay a pair of spotless white gloves. The officer reported the fall of Queretaro and the capture of the Emperor. He then conveyed Maximilian's request that only he be punished.

Juárez calmly examined his hands and pulled on the gloves, smoothing out any creases.

'Archduke Maximilian intervened in the internal affairs of Mexico,' he said. 'This contravened the act of 1862 and carries the penalty of death. His intervention has caused the deaths of thousands of Mexicans. He must stand trial before a military tribunal.'

'And what of his generals, Mr President?'

'Miguel Miramon and Tomas Mejia stand trial with him.'

The officer saluted and was about to depart when Juárez added, 'Give my compliments to General

Escobedo and inform him that General Diaz has taken Mexico City. The Empire is truly over.'

Escobedo, when he learned that Maximilian together with Miramon and Mejia were to go before the tribunal, moved them to the more secure confines of the Convent of the Capuchins. Before he left La Cruz, Maximilian asked to see William. The two stood alone in that austere room with its bare, whitewashed walls.

Maximilian bent forward and whispered, 'William, ambition is the enemy of true joy. Believe me, I know. Go home to your Martha.'

He stepped smartly out into the corridor and was marched off to his new prison.

Martha, William thought. She can only think me dead. I must write to her. Maximilian's advice was right; he would get a discharge and head for home.

Dobson's men, after tarrying awhile on the Mexican side of the border, pressed on to the nearest town in Chihuaha province. There they spent a few hedonistic days in a flyblown dive that served as a drinking house and brothel. Surfacing, they realised that Dobson and William had not caught up with them. Unshaven and wearing only their filthy long johns, they lolled in Haig's room and considered their predicament.

'The situation is serious,' Jones wailed. 'Isn't it?'

'I find the situation idyllic,' Haig said, scratching his large belly. 'Plenty of whisky and somewhere to park your weapon when nature calls.'

'Sober up, Haig,' Taylor said. 'Taffy's right. Something must have happened to them and without Stiletto we can't buy cattle.'

306

'Yes indeed,' said Jones. 'And the money's running short. Isn't it?'

Haig glared around and said, 'Well, what do we do?'

Taylor said, 'Only one thing we can do. Retrace our steps and try to find them.'

'I feel in my bones they're doomed,' Jones said mournfully. 'Stiletto always was one for a fight and young William wouldn't have been much help in a scrap.'

'Shut it, Jones!' Haig snapped. 'Some of the dampness from that rain-soaked hovel in Wales must have soaked into those precious bones of yours.'

Jones retorted indignantly, 'I'll have you know, I was brought up on the Gower coast, one of the sunniest places on God's earth. Isn't it?'

'For God's sake, stop it you two,' Taylor said. 'We'll go back to El Paso, seeking news as we go.'

'And if we don't learn anything?' Haig asked.

'We'll meet that problem when it comes,' Taylor answered.

Within the hour they had saddled up and headed back towards the Rio Grande. All along their route over the bare desert, they found no trace of the missing pair. They forded the river and rode to within sight of El Paso.

'We should ask at the saloon,' Taylor said. 'That's were they were heading when they left us.'

'Don't think we'll be welcome there somehow.' Haig said. 'Especially if Stilletto made trouble.'

'If we're ever going to find the truth, it will be there,' Jones said. 'You two wait here. I'll ride in and ask. Pretty nondescript fellow, me. They won't remember I was ever there. Isn't it?'

Before the others could reply, he dug his spurs in and rode off at a gallop. Dusk was falling when he returned. Taylor and Haig could tell by the way he sat on the saddle that the news was not good.

'Well?' Haig demanded.

'You were right, Haig,' Jones said sombrely. 'Stiletto started a fight. Isn't it? Accused the banker of cheating and, when the fellow drew a gun and fired, Stiletto reached for his knife. You know the end of that, the banker lying on the floor with six inches of cold steel in his heart. In the confusion Stiletto and William got away and headed for the desert, but the barman thinks that the banker's shot found its mark in Stiletto's stomach. A posse took up pursuit but lost them in the dark.'

'That's it then,' said Taylor. 'A stomach wound would prove fatal and William would never survive on his own in the desert.'

'Yes indeed,' Jones said. 'Their bones are now whitening under the desert sun.'

'For God's sake, will you listen to Cassandra there!' shouted Haig.

'We go back to Kansas,' Taylor said. 'Abraham will know what to do. He always was Stiletto's confidant. He'll be the boss now.'

When the three rode wearily into the ranch at Kansas and told Abraham their sad tale, his large cheerful face crumpled and they could have sworn he turned pale. Taylor was correct, Abraham and Stiletto had been very close and Abraham slipped effortlessly into the role of leader.

On the journey back to the ranch the three cowpunchers had talked about William and Martha. The poignancy of a young girl waiting patiently in Chicago for a betrothed who would never return pierced the carapace of even their tough hides. When they discussed this with Abraham, he said that, because of Stiletto's death, he would have to go and settle certain legal matters with the authorities in Chicago. He offered to contact Martha and break the news.

Martha had been bearing the hurt of William's absence by nursing in her heart the joy that she and William had found in each other. She looked forward to the loving home they would share and the children they would rear. As the time approached when she expected Dobson and his men to bring their cattle to the Chicago stockyards, her excitement mounted. She was working in the linen room when the housekeeper told her that a Negro was in the lobby and had a message for her. Thinking that he might be carrying a letter from William, she flew down the stairs to the lobby where Abraham waited. She spotted his tall bulky figure and ran eagerly towards him, then something in his face made her stop and tremble.

He took her hands and said gently, 'Miss Martha, it would be better if you took a seat.'

'No,' she cried. 'Tell me. I know. William is hurt.'

'William is missing, but I fear he may be dead.'

He guided her to a chair and told her the whole story.

She listened calmly and when he had finished she looked up at him through eyes glistening with tears and said, 'He is not dead – not my William. I will hear from him soon. He and I are destined to go through life hand in hand.'

She rose, thanked Abraham for his trouble and walked up the stairs to the linen room.

On arrival at the Convent of Chapuchins, Maximilian, Miramon and Mejia were placed in separate rooms that opened out on to a common balcony, overlooking a small courtyard. While preparations for the trial proceeded, the prisoners had few visitors.

Among them was a young American woman. She was the wife of Prince Salm-Salm. The Prince was held in the city's casino, along with all prisoners who were not facing trial. Princess Salm visited Maximilian every day and brought him clean linen, bread and cakes. Despite his gaunt and pale appearance he was in good spirits and was convinced that Juárez would never allow him to be executed. He spoke of how after his release he would rejoin Charlotte at Miramar and spend his time sitting in the beautiful gardens writing his memoirs. He was so confident that when the tribunal convened he refused to appear before them.

The trial took place in the auditorium of the local theatre. It was June and the air in the crowded courtroom was fetid and swarming with flies. The members of the tribunal, all young inexperienced officers, sat on a dais at one end of the room. Facing them were the tables occupied by the lawyers and, set at right angles, the dock containing Miramon and Mejia. The rest of the room was crammed with spectators, among them Princess Salm, Mejia's pregnant wife and Miramon's wife. Miramon and Mejia sat in lofty silence, refusing to recognise the jurisdiction of the court. Miramon still wore a bandage over part of his face to cover the wound he had sustained when captured.

The defence lawyers claimed that, since Maximilian had raised the white flag of surrender, he and his men were prisoners of war and it would be illegal to shoot prisoners who had surrendered. The prosecution argued that Maximilian's intervention was illegal and that he and his officers could be held directly responsible for the deaths of thousands of Mexican citizens. The court adjourned and said it would announce the verdict the next morning.

The three men were found guilty and sentenced to death by firing squad, the executions to take place at the Hill of Bells on June 16. On hearing the verdict, Princess Salm hurried to Maximilian's cell and told him of a scheme she had for bribing the guards and effecting his escape to an Austrian ship lying at anchor in the bay off Vera Cruz. Maximilian recoiled from the idea and told her that it was his duty to die but he would send a plea to Juárez that he spare the lives of Miramon and Mejia. When Juárez learned that lawyers were travelling to San Luis Potosi to plead for mercy, he ordered a postponement to June 19. He had been greatly troubled by a stream of interoceanic cables from the crowned heads of Europe asking him to spare the life of the brother of the

Emperor of Austria, and he wished to show that he was not some bloodthirsty monster.

When the lawyers arrived, Juárez was taken aback to find that they were accompanied by Princess Salm and the wives of Miramon and Mejia. He listened to the lawyers' arguments and dismissed their semantics with contempt. He paid careful attention to the wives' entreaties and in reply spoke gently of how he understood their suffering but he had a duty to all those who had died in the war. These executions would be the atonement for those lost lives.

When Princess Salm went down on her knees and begged that Maximilian be spared, Juárez told her that Maximilian would be a rallying point for the Conservatives as long as he lived. To ensure future peace he must die. Maximilian, on learning of Juárez' decision, sent him a telegram asking that the death penalty on Miramon and Mejia be revoked and that he, Maximilian, be the sole victim. He ended with the words: '*Let the bloodshed end with me.*'

Juárez did not reply.

Maximilian prepared for death. He wrote to his brother a short formal letter in which he apologised for any harm his actions had done to the Austrian crown. In the letter to his mother Sophia, he made a reference that she would find full of nostalgia and hidden significance – '*I trust that in the conduct of my life and the manner of my death I have proved true to the memory of an exemplary father and an illustrious grandfather.*'

Sitting alone in his cell as dusk fell on the evening of June 18, Maximilian steeled himself to write his farewell to Charlotte:

'My darling Charlotte,

'I pray that God has restored you to health and you are able to read and understand these last words of mine. Fate has been cruel to me in the months you have been away. All our high hopes are destroyed and death will come as a happy relief. I will die like a king. I thank God for the years we had together and when God calls you to him, I shall be waiting at his side and we shall be together again. Forgive me, Charlotte.'

He signed the letter '*Your ill-fated Maximilian.*'

Earlier that day Captain Gonzales had mustered his company and, walking down their ranks, picked out twenty-one men whom he ordered to report to him at dawn the following morning for special duties. William was one of those chosen and realised immediately what those special duties entailed. After the company was dismissed he walked around the yard in an agony of indecision and then headed for the captain's room. He knocked timidly on the door and, hearing Gonazales bark something unintelligible, entered.

Gonzales had settled down to some serious drinking and was annoyed at being disturbed, but when he saw it was William his manner changed. He had no family of his own and he had grown to like this young Englishman.

'Oh, it's you, Dawson,' he said. 'Sit down and have a drink.'

'I'll take a seat but if you don't mind I'll forgo the drink, sir.'

Gonzales laughed and said, 'Relax boy, the drink isn't compulsory.'

'Permission to ask a question, sir.'

'Granted.'

'The men you picked out, are they the firing squad for tomorrow?'

'Yes. What of it?'

'But I can't be a member of it.'

'Why not?'

'You know, with your permission, I spent hours talking to the man. We practically became friends.'

'I know,' he said. 'That's the reason I picked you.'

'I'm afraid I don't understand.'

'Believe me, when a man faces death the one thing he craves in those final moments is the sight of a friendly face. There is nothing worse than dying amongst the indifference of strangers.'

'You're sure of this?'

'I chose you to help Maximilian through his ordeal. Don't let him down.'

Shaken, William stood up and saluted to signify his acceptance. Gonzales got up and placed an arm across William's shoulders.

'William, have you thought of what you'll do with your life?' he asked.

'Return to Chicago and marry Martha,' William answered without hesitation.

'Think carefully. I could get you a commission and the prospects for a man who shot the Emperor are limitless. You could be on the threshold of a glittering career.'

William spent a restless night – his sleep was a succession of grotesque images. A monstrous Ann Wilson towered above him, perched precariously on a stile, her petticoat and long frilly drawers filling the sky. Oliver's vulnerable naked body lay trembling on a drape of green velvet. From the darkness of an alley a mouth smeared with lipstick mouthed obscenities. A bundle of rags wriggled in his arms and turned into a baby with withered limbs and hurt, bewildered eyes. Ted's face, a silent scream, disappeared beneath dark waters. Mary Surratt, shrouded in black and with a noose around her neck, grinned mirthlessly. John Wilkes Booth strode towards him blood streaming from a gaping hole in his neck. A crude mound of stones, surmounted with a simple cross fashioned from branches, burst asunder and Stiletto rose from the rubble, rotting flesh dribbling from his bones. Martha was standing in the road waving and he watched in horror as she crumbled into dust and a wild wind swept her away. William woke and shivered in the cool morning air.

Maximilian sealed the letter to Charlotte and flung himself down on the bed to face his last night on this earth. Strangely, he fell into a deep sleep. It was his wedding day and Charlotte was gliding down the aisle towards him. Her dress of white satin billowed out behind her and her lace veil rose slowly to reveal the face he loved. The image faded and he found that he was staring at a wooden screen decorated with a painting of the most beautiful females, all streaming hair and flowing draperies. Charlotte emerged, flushed and embarrassed, from behind the screen enveloped in an absurdly voluminous garment. He gathered her up in his arms and laid her on the bed. He gently removed her clothing and pressed his face between her breasts. Her heart pounded wildly and she dug her fingers in his back.

Maximilian woke, ready to face his fate.

It was six o'clock when William and the rest of the firing squad reported for duty. The streets were silent and deserted as Captain Gonzales marched his men to the top of the Hill of Bells and stationed them in front of a low adobe wall. Outside the Convent of Chapuchins a small group kept vigil – Princess Salm, Miramon's wife and her three children and Mejia's wife with her newborn baby in her arms.

The silence was broken by the sound of the Dead March as a military band slowly moved up the street followed by three closed carriages. The procession halted and the band ceased playing. Silence returned to Queretaro. When the three men emerged from the convent, the women rushed forward but were brutally pushed back into the gutter. Maximilian, Miramon and Mejia were bundled into separate carriages. The band struck up and the sad cavalcade of death moved off, to slow march through streets lined with Escobedo's soldiers. The citizens of Queretaro remained inside their shuttered houses. When the cortège reached the foot of the Hill of Bells the carriages were pulled to a stop and the condemned men alighted.

From his vantage point William saw three men walk slowly up the hill. Maximilian stood out from the others. His tall figure was clothed entirely in black and he wore a large white sombrero. When they reached the top of the hill, Escobedo stepped forward.

Maximilian smiled and, looking up at the cloudless blue sky, said, 'Who could want a more beautiful day to die?'

Taken aback, Escobedo asked, 'Sir, do have any last request?'

'Only this, that President Juárez care for the families of General Miguel Miramon and General Tomas Mejia. Men of such courage and loyalty deserve that, no matter what master they serve.'

'I swear on my honour as a soldier that I will convey your wishes to the President. Have you any other request?'

'I wish to speak to the firing squad.'

Escobedo called Captain Gonzales forward and presented him to Maximilian. Gonzalez then conducted Maximilian along the ranks of his men. When Maximilian drew level with William he stopped and his eyes filled with tears.

'William, my boy,' he said, his voice full of emotion. 'What a comfort it is to see a friendly face as I pass into the shadows.' Then he whispered, 'Aim for the heart, there's a good fellow. Aim for the heart.'

He moved on and Gonzalez gave William a grave and knowing look.

The inspection over, Maximilian addressed the men, 'You are soldiers and must obey your orders. I absolve you of all blame.'

Maximilian asked that Miramon be given the place of honour in the centre while he stood on

Miramon's left and Mejia on the right. Maximilian handed his sombrero to Gonzales and spoke for the last time.

'Here is where I wished to plant the standard of victory,' he said, his voice steady. 'Instead it is where I am going to die. May my blood give succour to this land. Long live Mexico!'

Miramon and Mejia cried, 'Long live the Emperor!'

He stepped back against the wall and folded his hands over his heart. The firing squad raised their rifles. William took careful aim at those folded hands. There was a roll of drums.

Captain Gonzales shouted, 'Listos…Apunten…Fuego!'

The following day, June 20 1867, Lieutenant William Dawson marched with the victorious army along the road to Mexico City. He thought contentedly, 'Three years ago to this very day I arrived in New York a frightened, helpless immigrant, and now I've shot an Emperor and I'm marching to establish a Republic.'

Martha would have to wait.

EPILOGUE

Marshal Michel Ney

During the Battle of Waterloo, Ney had four horses shot from under him and, when his men failed to respond to his challenge of yet another desperate charge, he was forced to leave the field. Unable to face exile he took refuge in an isolated château near Aurillac, where he was found and arrested. The restored Bourbon government brought him to trial and he was condemned to death. On December 7, 1815, he appeared before a firing squad at the Carrefour de l'Observatoire in the Jardins du Luxembourg. He met death in the same fearless manner in which he had lived his life – giving the order to fire himself.

Marshal Emmanuel de Grouchy

Grouchy successfully extricated his troops from the battlefield at Waterloo and returned to Paris. On hearing of Napoleon's abdication he fled to the United States of America where he settled in Philadelphia. He was pardoned in 1820 and returned to France. He died at St Etienne on May 29, 1847.

Grouchy has been blamed for the failure of his army to make any contribution to the Battle of Waterloo. It is true that he stuck too rigidly to the letter of Napoleon's orders and was slow to respond to his second in command's plea to head to the sound of the guns. But it must be remembered that it was Napoleon who had sent him off on a route that led away from the battle.

Napoleon I

In 1840 Napoleon's body was brought back to Paris from the island of St Helena for burial in the chapel of the Hôtel des Invalides. On December 15, in a blinding snowstorm, the hearse proceeded from the Arc de Triomphe down the Champs-Elysées across the Place de la Concorde to the Esplanade and finally to the Hôtel des Invalides. The sarcophagus of red porphyry, which was not completed until 1861, lies directly under the golden dome of the chapel and rests on a pedestal of green granite. Napoleon's body, dressed in the uniform of the Chasseurs de Garde, is encased in six coffins, one inside the other. Twelve marble statues of winged Victory surround the tomb. The massive edifice bears brutal testimony to the awe in which the people of France held him.

Among his lasting achievements must be listed the Code Napoleon, which has influenced the laws of many nations other than France. The Code was founded on the premise of purely rational law, free from ancient custom. Under the Code, all citizens are equal; class privileges are abolished; institutions are emancipated from ecclesiastical control; the freedom of the individual and the inviolability of private property are protected.

Few will question the verdict of history that Napoleon was a soldier of genius and the creator of modern Europe.

Brooklyn Bridge

Work on the construction of the suspension bridge commenced in 1869 and took fourteen years to complete. John Augustus Roebling died as the result of an accident early on in its construction and his son took over as chief civil engineer. At the time it was the longest bridge in the world.

John Surratt

After Lincoln's assassination he escaped to Canada and then to Europe. He was captured abroad and extradited to stand trial in a civil court in 1867. The jury failed to reach a verdict and John Surratt was released. He died of pneumonia on April 21, 1916 at the age of 72 and is buried in Baltimore.

Anna Surratt

Four years after her mother's execution, Anna made a successful request to the authorities for her mother's body. Mother and daughter lie side by side in Mount Olivet Cemetery, Washington DC.

Dr Mudd, O'Laughlen and Arnold

President Andrew Jackson pardoned these three conspirators in 1869.

Boston Corbett

Corbett had been born in England in 1823 and had come to America with his family at the age of seven. He became a hatter in Boston and joined the Union army at the start of the Civil War. He returned to Boston after killing Booth and resumed his trade as a hatter. Later he moved to Concordia, Kansas and lived in a dugout cut into the side of a steep hill. In 1887 his wild, eccentric behaviour resulted in him being declared insane and sent to

Topeka Asylum. He escaped within a few months and was reported as heading towards Mexico. He was never heard of again.

Abraham Lincoln

Lincoln's assassination occurred on Good Friday and many Americans saw significance in the fact that this day was crucifixion day. One declared, 'Jesus Christ died for the world; Abraham Lincoln died for his country.'

In Washington DC, on May 30, 1922, a stately monument honouring Abraham Lincoln was dedicated. Thirty-six marble columns surround the building, one for each state that comprised the Union in Lincoln's time. The colossal seated statue of Lincoln, composed of Georgia white marble, dominates the interior of the monument and looks eastward across a reflecting pool at the Washington Monument and Capitol. On the South Wall is inscribed Lincoln's Gettysburg Address and on the North Wall his Second Inaugural Address.

A man revered for his tolerance, honesty, resolution and insight has passed beyond history into the land of legend.

President Andrew Johnson

Johnson's Reconstruction policies met bitter congressional opposition and in 1868 the House of Representatives voted articles of impeachment against him – the first, though not the last, such occurrence in US history. In a trial before the Senate the key votes fell one short of the two-thirds necessary for conviction and he was exonerated.

He retired to Tennessee when his term as President expired and he was elected a senator in 1875, shortly before he died.

William Henry Seward

Seward's support for Johnson earned him a share of the vilification directed at his chief. He retired from his post of Secretary of State in 1869 and died on October 10, 1872 at Auburn, New York.

Seward will be remembered as the man who bought Alaska from Russia in 1867.

General Ulysses Grant

In 1869 Grant stood as the Republican candidate for the Presidency and was elected with a small majority. He won re-election in 1872 with a far larger majority but his second term of office was compromised when it was discovered that prominent Republic politicians were involved with a corrupt financial corporation. He died on July 23, 1885 at Mount McGregor, New York.

Phillip Henry Sheridan

The presence of Sheridan's army along the Mexican border had hastened the fall of Maximilian and, as a reward, he was made military commander of Louisiana and Texas. His harsh administration, however, forced President Johnson to remove him from this post. He spent the remaining years in Western command, was promoted to lieutenant general and became general-in-chief in 1883. He died on August 5, 1888 at Nonquitt, Massachusetts.

General John Schofield

John Schofield was Superintendent at West Point from 1876–1881. After serving in many departments he was made general-in-chief in 1888. He died in 1906.

Schofield recommended that the United States establish Pearl Harbour, Hawaii as a military base.

José Hidalgo and Gutierrez de Estrada

These two schemers, who were primarily responsible for persuading Maximilian to take the Mexican throne, strangely chose not to accompany him to Mexico. They spent the rest of their lives in exile from their beloved land. Hidalgo, for a short time, was the Mexican ambassador to France while Estrada retired from public life. Both died in poverty and obscurity.

Pope Pius IX

In 1870, after a plebiscite, Rome was incorporated into the Kingdom of Italy. Pius IX was allowed to retain authority within the Vatican itself and a small district around it. Although this loss of temporal power over part of his domain in no way diminished his spiritual authority, Pius considered himself a prisoner inside the Vatican for the remaining eight years of his life.

His long pontificate is noteworthy for the declaration of the Immaculate Conception and the convening of the first Vatican Council at which the doctrine of Papal Infallibility was defined. Pius presided over the creation of the modern papacy.

Marshal Achille Bazaine

In 1870, after the first major battle of the Franco-German War, Bazaine was appointed commander in chief and took field command of the Army of the Rhine, which comprised the left wing of the French army. After fighting a number of inconclusive battles, during which he was wounded, he withdrew to the entrenched camp at Metz, where he was besieged by the Germans. He negotiated with Otto von Bismarck and surrendered with his army still intact. For this action, a military court sentenced Bazaine to degradation and death. Marshal Patrice de Mac-Mahon, then president of the French Republic, commuted the sentence to twenty years' imprisonment. Bazaine escaped in1874, and died in exile.

Prince Salm-Salm

In 1870, Salm died as he would have wished, gallantly leading a Prussian charge against the French in the Franco-Prussian war.

General Leonardo Marquez

Marquez had escaped from Queretaro with the avowed intention of mustering a force to raise the siege of the town. On reaching Mexico City he recruited men and collected money in the name of the Emperor. He spoke constantly of going back to Queretaro with reinforcements but he remained rooted in the capital. When General Diaz approached the capital, Marquez fled to Havana. He was eventually allowed to return and end his days in Mexico City.

He had been a cruel and murderous soldier but as he neared death he underwent a metamorphosis and became deeply religious; a phenomenon that is often to be seen in the lives of other vicious and disreputable characters.

Benito Pablo Juárez

Juárez returned to Mexico City as President and in 1871 was elected for a second term. However, there was much resistance to him and he spent the remaining months of his life fighting a rebellion. He died of apoplexy, in Mexico City, on July 18, 1872. He was the first President of Indian descent.

Juárez possessed extraordinary qualities that enabled him to overcome the prevalent social attitudes towards his Indian background. He remains, for most Mexicans, the pre-eminent symbol of nationhood and the hero who led their fight against foreign intervention.

Porfirio Diaz

Diaz welcomed Juárez to Mexico City but in 1871 led an unsuccessful rebellion against the election of Juárez for what he considered an unconstitutional second term of office. He was forced to flee to America but he returned in 1876 and was elected President a year later.

Napoleon III and Eugenie

News of Maximilian's execution came when the Emperor and Empress were attending the Great Exhibition in Paris. They hurriedly left and returned to the Tuileries, where Eugenie collapsed and was put to bed.

The Emperor's failures in foreign affairs strengthened the opposition at home and led to his downfall. In 1870 he went to war with Prussia over the candidature of a Hohenzollern prince for the Spanish Throne. Napoleon, in an effort to emulate his renowned uncle, led his troops at the Battle of Sedan. He was forced to surrender and was deposed.

Napoleon was released by the Germans and exiled to England, where he lived a simple life. He died in 1873, at Chislehurst, Kent, from a bungled operation to remove his bladder.

His despotism was relatively benevolent and he introduced valuable social and economic reforms. In the field of foreign affairs, the threat from Prussia was perceived too late and caught the French unprepared when war came in 1870. However, he was not solely responsible for the military failures of his regime, and he gave France two decades of prosperity and stable government.

Eugenie lived on, dividing her time between homes in England and France that were filled with memorabilia of lost glory.

Francis Joseph

Francis Joseph received the news of his brother's death calmly and did not allow it to affect his routine. He considered that he had been correct in his attitude to Maximilian and that he bore no blame. He arranged for a shrine to be built on the spot where Maximilian and his two generals were executed.

Francis Joseph formed an alliance with Prussian-led Germany, and in 1914 his ultimatum to Serbia led to World War I. He died at Schloss Schönbrunn in 1916.

Francis Joseph was a model of meticulousness, devotion to duty and justice. His unapproachable bearing meant that he was revered more than loved. He occupied the throne for sixty eight years and the social legislation enacted during his reign will stand as his main achievement.

Maximilian

In 1868 Maximilian's body was returned to Austria and interred in the sepulchre in the Capuchin Crypt of the Augustiner Church of Vienna, where it lay alongside the coffin containing the remains of the Duke of Reichstadt, whom many considered to be his father.

History has portrayed Maximilian as being noble but naïve. This is not strictly true. Before accepting the Mexican throne, he insisted on being given proof that the majority of Mexican people wanted him. That adventurers like José Hidalgo and Gutierrez de Estrada faked the proof does not alter the fact that Maximilian demanded it. As Emperor he did not rely solely on French troops but tried to create an efficient army composed of native Mexicans.

He faced death with courage and dignity.

Archduchess Sophia

Maximilian's mother never recovered from the news of his death. The knowledge of what she had written in her last letter to him haunted her for the rest of her life. The night when they interred Maximilian in the Capuchin Crypt, Sophia entered the sepulchre and fell on her knees. She stayed there until dawn weeping over the corpses of her lover and son.

In 1940 during the German occupation of Paris, Adolf Hitler had Reichstadt's body removed from Capuchin Crypt and reburied alongside his father in the chapel of the Hôtel des Invalides.

Charlotte (Empress Carlota)

Charlotte's brother Leopold II, King of the Belgians, and his wife Henriette felt that the family should take over responsibility for Charlotte's welfare. Therefore in 1868 Henriette travelled to Miramar and brought Charlotte back to the family palace at Laeken. No one had yet dared to tell Charlotte Maximilian's fate, so Henriette arranged for her to be told how Maximilian had died a hero's death. The news at first induced a great calm and she spoke lovingly of Maximilian and of the life they had spent together but this soon past and the cruel curtain of madness again descended between her and those who cared for her. Charlotte was fated to live for another sixty years tormented by a grief she could not comprehend. She was buried in the crypt of the Church of Our Lady in Laeken, alongside her father King Leopold I and her mother Louise Marie. The coffin was draped with the Belgian flag and the colours of Imperial Mexico.

William

What did fate have in store for William as he marched triumphantly with the victorious army from Queretaro? Did he return to Chicago, marry **Martha** and pursue a prosperous but prosaic career in the hotel industry? Or did he seek a more illustrious future as a great soldier – a man who would hold the fate of nations in his hands?

Well, that is another story.